THE HEAD TEACHER

H.M. LYNN

This was a good one x

B

Boldwood

First published in Great Britain in 2024 by Boldwood Books Ltd.

Copyright © H.M. Lynn, 2024

Cover Design by Head Design Ltd

Cover Photography: Shutterstock and iStock

The moral right of Hannah Lynn to be identified as the author of this work has been asserted in accordance with the Copyright, Designs and Patents Act 1988.

Every effort has been made to obtain the necessary permissions with reference to copyright material, both illustrative and quoted. We apologise for any omissions in this respect and will be pleased to make the appropriate acknowledgements in any future edition.

A CIP catalogue record for this book is available from the British Library.

Paperback ISBN 978-1-83603-761-3

Large Print ISBN 978-1-83603-762-0

Harback ISBN 978-1-83603-760-6

Ebook ISBN 978-1-83603-763-7

Kindle ISBN 978-1-83603-764-4

Audio CD ISBN 978-1-83603-755-2

MP3 CD ISBN 978-1-83603-756-9

Digital audio download ISBN 978-1-83603-759-0

Boldwood Books Ltd
23 Bowerdean Street
London SW6 3TN
www.boldwoodbooks.com

To Amy, for being the first ever person to recognise me as an author in public (and possibly my first stalker).

PROLOGUE

When the curtains catch alight, it's instant. The flames engulf the fabric. They rise towards the ceiling before spreading out sideways and meeting in the centre of the window. It's a perfectly framed border of flames and, for a split second, I pray that the fire is going to stay there; contained and controlled enough for me to get out of the house and call the emergency services. But my home stank of whisky from the moment I stepped inside. Now I understand why. It was planned to the last detail. A trail catches light down the side of the wall, leading straight towards the sofa. If that goes up, the entire wall behind it will be gone too, and I'll be trapped. We both will. I need to move fast, only I don't know if I have enough strength. Not to get both of us out.

I stand there. The smoke stinging my eyes and burning my lungs. This can't be where it ends. It just can't...

1

Every morning, I wake up four minutes before my alarm. Exactly four minutes, every bloody morning. And I hate it. If I wanted to wake up earlier, I would set my alarm earlier, but I don't. Instead, I wake up, lying there in my bed, wishing I had hours left to sleep, but knowing instead that any second, my silence is going to be shattered by a high-pitch squealing and I'm going to be thrust into the real world. Dealing with entitled and angry parents and upset children and teachers who don't have enough time to do their job because I don't have enough money to fund their department. I know that every mistake I make is going to be lauded over me, while every achievement is instantly forgotten. I'll admit, when I first got the job, I didn't imagine I would take it all so personally. I thought I'd be able to compartmentalise a little more. But it's harder than I'd expected.

So, for those first four minutes of the day, when I lie there with no one expecting or demanding anything from me, I dream of what it would be like to have a job where there's no responsibility, no pressure, no infringement on my family time or mental health. But then I remind myself that I'm the one who wanted this. I'm the one who wanted the bigger mortgage, not to mention the accolades that go with the title of head teacher. I'm the one that wanted to be making the rules, rather than having to abide by them. That's why, when the alarm pierces through my skull, I roll out of bed and walk automatically over to the shower, ready to start another day as head teacher of a prestigious Catholic school.

It doesn't matter what time of year it is, that moment when I turn off the main road and first see St Anne's in the morning light, at the end of the long, meandering driveway, always takes my breath away.

The grounds of St Anne's are unlike any other school I've worked or trained at. The main house is the type of thing you see in a period drama, complete with large bay windows and carved reliefs in the brickwork. It had been a private home until the 1940s, after which the owner died and the house passed – much to his relatives' distress – to the Church, who promptly turned it into a school. Since then, it has gone through countless renovations. In fact, it always seems like it's going through some work or another. It's a disadvantage with being in an older building, with hand-carved brickwork and solid wood flooring laid over a hundred years ago. Not that there aren't plenty of advantages to it. My office, which looks out across the sports field, has a working fireplace, and double doors that open fully onto a first-floor balcony. With genuine oil paintings on the wall, and original Turkish rugs that probably cost over a month's salary, it's a long way from some of the state schools I worked at early in my career. It doesn't even look like an office. It looks like a very posh living room. Or a drawing room, maybe? Is that what rich people call rooms where they have sofas and desks? I don't know, but, either way, with its powder-blue armchairs and marble mantle-piece, it's my sanctuary. The one place I get to control what goes on. But to get there, I have to make my way from the car park through the rest of the building.

'Morning, Liz.'

'Morning, Angela.'

'Good morning, Mrs Croft.'

'Morning, Darren.'

'Good morning, Liz.'

'Morning, Chris.'

By the time I reach my office, the breakfast of toast and black coffee I wolfed down with my husband and daughter only thirty minutes before feels like a distant memory. I've normally greeted close to thirty people by this point, and I know it's just the start of it. But it's even worse than normal today because this is the first day of a new school term. There's going to be so much smiling, my cheeks are going to burn. I'll get through it, though.

I won't deny my upbringing played a role in me getting this job at St Anne's. The governors would have never given it to someone who hadn't been through Catholic education themselves.

They don't need to know how much I despised it.

From the age of four to eighteen, I played the role of the perfect, doting Catholic girl. I attended every mass, memorised every prayer. Never missed a deadline for school or a choir practice or even considered rolling up my skirt so it was more in line with fashion.

It was easier that way.

Though it was all a lie.

I knew before I'd even hit my teens that this wasn't me. I couldn't bear listening to teachers preaching the values of virtue, while you knew from the school grapevine they'd spend Friday night out in town, getting so drunk, they could barely stand. Don't get me wrong, I didn't judge them for drinking. It was the hypocrisy I judged them for. As I sat there in sixth form, listening to lectures on how it was my duty to God to save myself until marriage, I promised myself that once I left that school – and my hometown – I would never call myself religious again. And I stuck with it. For years and years, I rebelled against my upbringing and did a lot of things that were not in keeping with the values the school tried so hard to impress upon me. A lot of things that would definitely have stopped me getting this job if they were ever made public. But it's not like that's ever going to happen; after all, it was before camera phones captured our every movement, and we posted our entire lives on social media, thank God.

So, for the longest part of my life, I ignored my religious upbringing altogether. That was until the job came up at St Anne's. One of the best schools in the entire district, with a proven track record and a position that was so perfect for me, I could have written it myself. But, as I scanned the application, I saw a preference in the criteria, clear as day. Catholic. Guess who's the hypocrite now?

As the thought rises in my mind, I try to negate it with justifications.

St Anne's is a long way from my convent school upbringing. Our aim here is to raise well-rounded, compassionate young people who can go out into the world and make a positive contribution to society in whatever manner they see fit. That's what the school manifesto says, and that's what I'm sticking to.

2

For some reason, this school year starts on 31 August, which has pissed the staff off no end. There's this unwritten rule in teaching that August is officially a holiday month. And most years, it is. It's just, now and then, the calendar has to be shifted because of some religious event we've got to pay homage to, and we're back here before the start of September.

As soon as I step into the staffroom, and face a sea of overly tanned, overly talkative teachers, it's clear I'm going to have a battle on my hands. At least until we all get into the swing of things. As soon as the children arrive on Wednesday and they're back in the classrooms, teaching the subjects they love, it'll all be fine. But I've got two days of uphill battles to get through before then.

'Good morning, ladies and gentlemen, I hope you've all had a wonderfully relaxing holiday and are ready to hit the ground running. We've got a busy term ahead of us.'

I position myself just to the left of the door so I can get out as quickly as possible once I'm done. I've got so many emails to respond to, I want to get started on them straight away. So I fix my face in a smile, and clear my throat loud enough for everyone in the room to know this meeting has officially started and that they should be paying attention to me, not chatting or scrolling through their phones.

'I want to keep this meeting short, as I know you have a lot of work you want to get done before your classes arrive on Wednesday,' I say. 'So if I can have your full attention please, that would be appreciated.'

As I speak, the last couple of heads roll towards me. Not to mention a fair few eyes. It would be the same anywhere, I remind myself. You are always going to have people who think they don't need to listen to you, no matter how far down the ranks they are. Besides, it *is* the end of the holiday. I've no idea what people have gone through during the previous month. I make a note to remind myself of that when I talk to people. After all, I always promised myself that, when I ran a school, it would be with a carrot, not a stick.

Trying to adopt a softer smile, I carry on with my notices.

'We've got a few big dates coming up in the next couple of weeks,' I say, 'so can everyone make sure you've got your calendars up to date? If you have any problem syncing them online with the whole school calendar, then please ask tech support for help. Digital calendars went wide last year, so there's really no excuse for anyone not using them now. It will help you in the long run, believe me. And I was as sceptical as the worst of you before I embraced them.'

My eyes instinctively dart across to Alice, who's sitting on one of the Chesterfield armchairs to the right of me. She's always my go-to when I worry about sounding overbearing. Or rather bossy. That's probably what I should say. That's the word us women get, right? I'm sure if the previous head had tried to introduce something like this, the old boys' club would have said how innovative and inspirational he was. It's ridiculous how many people didn't see the extent of his inability. There are still so many here who think he was God's gift to the school and I'm the tyrannical usurper. Last year, particularly during my first term as head, I woke up nearly every morning in cold sweats, which were always at least half to do with the school. Every new idea I tried to introduce, half the staff rebelled against it just out of principle. Or perhaps because they thought I was making extra work for them all, although that's exactly the opposite of what I was trying to do. Either way, I ended up folding half of my ideas before they'd even had a chance to take off. It's getting better now. Most of the staff have learned I'm only doing what I think is best for them and the children. There's still a core who don't want me in that office, though. Some of them are misogynistic pricks who just don't like having to answer to a woman. Others thought the sun shone out of the old head's arse. But, quite frankly, I'm now at a place where I just think, screw the lot of them.

I look at Alice and she presses her lips tightly together, offering the most minuscule of nods. It's a sign that I'm doing okay, but not to push it any further.

Reading the message loud and clear, I flash a smile and carry on.

'So, dates. We had a full week of insets at the start of last year, but that is not the case this time. Children arrive Wednesday and they know that. Any absences need to be recorded as unauthorised unless admin has told you otherwise. We are not accepting parents not reading newsletters and bulletins as a reason for their child not being in school. We have Year 7 and new parents' evening on Thursday next week. Now I know you probably won't know half the new children's names by then, but, please, try to give it a go. It makes all the difference. Print off a class photo list to help you in those first couple of lessons. Use seating plans if you need. Whatever works for you; we just want to make the best possible impression. We want to show the parents they were right in selecting St Anne's for their children, right?'

The moment the question hangs in the air is the second I realised I pitched it wrong. I went too peppy. Too 'go get 'em'.

Hurriedly, I try to reel it back in.

'So, more dates... we've got twilight training on three Mondays before half-term, the dates of which are all on the online calendar. These are looking at the changes in exam systems for next term and so are compulsory for everyone, even those not currently teaching exam classes. While we're on the subject of exams, Year 11 mocks begin on Friday next week. I know it's an awkward day to start, but it's what we have to do to fit everything in with the timetabling. Letters and emails were sent home at the end of last term, so please don't believe the students or parents when they say they didn't know. We are not changing the dates because we need the auditorium to start rehearsals for the autumn-term play as soon as they finish. Year 11 tutors, if you have any issues, please let me know. Talking about the school play, I'm assuming there will be emails sent home about auditions soon? Alice?'

I give her a look that tells her it's time to speak. Flashing me a smile, she stands up.

The pair of us have been friends for over twenty years, which nowadays officially counts as forever. We met when we were doing our teacher training, in what was undoubtedly the wildest phase of my life. The day I graduated from my degree was the same day my boyfriend of two years told me things were over, and I wasted no time making up for all the adventures I'd missed while I'd naively been playing a doting wife. Alice had been single a few months longer, and we were each other's wing woman. When that bell rang on a Friday, we were down the pub before we'd even taken our pencil skirts off, drinking into the early hours of Saturday morning, then sleeping for the rest of the day – normally on one another's sofas – so we could spend Sunday planning and prepping all our lessons for the upcoming week. Were we the greatest role models for young minds? Possibly not. Did we have fun? Absolutely. And now she's the Head of Drama, single again, after an unusually swift divorce a year ago, during which her husband simply upped and moved to another part of the country. Despite her daughter leaving for university at exactly the same time, Alice has never been better. She's putting on whole-school productions left, right and centre, while she manages a team of young, enthusiastic teachers who don't mind giving up their weekends to learn all the choreography for *Willy Wonka* or whatever else she has in store for them.

'Yes, so this year's school production is *Sweeney Todd*,' Alice says, turning slightly as she speaks so she can address the entire staff room. Her drama training means she's far better at talking to large groups than I am. She's probably better at charming the parents and sweet-talking the governors too, but she's climbed as far up the ladder as she wants to go. Still, I'm always a tiny bit jealous when I see her speak like this, without the slightest hint of nerves. 'As always, the production is open to all the senior school children,' she carries on flawlessly, 'but we would encourage our exam years to think carefully before auditioning. It takes a lot of time and, with exams looming, they really should be focusing on their academics. I'll send the audition pieces and times after this in an email, and if tutors can pass the information on, that would be amazing.' She looks at me and flashes another smile. 'That's me done.'

'Great,' I say, taking back the reins. 'Now, I know we've all got departmental meetings to get to, but are there any other quick notices people want to share?'

You can tell it's the beginning of term when more than three hands spring up into the air. Later on in the year, everyone will just want to get out of the place as quickly as possible, regardless of what information they should be sharing.

The first two people to talk are both PE staff, who tell us about their different teams, try-outs, away fixtures and ask for staff volunteers to help drive the minibus. I add some brief line about community spirit while trying to work out which weekends will be best for me to help. In some ways, I've done my dues. When I was newly trained, I gave up every other weekend running trips here, there and everywhere. But things change when you've got a family, and now it's a careful balance to make sure I do enough that no one thinks I'm slacking, but not too much that Jamie and Sasha get annoyed with all the time I'm away from home.

After PE, it's a notice about lost property, after which June, the history teacher, raises her hand. June's the same age as me, give or take a couple of years, but she looks at least a decade older. She's one of those who believe the old head could do no wrong and that he was pushed out unfairly, but our lack of friendship goes further back than that. The moment I came to work here, there was an immediate mutual dislike. I thought she was old fashioned – which she was and still is. She thought I was brash and trying to work my way up the ladder. Which I was and have. Fifteen years on, not much has changed except I'm as far up the ladder as I can get – here at least. I'll admit, though, beneath all her fuddy-duddy-ness, she's a pretty spectacular teacher. That's why she's an assistant head and the person in charge of the school's teacher-training programme.

'I just want to remind people we will have our trainee teachers arriving at the school tomorrow,' she says, in a voice that's so soft, it sounds fake. 'It'll give them a chance to see the place before the students arrive. They'll be with us for twelve weeks before moving on to their new placement. Please try to make them feel as welcome as possible. I will send out details to the teachers it affects over the next twenty-four hours, so keep your eyes out for that.'

She offers me a tight smile that could be an attempt at genuine human connection but could also be trapped wind.

I offer her a similar gaze before addressing the rest of the room.

'Okay, guys, that sounds great. So, if there's nothing else...'

The moment I speak, I hear his throat clear and my stomach sinks. I should have known he wouldn't raise his hand with the rest of the staff the way general etiquette dictates, because that way, I might have asked him to give his notice earlier on. And he wouldn't like that. Not one bit. Because Nathan Coles always has to have the last word.

3

At thirty-five, Nathan Coles is nearly a full decade younger than me, and has been hankering for the headship since the moment he swaggered into the school four years ago. And, believe me, he swaggers. He's charming and moderately competent, but it's the fact he slicks his hair back and wears shirts tight enough to see his abs that has all the female staff and parents eating out of the palm of his hands. I'm not denying he's a good enough teacher – but he's not on June's level, or mine for that matter – and the kids like him, but he needs to earn his stripes in this job. St Anne's is a walk in the park compared to some schools I've worked in and he wouldn't last a day in one of those. No, I'd like to see how he'd handle those parents as they swore at him and threatened him and made his life a living hell. I doubt his tight shirts would help him then. Unfortunately, he's my other assistant head, but, unlike June, he still wants to climb the ladder to the top.

Obviously, when the headteacher's job was advertised, Nathan applied for it too, and he's been waiting on the sidelines for me to fail ever since. At the beginning of last year, when things were so tough, both here and at home, his smug face was one of the reasons I didn't quit. I just couldn't give him the satisfaction.

'Nathan,' I say, my cheeks aching as I force my lips to curl upwards. 'Sorry, I didn't see you there. You have a notice?'

He flashes a smile, and it really is a flash. Like a camera going off, his teeth are so damn bright. I can't imagine how long he spends whitening them, but it doesn't look natural at all.

'Yes, thank you, Liz.' He takes a step forward so that he's standing in front of me. Blocking me out from my entire staff.

'I know it's the beginning of the year, but I hope you are all feeling refreshed and ready for a great start to the term...'

I frown. I'm pretty sure that's how I just started my speech. As the head. So he's starting the term making it clear he still wants my job. I could spit I'm so angry, but that wouldn't be a good look. Still, my fingers twitch at my side. All eyes are on him as he carries on.

'...but the last thing I want is for us to get complacent about our mental health. Burnout is more prevalent than ever in our profession. Which is why I am going to be offering group mindfulness sessions three times a week. Tuesday and Wednesday at 7 a.m. and Thursdays after school. If you can't make any of those, then please drop me an email and I'll see if I can slip in a couple of one-on-ones. Remember, you're the cogs that keep this place turning. If you stop working, the whole machine falls apart.'

Arsehole, I think. It's not a great managerial thought to have, but it's deserved. Nathan knows that any clubs or activities offered to the staff or children must pass through me for timetabling. Just to make sure we're not cramming too much into the week. Now he's announced that he's using not just one, but three of our slots, and I can't even call him out about it, because they're focused on wellbeing. If I try to cancel any of them, it's going to look like I'm a bitch who doesn't care about my staff, which is absolutely not true. If anything, his stunt now means I'm going to have to put meetings on Monday or Friday. People's least favourite days for staying late. But, of course, he knows that. It's all planned.

'Well, that's great,' I say, my back teeth grinding together with annoyance. 'Well, ladies and gents, I know you've all got year group and departmental meetings to get to, so I'll let you go. And, don't forget, my door is always open.'

They don't need telling twice. Immediately, the double doors swing open and people disappear outside, off to their classrooms. Only a couple of old staff hang about, heading to the kettle to fix their third coffee of the day. I consider grabbing myself a drink too, just so I can try to shake off the bad mood Nathan has put me in before I head back to my office, but, before I can move, Sandra is standing in front of me.

Sandra is my PA and firmly in June's camp of wishing I hadn't got the job. She's made no qualms about saying she thought Nathan would have been a better fit, although the only thing he has over me is a Y chromosome. Unfortunately, she's one of these old-school women who acts like feminism is a dirty word, because why would she want equal rights to her husband? She's infuriating, and everything I don't want at St Anne's, but I can't get rid of her until she screws up. Annoyingly, she's highly efficient. She knows every single thing about every member of staff, and what she doesn't know she makes it her business to find out. And not just the staff, but their family, too. Of course, part of that isn't efficiency; she's just a damn nosey old gossip. It's like she has a thousand spies, placed across the county, who filter all their knowledge to her. She knew I'd applied for a place for Sasha to move schools before I'd mentioned it to anyone here. Thankfully, that was where her knowledge on the matter ended, not that she didn't try to dig a little.

'Elizabeth,' she says, because she can't possibly call me Liz like everyone else. 'You need to come down to reception. There's something you have to see.'

* * *

Being summoned to reception is never a good thing. Not even for the head. And as we're walking down the stairs, I rack my mind, trying to work out what could have happened that would require my attention before there are even any students at school. It can't be a fight – not that we have many of those here – or a parental complaint this early on. Issues with timetables could be something, but Nathan handles teaching allocations, so they would normally ask him about that.

I'm still trying to work out what it could be when I step into reception. A loud laugh escapes my lungs.

'He did not?' I say.

Jo, who is sitting behind the reception desk, is the antithesis of Sandra. The spry thirty-something with bleached blonde hair doesn't attend staff meetings, but stays put by the phone to take any calls while we're busy. Several times I've debated if there was some way I could exchange their roles and have Jo working directly with me, rather than Sandra, but I'm not sure how I could do it without it simply looking like I don't want Sandra near me.

'He did.' Jo grins back.

Sandra, on the other hand, is not grinning. There's not even a hint of a smile on her face.

'I don't think it's appropriate,' she says snootily. 'Personal declarations like this are for the home, not the workplace.'

Both Jo and I ignore her.

There on the front desk is an enormous bunch of red roses.

At least two dozen, beautifully hand-tied and open in full bloom. I don't care if people think roses are a cliché. Or that personal declarations should be kept at home. The whole thing is perfect. And the smell is divine.

Stepping up to the desk, I pull the little note from between the blooms and open the envelope.

Have an amazing first day. Knock 'em dead.
    J x

Jamie. My husband of nineteen years.

Sometimes I struggle to believe that it's true. Nineteen years married and I can honestly say that I love him more now than when I said, 'I do'. But then we've been through a lot. What we went through last year either breaks a couple or makes them freakishly strong. The fact he sent roses on my first day back at work is a clear sign we made it through tougher than ever.

'You've got a good one there,' Jo says as I slip the note back into the flowers.

'Yes, I do. But I had to kiss a couple of frogs first,' I tell her, partly because it's true – my trainee year is testament to that – and partially because I know it's what Jo needs to hear. For a lovely young woman, she has the worst luck in love and the last thing I want is to appear like I'm gloating, just because I married the best man in the world.

'I think you should take them up to the office,' Sandra says, pointedly. 'We do have people visiting today. It doesn't give the most professional impression when people enter the school.'

'You're right,' I say, a smile still warming my insides. 'Can you take them up for me? I've just remembered I need to pop back to the staffroom.'

She looks like her blood is going to boil, but there's no way she'd ever say no. Definitely not with Jo there. A moment later and she's heaving them into her arms, and I'm wondering if I've made a mistake. After all, I wouldn't put it past her not to drop them out of spite.

'I'll see you later,' I say to Jo. 'And make sure you take a proper lunch break, okay? It doesn't matter if one or two calls go to voicemail. That's why we pay for an answering machine.'

'See you later,' she says, then her head is back at the computer and I'm walking back to the staffroom with the sole intention of making myself a cup of coffee. The bad mood Nathan put me in has notably diminished. Maybe it'll be a good day after all.

4

By the time I leave work, I feel like I've been in school for at least a week and a half. It's impossible to believe that it's only the first day of term, and the kids aren't even back yet. There was a constant stream of issues from the geography field trip, which needed to change locations, while a new member of staff had accepted a job abroad without telling us, and therefore not turned up. I also had to field an angry telephone call from a parent whose child didn't get the exam results they needed and blamed the school entirely, although we'd told them several times that the child was not doing enough work. I know it could be easy to judge the parents in a situation like that. After all, if they'd done like we'd advised and monitored their child's evening activities, this would never have happened. But I know better than anyone how things can happen with your child right beneath your nose. Even when you think you know everything about them.

But that stage of our life is past now. Of that, I'm certain. After all, what Sasha put us through wasn't half as bad as what she put herself through. And I'm speaking from experience there.

Thankfully, when I unlock the front door, I'm hit by an amazing aroma. In that moment, it's like school and worries are just washed away.

'Did you get takeaway?' I call into the house, my mouth already salivating. 'Please tell me it's Thai?'

'It's Thai,' Jamie calls back. 'I got you a massaman chicken curry and sticky rice.'

'And did you get spring rolls, too?' I say as I walk into the kitchen and drop my laptop bag on the ground by the shoe rack.

'As if I'd forget a thing like spring rolls,' he says, before turning to the fridge and pulling out a bottle of wine. 'Rosé?'

'A big one, please.' I can't help but let out a yawn as I wrap my arms around Jamie and breathe in his scent. Nineteen years later and, I swear, he still smells exactly the same. There's a deep earthiness to his skin with the most delicate undertones that just draws me in. Even though he's still holding the cold wine bottle and I'm sure it must be freezing for him, I can't help but press my lips against his and sink into a long, hard kiss.

'Those roses were ridiculous, you know,' I say, when I finally break away.

'I know, but they were good, right?'

'Very good. But the expectation is high now. You know I'll be expecting these at the start of every year?'

'Obviously.'

After pouring the wine, he puts the bottle back, then takes some plates out of the cupboard and places them on the worktop. There are only two, though.

'Where's Sasha?' I ask.

'She already took her phad thai up to her room. I told her she could eat there. She's got some video lessons or something she wants to watch.'

'Fair enough,' I say. The start of the year can be stressful for all kids, but particularly for Sasha. After all, this time last year we were in a very different situation. I don't want to push her. Not if she's not ready for that. 'How was her first day back?'

'I'm not sure. All I got out of her was grunts and a food order. I think she's pretty shattered. But you never know, she might tell you more.'

'I'll head up after dinner,' I say.

Until last year, Sasha went to St Anne's. It was easy; she'd come with me in the morning, then hang around after school, finishing her homework in the library until I was ready to leave. But then, in the summer of last year, all that changed. I guess it was a good thing it happened during the holidays, really. That it wasn't part way through the school year. That could have made things even more complicated. Unfortunately, there were no places in any of the nearby state schools so Jamie and I had to fork out for the local private. Sasha got a music scholarship, which cut the fees down, but really it's hard not to laugh at the irony. There was a reason she got so good at playing the oboe, and *he* was the reason for all the mess, too.

Still, she started her new school on the first day of term, everyone oblivious to what she had gone through only days beforehand.

The lie was simple; she didn't want to be at the same school where her mum was now head. No one batted an eyelid at the transfer, even though she was halfway through an exam course. But the change wasn't quite as straightforward as we'd hoped. Sasha had healing to do, and she needed people she felt safe around, even if she didn't want to tell them what had happened. Kids in private schools like the one she goes to now have been together forever. Some of them since nursery, some of them even while their mothers were attending their pregnancy massage sessions and interviewing doulas. Sasha immediately felt on the outside, and it didn't help that every little win was followed by a fast dip down. Getting a place on the hockey team was quickly followed by girls bitching, saying she'd taken someone's spot. The same thing happened when she got her role in the school play, or a position on the school debate team. It was like she couldn't win. And given how my job was going at the time, I knew exactly how that felt.

'I can remind her to bring her bowl down from upstairs while I'm there,' I say.

'Just go easy on her, okay?'

'What's that meant to mean?' I can hear the tone in my voice. One I try never to show at school, even with pricks like Nathan. But Jamie just raises an eyebrow.

'It means go easy on her. That's all. First day in sixth form has got to be exhausting,' he says, knowingly. 'You're tired. And when you're tired, you get snappy. Particularly with Sash.'

There's no point denying it. Jamie would never gaslight me into thinking something that isn't true, and I feel bad that he and Sasha are the ones that always get the brunt of my exhaustion.

'You're right. Don't worry, it's a check-in, that's all. And I'll take some chocolate up to her. That'll win me some Brownie points.'

5

From the moment Sasha was born, I felt certain I was meant to have a daughter. I'm sure I would probably have said the same if I'd had a son, but, the instant I held her against my chest, I felt like this was the way my life was meant to be. Like she and I were always destined to be together. I felt the same way during her early childhood years and school days, even those early teens.

But, then, Christopher happened. It's fair to say, I didn't respond the way Sasha would have liked me to, but any mother worth her salt is going to blow up if she discovers that her fifteen-year-old child is in a relationship with an adult man six years older than her. When the shit really hit the fan, I threatened him with the police. Only it wasn't a threat. I would have seen them lock him up and throw away the key if I hadn't known what it would do to Sasha's and my relationship. I guess I was a coward and I still have to live with that. Thankfully, she put all that pain into focusing on the future, and I don't think she's said his name in nearly a year.

Music is coming from her room, though it's not the type of

music you'd expect from a sixteen-year-old's bedroom. This is classical. An oboe concerto, probably by Mozart. That would be my guess, anyway. I don't really know. It could be Bach, or Strauss, or even Vaughn Williams. I struggle to tell the difference most of the time. But I keep trying, just like I did with the Christopher situation, although I'm far happier that the classical music is here to stay.

I knock on the door, but there's no reply, so I knock again, this time a little harder.

'Sash?' I push the door open a little. Just enough to see her lying on her bed, working away on her laptop. She has a perfectly good desk in the corner of the room. One she insisted we buy. And yet she never uses it. It's piled so high with sheet music, you can't even see the wood beneath it. Knowing our luck, she'll probably end up complaining about her back at some point and I'll be forced to fork out for a chiropractor.

'Hey, everything okay?' I say as I walk inside the room. I figure I've knocked and asked enough for her to have refused if she didn't want me to come in. 'Mind if I take a seat?' I say, gesturing to the end of the bed.

For the first time, Sasha lifts her head up and looks at me.

'Did you want something?' she says.

'Just to know how your day went, that's all?'

'You mean...'

She pales slightly as she looks at me.

'I mean, you're in Year 12 now. The start of A-Levels. It's a big deal, and it's completely okay to feel a bit overwhelmed at first.'

Her face flickers away from me, and she inhales so sharply, there's a hissing sound. For a second, I think I've said something wrong, but then she turns back to me and starts speaking again.

'You know, at Uncle Tony's school, the students actually start some of their A-Levels a year early? Their GCSEs too. It gives them more time to focus on the extra-curricular activities they need to get into university. It's a good idea, isn't it?'

'You can't possibly be worried about getting into music college,' I say in surprise. It's what she's been working towards since she was thirteen, and was why we sent her to a joint venture youth orchestra with one of the local colleges. Unfortunately for us, it was the one Christopher attended.

'I'm just saying that schools like that have it all wrapped up. You know, they have a full orchestra. They're doing "Lark Ascending" this term.'

Jamie's brother Tony is in education too. He's an assistant head at a school in Singapore, and we spent three weeks in the summer visiting him and travelling around Southeast Asia. The full-size concert hall was all it took to have Sasha desperate to attend a place like that, but she's only two years away from music college, and the way she's going, she'll have her pick of conservatoires in London. I'm about to say as much when she speaks again.

'So, how was your first day back?' she says. 'I heard Dad sent you flowers. I assume that was cringe.'

'No, not cringe. Romantic,' I say.

'Until they wither and die on your desk.'

'Wow, this is a cheery conversation. Talking of which, Aunty Alice is putting on *Sweeney Todd* this term. You know she loves her gruesomeness.'

'That'll be good. Maybe I'll come and see it.'

'I'd like it if you did,' I say, surprised she'd offer such a thing. Sasha cut a lot of ties when she was with Christopher, then more still when she moved school. Over the summer, she started messaging some friends again, but her coming to visit St Anne's would be a significant step forward.

'Of course you would...' she replies, with an animosity I hadn't expected.

All of a sudden, something more is hanging in the air. A tension building, but I can't think why. It's that typical teenage situation where I've somehow ended up in the doghouse because I've come to talk to her. Perhaps I should have stayed downstairs. That was the way it went for a while and sometimes I think that's how she'd like it to be again.

'So, I should probably do some practice,' Sasha says, gesturing to her oboe beside her. 'After all, tomorrow is a big day for me.'

For a split second, that tension's there again so intensely, I feel the hairs rise on my arms, but in a heartbeat, Sasha is back, staring at her computer and I'm wondering if that moment ever happened.

'Don't stay up too late, and no practising after nine,' I say before kissing her on the head.

Downstairs, Jamie has already cleared up the takeaway and loaded the dishwasher. I wrap my arms around him and squeeze him tightly.

'How did everything go?' he asks.

'Honestly, I don't know.'

He nods, and there's a similar solemnity to Sasha in his eyes. What the hell is it I'm missing? I'm about to ask when my phone buzzes in my pocket. A quick glance at the screen tells me one of my head-of-years just handed in their notice. The children aren't even in school yet. Why the hell would anyone do that?

With a deep groan, I offer Jamie an apologetic smile.

'I guess I should head upstairs to the office for the night,' I say, grateful again that we got the house with two spare bedrooms so that I can work at all hours of the day.

Jamie nods. He knew this was coming. An hour for dinner together is a luxury we don't normally get.

'Don't work too late,' he replies, like I actually have a choice in the matter.

6

Once again, I wake up four minutes before the alarm goes. A sinking dread circles my stomach before I push it down. There's no need to be feeling this way, I remind myself. Everything is fine. School went well yesterday. I did my job well yesterday, just the same as I am going to do every day this term.

I turn over and see Jamie there, still snoring softly next to me. He never wakes up before the alarm. Sometimes, he doesn't even wake up with it. I love him, but he could sleep through a typhoon. Still, I use the moment of silence to think through the day ahead. My list of jobs is endless, and the amount of paperwork I have to read through each day makes my eyes sting. And I have to actually read it. Every sentence. It's not like when I was younger and I'd be handed something to sign. In those days, I'd scan whatever I'd been given so quickly, I probably took in less than half before scribbling my name at the bottom. But everything at St Anne's has my signature attached to it. I'm the one the buck stops with, and the thing about working with children is it's like working with animals. They're unpredictable. You might think you've covered every base, but something can always happen that you haven't predicted. And it's terrifying. As Jamie lets out a snuffly snore, my mind flicks away from school and to my family. First to the roses Jamie sent, then to Sasha.

She was odd last night, and it's worrying. It was like she was expecting me to say something and I failed her. In terms of life, failing Sasha is my greatest fear of all, and I already did it once. I won't let that happen again.

As I'm thinking about the year before, there's a click somewhere in the back of my mind, like the neurones I need are finally firing together. Unfortunately, it's at the exact moment as the alarm blares out into the air. And that's it. I'm automatically rolling onto my feet. Ready to start the day again. Whatever thought it was has been lost.

* * *

'Morning, Liz.'

'Morning, Jo.'

'Good morning, Mrs Croft.'

'Morning, Darren.'

'Elizabeth.'

'Sandra.'

Tuesday is the last day the teachers have to get sorted before the students arrive, and the last thing they need is me holding unnecessary meetings reminding them how to suck eggs. I've still got to run a couple of sessions, though. Safeguarding and child welfare need to be covered every year and obviously, I'm the one who has to run those. There's also another session on the school registration system that Nathan is leading, and it's almost a one hundred per cent pointless me being there. The only time I ever take a register is when I'm covering a lesson and they only ever use me as a last resort. It's not that I don't like doing it. I love teaching. More than being in an office. Several times last term, I had to go into the classroom and it gave me a chance to connect with the students in a manner I don't get to do very often anymore. But me being in a classroom means time away from my endless to-do list and means I lose even more of my evening time with Jamie and Sasha. Still, I need to show my face at these things, and pay attention too. I can't expect them to follow my example otherwise.

Theoretically, the afternoon is mine, but I've only been in my seat for twenty minutes when there's a knock on the door.

'Come in,' I say.

A second later, June's head peers around the door.

'Is it all right if we come in?' she asks.

I know it's unfair that things like that grate on me, but she just heard me say, come in. That's why she opened the door. Why does she need to ask again? She always does it, though, the same way Sandra always opens the door before I've spoken and Nathan always remains standing even when I tell him to take a seat, because he enjoys looming over me. I guess they'd all say I've got foibles too, but I can't imagine what they are.

'Of course.' I smile politely, only noting the *we* in her previous question when four other people trail in after her.

'These are our trainee teachers who are going to be with us for the next week,' she says, holding out her hand as she presents the group to me. 'I was just giving them a little tour of the place, and wanted to introduce them, just so you know who's wandering around the school.'

There's an extreme mixture of people standing in front of me, about to embark on their teaching careers. The oldest of the group is a balding man who must be nearly sixty, while the youngest is also male, but doesn't look much older than some of the sixth form, although I know he has to be. I remember those days, when people would mistake me for a student and ask why there was no teacher in the room. Though that was a very long time ago. There are also two women in the group. Again, one is young. She's wearing a sharply tailored suit with her hair tied back in a severe bun, probably hoping the outfit makes her look older. It gives the impression of someone dressing up in their mother's work clothes. The last woman looks somewhere in between. Probably late twenties or early thirties. Unlike the others, she's dressed in a far more relaxed manner, with wide legged trousers, a patterned shirt and lilac manicure. I stand up before I speak to them.

'Welcome to St Anne's. I hope you find the time here really beneficial. I remember how scary these first few weeks can be, but our students are lovely and you're in safe hands with June here. She's one of the best teachers we've got.'

June smiles at this comment, but it's thin-lipped, like she doesn't believe the compliment. Seriously, there's no winning with some people.

'Just to give you all a quick introduction.' June takes over. 'Obviously, Mrs Croft is our headteacher here. You shouldn't have any reason to contact her directly, but I'm sure you'll see her around.'

'You never know, I might observe some of your lessons when I'm doing my rounds.' I try to sound as friendly as possible as I say this, yet the younger of the women's eyes nearly bulge from her head.

'You do that? You observe us?'

'Observations tend to happen with your subject teachers only,' June says, shooting me a look.

Now she's made me look like an idiot and the last thing I want is to leave these student teachers with the impression that I don't know how the system works, which is why I speak again.

'So, what subjects are you all training in?' I ask.

Both of the men are training in science – one biology, one physics – while the young woman in the suit is doing maths. Clearly, the outfit is aimed to imply intelligence and age. The other woman's more relaxed outfit also makes sense when I discover she's training to be an art teacher. There's something about art teachers that makes them think dress codes don't apply to them. I dated one when I was training – well, date is a loose term – and it's probably clouded my opinion of them since. After all, it's not like this woman's outfit is unprofessional.

'Well, my door is always open,' I say. 'And don't be afraid to say hi and let me know how you're getting on if I see you about.'

Thankfully, June knows me well enough to know when she's been dismissed and offers me one more tight-lipped smile before ushering them out and leaving me with a load of documents to read through and sign, because tomorrow is the big day.

* * *

On Wednesday, the students finally arrive and guess who has to be at the gate to greet them? Yup. Me.

Three times a week, I'm on the gate in the morning offering wide smiles while correcting uniforms: insisting ties are done up and hoodies off. The other two mornings, June and Nathan split, but they also do the afternoons, so I get off lighter than I could. After all the meets and greets, it's time for assemblies, but, as the auditorium isn't big enough for the whole school, they're split into year groups, which means five times, I have to stand on the stage and show the same presentation, talking about St Anne's and our values and hopes for the upcoming year. I try to make it personal and relatable, showing a few of my holiday snaps in the mix where it helps make a point. Like when our school values talk about taking risks, I show a photo of me on a forest skywalk in Malaysia, where we headed with Jamie's brother during our summer trip. I have to tread a careful line, though. Not all our families can afford holidays aboard, or holidays at all for that matter, and the last thing I want them to do is go back home and feel like I was gloating.

By the time I've finished all the assemblies, there's only two periods left in the day and I've done absolutely no admin, and it's still not the end of my presentations. I've still got the sixth-form assembly the following morning, although most of those students knew me when I was in the classroom, so I have a better relationship with them. Sixth-form assemblies often turn into a bit of a discussion, so at least it adds some variation.

With my throat so dry I don't know how I'm going to make it to the end of the week, let alone the end of term, I head back to my office, passing Sandra, who is typing away and doesn't even bother looking up and saying hello. I'm anticipating some time to get my head together, only, when I open my door, I find someone is already sitting in my office.

'Florence,' I say, my throat tightening. 'What a surprise.'

7

While I have no evidence to confirm it, I am one hundred per cent positive that our Chair of Governors, Florence Beaumont, was the sole inspiration behind J. K. Rowling's character Delores Umbridge. There are the tweed suits in sickly pastel colours. Today, it's a buttercup yellow but I've seen everything from mint green to fuchsia. Then there's that smile that sends shivers down my spine and her soft way of talking that makes June sound like a foghorn.

I leave the door open before I speak again. 'Sorry, Sandra didn't tell me you were here?' I say, glaring at Sandra as I do.

'I'm sorry, Elizabeth. Florence has been waiting for a while. I completely forgot.' Sandra smiles innocently.

A flood of rage surges through me, but in a heartbeat, it's gone, replaced instead by a twinge of satisfaction. Sandra might think she's got one over on me by letting Florence go straight into my space, but that only tells me she has no idea what she's actually done. She's going to find out soon enough, though.

Knowing that's something I'm going to have to wait until later to deal with, I close the door and turn to Florence.

'You've been waiting?' I say, not hiding my confusion. 'We don't have a meeting, do we?'

'No, no. I just wanted to drop in and say hello.' There it is. That sickly sweet voice that is so nauseating. 'You know how it is. I wanted to see if there's anything you need to start the term? It all looks like it's off to a good start. Obviously, you're busy. Too busy to be in your office.'

'Oh, yes. It's been a very good start,' I say, ignoring the dig. She has no fucking idea what I do.

Her smile broadens.

'Stephen will be pleased,' she says. 'As will all the governing board, obviously.'

My jaw locks as I hold my smile there. So that's the reason for her being here. Talk about a conflict of interest. Stephen is Florence's husband. He's also the old head. It was ridiculous. Anything he wanted automatically got the governors' approval because she would give the say so. They should have asked her to step down when he was forced into early retirement, but there was no way she was doing that. And so now she periodically drops in so she can feed back to Stephen how she thinks things are going on ground level. And, obviously, she and Sandra get on wonderfully.

'Was there any official capacity you need to see me in?' I ask, trying to find the fine line between pointed and polite. 'Only I know the governors want the long-term expenditure plans at the next meeting, and I was going to use this time to write it up.'

It's a lie. I've a hundred jobs higher up my to-do list than that one, but she doesn't know that.

'No, no, it was just a wellbeing check,' she insists, then stands up. 'I'll let you get to it. Remember, I'm just a phone call away if you need anything.'

'Thank you, Florence. That's ever so kind.'

I shake her hand before opening the door for her. With a smile so fake, I could scream, she totters out in her patent Mary Janes, and I can tell she's going to stop at Sandra's desk, no doubt for a giggle at how they just blindsided me, but I beat her to it.

'Sandra, can you come into my office for a minute, please?'

The pair exchange a look before Sandra slowly rises from her seat and ambles over. Once she's inside, I don't bother closing the door and I don't offer her a seat either. I want to be as close as possible and able to look her right in the eye as she hears my words.

'People are not allowed in my office unless I am present,' I say.

'I understand, Elizabeth,' she says, with a voice almost as saccharine as Florence's. 'But Florence is the Chair of Governors. And she spent plenty of time in there alone when Stephen was head.'

There's no drop in Sandra's false smile yet, but I'm not done.

'Then that was an issue you should have raised then, too. There is sensitive information in here. Information about student welfare and having anyone inside here is a safeguarding risk.'

Her face pales by just a fraction, but she holds my gaze strongly.

'She's the Chair of Governors,' she repeats, as if that's going to get her out of trouble, but every schoolteacher and education worker knows that when the word 'safeguarding' is pulled out, it's trouble.

'I am well aware of what her position is, thank you, Sandra,' I say. 'And in that position, she has no access to student data whatsoever.'

'She didn't—' Sandra tries, but it's too late. I've got her, and she knows it.

'She didn't what, Sandra? Access files? Open folders? How

would you know as you not only allowed her in my room, without supervision, you even let her close the door behind her?'

'But that's just... she always used to...' Sandra is floundering, her cheeks going red. She knows there's no escape.

'It's just a good job I always lock my computer, otherwise what you would have done would be a sackable offence, you know that. It still could be if I discover she's even touched so much as a pen on my desk. And there's not a union or school board in the country who would disagree with me. Now get out of my office.'

8

I know it's wrong that the confrontation with Sandra gives me so much satisfaction. A better leader than me probably would feel guilty, rather than smug, for calling out a member of staff, but I'm well aware that our conversation is going to get straight back to Florence, and she needs to hear it. Florence and Sandra – and everyone else stuck in the past – need to hear that the old school ways, of letting things slide because 'it's not that big a deal,' the way they used to do time and time again, are over. They need to know that I'm not just going to roll over and accept their decisions the way I did last year, when I was struggling to keep my head above water. I was weak and let them make the call on far too many issues. This year is going to be different and, perhaps when they realise that, they might decide to remove themselves from the equation altogether. That would be better in a lot of ways, for all of us.

It's gone two-thirty when I finally sit down at the computer and open my emails. Just the subject lines of the first half-dozen are enough to make me want to hit my head against my table.

Cold pasta at lunch.

Uncomfy chairs in English.

These are the things the parents send me, the head teacher, and their children haven't even been back at school for a full day yet. This is why I hate today's mobile culture.

Emails like this are a ridiculous draw on my time. I don't understand how these parents think that the temperature of their child's meal is an issue worthy of messaging me over, when, in truth, I have children who don't get meals outside of school. Ones who are being made homeless through absolutely no fault of their own or their parents. Not to mention I'm getting my budget squeezed from every corner so I'm going to have to strip support from those children who need it the most. Chances are, their child's pasta was cold because he was late to lunch, or had been talking to their mates for twenty minutes before they started eating. And obviously, if it had been too hot, I would have got an email about that too – it being dangerous to serve children hot food and that type of nonsense. There is literally no way to win. Had it been another day, I'd have asked Sandra to draft some emails for those, but, right now, I have no idea what she might send. Certainly nothing I couldn't pull together in half the time.

Between all the emails that make me want to pull my teeth out, there are also an equal number of genuine ones, and by the time I next check the clock on the wall, it's nearly five. I don't know how; I didn't even hear the school bell ring.

Deciding to just get home and carry on after dinner, I pack up my things and lock the door.

Sandra is still sitting at her desk.

'Elizabeth – Liz,' she says as I pass.

I turn to look at her. 'Yes. Is everything okay?' I say. 'I'm just off home.'

My voice is absolutely neutral. There's no harshness or animosity in my tone, but it's far from the overtly friendly option I usually use with my staff. She can feel it.

'I just wanted to say again how sorry I was about that misunderstanding earlier,' she says, which is unexpected, because she didn't actually apologise in the first place. But I don't say that.

'Don't let it happen again.'

'I won't. Have a good evening. And give Jamie and Sasha my best. Those roses he sent you really are beautiful.'

God, she's a creep.

* * *

I turn into the driveway at exactly the same time as Jamie. To be honest, I'm surprised. We normally get home around the same time, but it's usually an hour later. We are one of those ridiculous couples who have the same car. Exactly the same. Year, make, model, even colour. Jamie got his first, about two years ago, and after three months of having it, I was hooked. It's far fancier than I need, with its multiple sat nav programmes, voice recognition for telephone calls and hundreds of blinking lights on the dashboard that I don't understand. But it's also got crazily comfy heated seats and drives like a dream.

What surprises me more than seeing Jamie back so early is seeing Sasha climbing out of his passenger seat. Most nights, she gets the bus home. The only time Jamie ever picks her up is when she has a counselling session, but those are normally Thursdays, not Wednesdays. As they both climb out, I'm about to ask why they're together, when I realise what the date is.

'Sasha...' I say, guilt billowing through me as I slam my car door closed. 'Are you okay, baby? I'm so sorry. Did you go see the counsellor today? What did she say? I'm so sorry darling, I just didn't think.'

She's got her key out and has opened the door as I ramble away. As the lock clicks, she turns to face me.

'Don't bother, Mum,' she says, before looking at Jamie. 'See, I told you she didn't even remember.'

A second later, she's thundering up the stairs and I'm desperate to follow, but Jamie grabs me by the arms.

'You need to give her some time to cool off,' he says. 'It was a tough one.'

He loosens his grip, but doesn't let go entirely. For over a minute, we just stand there in silence, my eyes locked at the top of the stairs, like Sasha might suddenly appear again.

'Am I the worst mother in the world?' I say, tears lodging in my throat.

'You've been busy these last couple of days,' Jamie replies, and I can't help but think how that's just a nicer way of saying yes.

9

I knock on the bedroom door a couple of times, but I'm not expecting her to answer, so I don't wait before opening it and stepping inside. Sasha is lying on her bed, but there's no laptop in sight like the night before. Instead, she's on her back, arms crossed over her belly, staring up at the ceiling.

'Hey, baby girl, are you okay?'

She doesn't speak, though her shoulders move in a slight shrug.

'I'm sorry. I should've said something this morning. Or last night. I'm sorry.'

'You didn't remember this morning, Mum,' Sasha says, still looking up at the ceiling. 'It wasn't a priority.' She states this with no apparent hurt or animosity; it's just a fact. 'I thought you'd remembered last night. I thought that was why you'd come in to talk to me, but then I realised you hadn't. You didn't have a clue. It's silly really, I don't know why I thought you would. That would require you to think about something other than your job, and we both know that's not possible.'

'Sasha, that's not fair.'

I want to pick her up and force her to look at me, but I can't. She's right – not that the job is more important than her, but it's the reason I forgot.

'It was the change in term dates,' I say, scrambling to find an excuse. 'I thought it all happened in the summer. Last year... it was in the summer. I'm sorry, you're right. I should have known it was the anniversary of... you know. It's just a lot has happened in the last year.'

'Please stop the excuses, Mum. You're sounding pathetic.'

Her words sting, and I want to tell her I'm sorry again, but I know they're just words. They mean nothing. It's actions that count and, right now, I've let her down. Big time. All I can do is squeeze her arm, and let her know I'm here for her now, not that I think she even wants that.

'Baby, I'm so sorry. You're right. I don't have any excuses. I know better than anyone what it's like to go through what you went through and I should've been there for you. I really, really should have. I'm so sorry. Do you want to talk about anything?'

She shakes her head. Still not looking at me. It's not a pose I've had to contend with in a while. The stoic, unemotional Sasha. To be honest, I thought we were past it, but I guess I've got no one to blame but myself right now.

There's another question I want to ask, and I'm sure she knows I'm thinking about it. If we were on good terms, I probably wouldn't bring it up, but given that she's already pissed at me, I can't see any reason not to. Still, it takes me a second to get the words out.

'What about him?' I say. 'Have you heard anything from him?'

At this, Sasha finally rolls over to face me.

'Can we not do this now, Mum? Not now. I just need some time by myself. Is that okay? Can I have some time by myself? Or do I have to listen to you ramble away now that you've decided you want to be a mother again?'

'That's not fair, Sasha. I did everything I could for you. I was there for you one hundred per cent of the way. And I would have carried on being, whatever you decided to do.'

'Yeah, it's just your compassionate side went away when the problem did, right?' She flips back onto her bed, staring at the ceiling, hands back across her belly.

An ache spreads in my chest. I don't want to leave her. I want to stay here with her, hold her and make all her hurt go away, like I did when she was little. I want her to stop being mad at me. To make her see that I don't even like my job. That she's the one I took it for, because I want her to have everything that she deserves. That I don't ever want her to struggle or feel pain the way she did last year. But I can't say that right now. She won't listen. So, instead, I stand up.

'Dad's putting the pizza in the oven now,' I say. 'I'll bring some up to you when it's done.'

'Don't bother,' she says. 'I'm not hungry.'

Knowing there's no point even trying, I leave the room and close the door behind me.

'Well, that was shit,' I say as I sit down at the dining room table.

There's a glass of red wine already waiting for me. I pick it up and take a sizeable gulp.

'How the hell did I forget?' I say to Jamie. 'Why didn't you remind me?'

He raises an eyebrow before dropping it again and letting out a long sigh.

'I know you didn't mean to forget. Sasha knows that too. But you're only one week into term. Less than that. Is this job really worth it?'

'What choice do I have? Quit?' I say. We had this argument so many times last year. It's practically the only argument we have. But it hasn't got any easier.

'Yes, you could quit. People do it all the time. They do it when their family is struggling. When their mental health is struggling. When their marriage is.'

This last comment catches me by surprise. Sure, this is the one thing Jamie and I argue about, but I'd hardly say that constitutes our marriage struggling. The summer in Asia was the most fun we've had in years. Then there's the fact he sent me roses to my workplace only two days ago. That hardly feels like the characteristics of someone who's not feeling secure in their marriage. I go to take another gulp of my wine, only to find the glass is already empty.

'It'll be better this year,' I say, reaching for the bottle to top myself up. 'I promise it will be better.'

But even as I fill my glass and take a well-needed sip, I can't help but wonder if that's a promise I can keep.

10

The next morning, I offer to take Sasha to school, just to drop her off, maybe have a little conversation, but she says she wants to get the bus.

I'll admit, I'm relieved. It's a ten-minute detour, and I have so much to do at work that I wasn't even sure I could spare the time. Besides, I don't think it would be the most pleasant journey.

All night, I wanted to bring up with Jamie what he said about our marriage struggling. I can't believe that's honestly the way he feels. We're the type of couple who talk through our problems before they can escalate. We always have been. That's the reason I've always considered us so strong. Deep down, I'm sure it was just a spur-of-the-moment thing for him to say. He knows how tough it was for me last year, and I know he only wants what's best for me. Adding to that how upset he would have been with the memory of everything Sasha went through, then it's probably not surprising he made such a harsh comment. But I need to bring it up at some point. Find out what I can do – short of handing in my notice – to prove to him that this year is going to be different.

As always, there are dozens of emails waiting for me when I get to school, from both parents and teachers, though I'm surprised to find there are none from Florence. Part of me thought there would be. Not an apology. No, she'd never go that far. Just something to let me know the message from Sandra had got through. Perhaps it's a good sign there isn't. Perhaps she's learned that her smarmy, saccharin words can't sway me anymore. That I won't be a pushover this year. I can't be. If my family is struggling because of the job I'm doing, then it sure as hell needs to be worth it.

Amongst the emails are several staff requests for leave. It's a school rule that these must come in during the first week of term, but, even if they're in on the first day, there's a good chance I won't be able to accept them. It's always crappy. Teachers are bound to their holidays, regardless of whose wedding or important event they have to miss. Six weeks in the summer is great, as long as you have enough in the coffers to pay double what flights would be at any other time of the year. And don't get me started on the amount of work we have to do in that time either.

Amongst the requests for leave, there's also news about one of our older members of staff. She'd been under treatment for much of last year, and we'd hoped that she was fully fit and ready to be back in the classroom this year. Unfortunately, less than a week in, and it looks like that won't be the case. The doctor has already signed her off work for the next two weeks and, if I had to hedge my bets, I'd say it's going to go on a lot longer.

Knowing I need to put something in place, I look at what options are available to us, only to fall down a rabbit hole of numbers and budgets, so much so that I forget what time it is, until the bell rings.

'Shit!' I glance at my watch. This sixth-form assembly, my last assembly for the week, and I know the kids will already be filling into the hall. Just like on the gate, I'm meant to be there, ready and welcoming them. Normally, I try to get in at least ten minutes early, so I can get the projector screen down and my computer set up. It doesn't matter how much of our budget goes on ICT; nothing ever works. I'm not saying I want to go back to the days of chalk and blackboard, but I can see it would have its advantages.

Making sure that the presentation I need is open on my computer, I pick up my laptop and rush through the building to the hall.

As I get there, the last straggling Year 12s and 13s are taking their seats.

'Looking good, miss,' I hear one of them mutter. I look around and they all turn quickly away, giggling to one another. I glance down at my outfit, wondering if maybe I've spilled something down me, but there's nothing on my clothes that I can see. It could well have been a genuine comment. The kids here can be like that. Say things that perhaps students at a normal state comprehensive wouldn't.

Deciding it must have been some off-the-cuff comment, I look up at the stage.

The projector screen is already down, and an image is taking up the whole side of the wall. But it's not the image from the Life After School Presentation I'd prepared for them. A presentation that is currently open and waiting on my laptop. It's a picture of a young woman, probably in her early twenties, with a pint glass in one hand, and a wineglass in the other. She grins at the camera. Or tries to at least. From the way her eyes are half-closed and head tilted to the side, it's obvious that she is completely inebriated. The drunken, partying atmosphere is a long way from the image of a responsible adult we promote at St Anne's, as is the attire she's wearing. The high-cut, hot-pink leotard is low plunging, and even with a pair of eighties leg warmers, the outfit leaves very little to the imagination.

But what's most alarming isn't the attire or the drinks. What's most alarming is that it's a picture of me.

11

For a split second, I stare at the photo, certain I'm mistaken, but I know I'm not. A photo of me, dressed in an utterly inappropriate outfit, and clearly drunk out of my mind, is on display to the entire sixth form. How? Why? What the hell is going on?

The questions flit through my mind, but they last barely a second. Within a heartbeat, I'm marching towards the stage, climbing up the steps and striding across to the podium.

George, the youngest member of the technology team, is there, but I can't tell what he's doing.

'George, what is this? Get that off the screen!' I hiss, trying to keep my voice at a level the students won't be able to hear, though given the way these old halls like to echo, it's unlikely.

'It's jammed. I can't get it off,' George says. 'I'm not sure what's going on. Someone's put it as a lock and home screen.' He's not the most forthright person at the best of times, but his voice sounds like it's about to crack.

'Then just pull the bloody plug out,' I bark.

There's no chance the students didn't hear that. Their chattering erupts to another level, but I don't even tell them to stop talking the way I normally would. Instead, my eyes are locked on the photo. It's not one I've seen before, even though it's definitely a young me on the screen. I stand there, trying to recall when exactly it was taken. It doesn't take long for the memory to hit.

It was part way through my teacher training. Alice and I were already pretty close then, and it was her birthday. We went to London on the train with several other women from our teacher-training group before we headed to our hotel, and got changed for the evening. Obviously, the theme was eighties.

The plan was a bar crawl, carefully mapped out to make sure we ended up back in a club in Camden that was within easy walking distance of the hotel.

The entire night had been filled with drinking and dancing. We needed to let our hair down. We were nearly two terms into our teaching placement and had already lost four people from the course who'd struggled to keep up with the constant pressures. It was nights like these that allowed us to recharge and keep going. Of course, it helped that social media wasn't really a thing back then. You could get drunk, do things a little crazy and not worry about it appearing all over the internet the next day.

But this night was memorable for more than just the eighties theme. We were a couple of bars away from the club when we bumped into a group of fully-trained teachers from our placement school. All men. They were there on a stag do, and all a fair bit older than us. The chances of it happening were so slim. I mean, of all the bars in London we could have been in, we ended up there with them. That was when the drinking and partying kicked up another notch. After all, they weren't students like we were. These guys had actual salaries. A couple were even heads of department.

We didn't leave until the club kicked us out, at which point, we staggered towards the hotel.

Alice and I had booked a hotel room to share for the night, and we did – just not with each other. That was the first night I spent with the art teacher. The night, the morning, the entire weekend... Things heated up between us pretty fast, and I saw him a couple of times afterwards, but it was never going to be anything long term. Not in the real world. A month later, I moved to my next school placement, and that was that.

But, as for the photo, I can't think how that would have ended up here, in my school hall. My heart is pounding against my ribs as I try to work out what the hell is going on. I don't doubt the photo is real. People always used to take digital cameras out with them in the days before phones and there are probably hundreds of shots like this, backed up on forgotten hard drives. But I don't think I even saw any of them from this night. I sure as hell didn't expect to be looking at them here, with two hundred sixth formers behind me.

'Got it,' George says and the screen finally goes black.

Even with the picture gone, I feel physically sick. That photo is the epitome of the behaviour I'm meant to be telling our students to avoid, not act as an ambassador for, and it's clear this gossip is going to be all over the school by break time.

I clear my throat, and a couple of them lower the chatting by a fraction. My palms are slicked with sweat as the enormity of what has just happened sinks in. My privacy has been violated. By George? Never in a million years would I imagine the geeky tech support worker doing something like that. Yet the evidence is there, plain as day.

I turn around, ready to launch into him and find out what the hell he was playing at, but he's already scurrying for the door, and I've got twenty per cent of the school looking at me. Waiting for me to respond. There's nothing I can do. Not while I'm standing up on the stage.

The only way I'd survive complete and utter humiliation is if they think it was something deliberate. That I somehow wanted to make this look like a stunt. A way to teach them a lesson. And so, taking a deep breath in, I step up to the podium.

'Morning, Sixth Form,' I say, addressing the students. 'You can see, I've got quite a lesson for you today. A lesson that people of your age need to know even more than young me up there with my dubious taste in clothing did. We are in a world where your footprint lives for ever in wires and electrons. Your actions will follow you wherever you go in the world. So you need to make sure that twenty years later, when you're applying for that dream job, or looking at adopting a family perhaps, there's nothing in that footprint that can come back and bite you.'

12

The minute the assembly ends, I'm straight down to the IT office.

It's over the other side of the school, in an area that was stable blocks when the building was still a house. Given the expense of items stored in the tech office, there is a keypad on the outside so only people with the code can get in. When I took over the job, I discovered that the tech department had kept this code a secret from everyone. Including the head. It was something I swiftly put an end to, though they dug their heels in, waffling on about expensive and delicate items, as if I was an idiot. So I made it simple. I explained to them that, as the head of the school, I needed access to every room on the grounds and, if they didn't agree to give me the code, I would move their office so it was next to mine. It wasn't a great way to start our relationship.

The plan had worked, and they gave me the code. However, when I popped in during the half-term holiday because my mouse had broken and I needed a new one, I discovered they had changed it without telling me.

I didn't bother treading lightly. Instead, I sent an email, CC'ing in the maintenance department, informing them all that the tech support team would be moving into the main building the following week. A desperate flurry of emails followed and in the end, I allowed them to stay where they were on a probationary period. That time came and went and I have been informed of every code change since.

With my blood pounding in my ears, I punch into the code and march into the office.

George is sitting behind one of six desks that fill the space. Six desks, although there has never been more than three members of the department. The other three are covered in junk. That's probably the wrong thing to say. I'm sure it's not actually junk. I'm sure they need all these keyboards and unattached monitors and other things that are scattered all over the place, but I can't for the life of me imagine why. Normally, Carl and Kevin are sitting at two of the other desks hiding away behind their screens, but right now neither are here, which is good, because I don't need any witnesses for the way I'm about to go off.

'What the hell was that, George?' I demand.

'I... I don't know,' he stutters. His bottom lip is wobbling as if he's never been shouted at before and is about to cry, but I couldn't care less. He's an adult who just exposed a private photo of me to all my sixth-form students. 'I don't know what happened, Mrs Croft.'

He sounds like a student, rather than a member of staff, but that doesn't come as a surprise. George used to attend St Anne's and was in his final year when I got my first job here. After that, he went away to university, but in his second year his dad died. Suicide. My heart bled for him.

He had a chance to do anything. Go anywhere. Instead, he came back here. He already knew how most of the systems worked from when he was at the school and when he came asking for help, there just happened to be a position open. Now it's like he feels this weird underling status to the staff because of it. Like he still can't call them by their first name. I think the only reason he's happy to do so with me is because I never actually taught him. But using my first name happens under normal circumstances, and this is anything but.

'What do you mean, you don't know?' I snap. 'It was your computer, wasn't it? Your computer had an image of me up on the screen. A completely private and inappropriate image.'

He shakes his head. 'No, no. It wasn't my computer. I just got a ticket saying that you needed help with the projector. That was all. I came down, and it was already on there. The computer and picture were already there.'

'A ticket?' That's what we call it when someone goes onto the system and says they need help with something ICT-related. It takes a fraction longer than an email to send, but it helps the tech department know where to prioritise and allocate their help. 'Show me,' I say.

He nods rapidly and taps away at his computer before sliding to the side so I can see his screen.

'It's that one, at the top,' he says, as I'm faced with a long list of things staff want sorting out. I knew a lot of our teachers struggled with ICT, but some of these requests are ridiculous. There are at least three asking for help setting up the online calendars, despite me sending step-by-step videos showing exactly how to do it. But I don't have time to consider the staff's incompetency at the moment. I'm looking at the ticket at the top. The one that says it's sent from my email.

'I didn't send you this,' I say. 'This hasn't come from my email. How has this happened?'

'I, I, I don't know... You just... you just put in a... an email on the ticket.' I didn't realise George had a stutter before now. I guess he only does it when he's nervous. 'They... they must have put in yours.'

He's right. I never understood why you had to put in an email for the tickets even though we were all on the school system, but it's the way it's always been. Which means anyone could have sent it.

George is still looking remarkably close to tears, which, considering he's nearly thirty, is not a look I expected. Which means he's either telling the truth or he's such a good actor that he seriously shouldn't be working in our IT office.

I let out a sound somewhere between a groan and a sigh. 'I want to know exactly who put that computer up there and who sent the ticket and I want to know now, do you understand?'

13

George tells me he'll look into it as soon as he can, but he has various tickets from teachers who can't get their interactive whiteboards and printers working. Do I want it to be a priority?

I grit my teeth. 'Do those jobs, then get on it,' I say. 'And come to my office when you find out who's behind this. I don't want you sending this by email, understand?'

He nods. I think he's too afraid to speak again.

Swallowing back the fury that's filling me, I turn around and march back towards the main building and my office.

I've been sitting at my desk for less than ten minutes when my door swings open. After the incident yesterday with Sandra, I can't believe she'd be as foolish as to walk into my office without even knocking first. As such, I'm ready to launch into her, when an entirely different face appears in front of me. Alice. The only person I don't mind walking into my office without knocking first, assuming I'm not in a meeting, that is.

'Did I just hear right: that you had a photo of you in your underwear on stage in front of all the sixth form?' She leans on the back of the chair as she speaks. 'My class won't stop talking about it.'

I press my fingers into the bridge of my nose, trying to rub away the headache I can already feel forming.

'It wasn't my underwear; it was a body suit. An eighties-style bodysuit, you know, from when we used to go out in fancy dress. It's from twenty years ago.'

Alice frowns. 'And why did you show that to them?'

The headache kicks up a notch.

'I didn't do it deliberately. I didn't do it at all.' I love Alice like she's a sister, but I can't deal with this now. 'Don't you have a lesson? Aren't you meant to be teaching?'

'I've got sixth form. Not that they can do any work. They're way too hyper after that assembly, so I set them a fifteen-minute improvisation task and told them I was going to the loo.' She shifts her position so she has one hand on her hip. 'So what the hell happened? Was it on your computer and you just forgot?'

'Of course it wasn't. Like I said, I didn't put it up there.'

'I don't understand?'

'You're not the only one,' I say, before letting out a deep groan. She's obviously not going to go until she gets some answers. Not that I have much to give. I glance at my computer, take a long breath in. 'I don't know what happened,' I say truthfully. 'When I came into the hall, the picture was up. I don't know whose computer it was, or where they got the photo from. It was just on there for everyone to see.'

'Seriously?'

'Yes, seriously.'

Finally, she seems to get it. Her eyebrows knit tightly together and her face pales.

'So someone planted it there?' Her voice is substantially quieter now. 'Why would they do that?'

I take a deep breath in. I don't know how to answer. It's the question I've been asking myself constantly and I genuinely have no idea what someone would think they could gain from such a stunt.

Before I can reply, a ping on my computer announces an email has come through. Almost immediately there's another, then another. The subject lines are all remarkably similar.

Inappropriate Attire.
Unacceptable Photographs.

At any other school, I could have hoped this could go by relatively unscathed, but I'm at a Catholic school. And while eighty per cent of the parents just send their kids here because of the grades we get, the other twenty per cent are far stauncher in their beliefs.

'Alice, I'd better deal with this. Hopefully, I can nip it in the bud before the shit really hits the fan.'

She looks at me, a deep dent between her brows where she's frowning.

'Good luck,' she says. 'Just call me if you need me.'

'I will do.'

As much as I want to get this shitshow sorted as quickly as possible, the next email that enters my inbox tells me that won't happen. It's from Florence and the subject says it all.

Concerning incident.

For once, I can't disagree with her. This is a seriously concerning situation, and no one wants to get to the bottom of it more than I do. Despite the title, the body of the email is scant. She doesn't even mention what the incident was, only that she wants a face-to-face. Although she turned up in my office entirely unannounced and unwelcome yesterday, she writes that she is currently unavailable until Monday morning. She has booked me in for 11 a.m. Anything else on my calendar is to be cleared.

Surprisingly, I'm relieved by this. It means I've got time to work out who the hell did this. And why.

14

I wait until 2 p.m. before I go back across school to speak to George. I know I could ring him. I've got the ICT office extension on a laminated piece of card by my phone, but I want to talk to him face-to-face. The situation is delicate, I don't want it to be overheard and, somehow, I don't think George would think of something like that. I could easily imagine him divulging a load of sensitive information about the situation with Carl and Kevin right there, listening in on every word.

Unfortunately, when I reach the office, Carl is the only person present. Carl, who is quite possibly the most unhelpful man in all existence. During my first couple of years at the school, I tried to get him onside. I thought maybe he was going through something, or that he just had difficulty communicating with people. It turns out he's just an arsehole.

He's been in the IT office longer than time itself. Or at least that's what it feels like. And I've no idea how he hasn't been sacked yet. He's rude to absolutely every female member of staff, while just being mildly obtuse with the men. More than once, he's changed the entire system's passwords because he decided

there was some sort of security breach, but didn't tell anybody.
Not to mention the fact that, for two weeks at the end of last year,
we couldn't access school data because he was doing a system
upgrade that was apparently going to help streamline the work-
load. He is up there with Sandra in terms of people I want to get
rid of. I figure another year, and George will be up to taking his
job, and I'll have enough information on Carl to get rid of him
without any backlash. And people think being a headteacher is
about looking after the students.

'Where's George?' I say, not bothering with niceties.

'The printer in the main building packed up again. He's
helping reprographics.' Carl doesn't look up as he says this.
Instead, he's typing away on his computer.

A surge of annoyance billows through me.

'Could you not have done that?' I say. 'I needed George to
work on something for me. Something important.'

'Aye, I heard. But the printer packed up. He's the one who
deals with that.'

Tension ripples down through my hands, and my fingers
twitch slightly, but somehow I stop myself from forming fists.

'I understand,' I say, trying to keep my tone neutral. 'What I
asked is why you couldn't have helped with that. Particularly if
you knew I needed him to work on something.'

Finally, Carl's head snaps up and his glare meets mine.

'I've spent the last half an hour sorting out the speakers in the
French classroom, because they wanted to do listening or something and the holiday cleaning staff had unplugged everything.
And I mean everything. Interactive whiteboard, hard drive, monitor. Before that, I was trying to get one of the trainees into their
computer because they'd somehow locked themselves out.
Before that, I was dealing with the new interactive assessment
tool the maths department are using, and that's before I've got

onto adding the new kids onto the system, and updating the firewall so someone can't just break in and steal all our information. And you've probably forgotten we've got an entire system update tomorrow, but you'll sure as hell notice if your damn email stops working.'

'Okay, I get it,' I say, though I'm torn between wanting to inch away from him and wanting to yell at him even more.

He drops his head back down to the keyboard and recommences his typing even harder than before. 'Like hell you do,' he mutters.

I stay there for a minute longer, almost mute at the disrespect this man has just shown me. I know I'm not alone. Carl is a dick to absolutely everyone, but you think he'd have a bit more respect for his boss. Apparently not.

A minute later, I clear my throat.

'Just tell George to come and find me,' I say, before turning and marching out the door.

It's gone three when Sandra buzzes through to tell me that George has come to the office. I tell her to let him straight in.

'So,' I say, standing up the minute he enters, 'have you found out whose computer it is? Or where they got the photo from.'

He flushes.

'The staffroom printer...' he begins. And I know just where this conversation is going.

Drawing in a lungful of air, I force myself to smile.

'It's fine. I know you were run off your feet today. We all are. It's the start of term. Just make it a priority tomorrow, okay? I'll email Carl and Kevin. Tell them you're off tickets for the morning. I need you to sort this out. Okay?'

He nods his head rapidly. 'Okay. Is that it then? Can I go?'

There's nothing else to say. I can't make him stay late just because I want answers, and it's not like I want to be here any longer than necessary.

With a slight sigh, I nod.

'Yes, it's fine. But you need to work on this tomorrow. Do you understand?'

'Yes, Mrs Croft,' he says. A moment later, he's gone.

15

I try to stay at work late. Keeping on top of things at the beginning of term is really the only key to not drowning in this job. There are several emails from heads of year, and heads of department, all needing clarification or support, but after answering the first couple – and taking three times longer than I normally would – I realise just how unproductive I'm being. Glancing at my watch, I give myself an internal pep-talk, telling myself to get my act together. Sometimes, it works. I've given myself a thoroughly hard kick up the arse on more than one occasion. However, when I'm still staring at the screen half an hour later, I know it's time to pack up and head home. Fingers crossed, I'll be in a better frame of mind to work there, though somehow I doubt it.

As I turn into the driveway, I wonder whether I should even broach the topic of the photo with Jamie. It feels like it will bring an added pressure into the house when that's the last thing we need. I definitely have no intention of mentioning it to Sasha, but as it happens, I don't need to. She already knows.

For the first time since term began, she's not hiding up in her room. Instead, she's downstairs, sitting at the dining room table, with her laptop open in front of her. She looks pretty focused, although the moment she sees me, she is on her feet.

'So, I hear you've been showing sexy pictures of yourself to the sixth form,' she says.

'How do you know about that?' I ask, a current of tension rising in me. Having a mum who is head teacher to all your old school friends is embarrassing enough, but this could be the next level of humiliation for her. Which is why I'm surprised when she rolls her eyes in the most typical teenage fashion and a slight smirk flickers on her lips.

'I do still have friends at St Anne's,' she says. 'And I'm in a lot of WhatsApp groups. So is your photo, for that matter.'

On the one hand, I'm pleased. Not about the photo being shared. No, that I'm not pleased about at all. But Sasha's response is far better than I could have dreamed. Twenty-four hours ago, she refused to even look at me. Now she's talking like everything's fine. Just like when we were travelling around Asia. Even with this relief, my sense of apprehension grows tauter. I know my daughter. I know she doesn't forgive and forget that easily, but maybe if she's acting like everything is okay between us, then that's probably how she wants things to be.

'What was it for?' Jamie says, coming and kissing me lightly. 'Sasha showed me the picture. It didn't seem very St Anne's of you to share it.'

'I didn't share it. I have no idea who put it up there or why.'

The smirk drops from Sasha's face.

'Are you serious?'

'Afraid so. I guess it was some kind of prank. Someone wanting to have a laugh at my expense. I've asked George to see if he can find out where it came from, and what computer they used, but he's been crazily busy today. I'm hoping he has time to find it out before the weekend, though, as the governors want a meeting on Monday.'

There are no smirks anywhere in the room now. Jamie is looking at me with his eyes wide, and I can tell he's got a load more questions he wants to ask, just not with Sasha in the room. I'm about to send her upstairs, under the guise of more oboe practice, when she speaks again.

'What do you need George for? It's just a basic reverse image search, right? I'm sure I can do it.'

'You can?' I say, not sure if I'm pleased by this or not. I want to find out where this photo has come from, but I don't want to get Sasha involved. Then again, maybe me letting her do this could be a way to build back some of the bridges I burned yesterday.

Which is why I slip into the seat next to her and say, 'What do you need?'

16

Sasha is a genius when it comes to computers, and that's not just her mother talking. She really is. She's been coding on children's programmes since she was six years old, defragging my old work PC when she was ten and now she regularly tries to talk to me about things like Python and GUI frameworks and I nod along, although I don't have a clue what she's saying.

The thing is, she's not that bothered about it. Just like she's not that bothered about maths, or science, or any other subjects, even though her teachers have told her she could go on and study any of her choosing. That doesn't mean she neglects them. She's a straight-A student across the board, but music has always been her thing. Orchestral music.

When she joined her first orchestra at nine, everything else paled into insignificance. I think it's the patterns. The rhythms, the notes. She tells me it's all so closely linked to maths and computers that they could almost be taught together. I don't believe her, but I still appreciate her skills. She's the one who taught me how easy it was to use digital calendars, and she's also set up a system that clears the history on my school laptop at the end of every evening. Apparently, it keeps the computer fast, and also means I can't accidentally bring up real-estate websites I was browsing the night before during a presentation to SLT. All teachers use their computers for personal use. It's a fact. But, as the head, I have to at least look like I don't.

Jamie leaves us to it, heading off to fetch a takeaway for dinner, while Sasha airdrops the photo across from her phone. A moment later, it's four times the size, taking up the entire screen of my laptop. Looking at it like this has my stomach in knots all over again. My cleavage is so revealing it's ridiculous, while my hair is slicked back from sweat. It must have been right near the end of the night. Or the end of the club, at least.

'Have you used this as your profile picture?' Sasha says, opening the internet and tapping away as she talks. 'That's the most obvious thing. If you've had it as your profile picture at some point, anyone online can scan back through all your previous profiles and find it.'

'That was what I thought but I checked. Besides, I don't think I've actually seen the photo before.'

'Seriously?'

'Seriously. Those aren't the type of images you share when you're trying to make a good impression teaching.'

Back then, I had only been at the very start of my career, but I knew from the get-go that teaching was what I wanted to do. That meant maintaining an air of professionalism. Then again, I was out with a bunch of teachers. Maybe I thought it would be okay?

'So you're one hundred per cent sure it didn't come from your Facebook?' Sasha asks.

'I'm pretty sure,' I say, my certainty already wavering. 'I had a look while I was still at school, and couldn't even find any from that night out. Unless I'm missing something?'

'There's a chance you could have archived the album,' Sasha says, already tapping away. 'Let me have a look.'

I've no idea what she's clicking on her screen, but she seems pretty confident. A few moments later, Sasha's talking at me again.

'Wow, there are some pretty bad pictures here,' she says. 'Why would you use that one for your profile? The entire horizon is wonky. And exactly how much eyeliner were you wearing here?'

I'm only half listening to her. I did exactly what Sasha is doing now while I sat at my school desk, and I came up empty. The more I think about it, the more I'm convinced I didn't use that photo on my profile. I was in that strange limbo between an irresponsible student and a responsible teacher. Irresponsible enough to drunkenly stumble into bed with another, far older teacher who worked at the same school, but responsible enough to keep any incriminating photos from that night hidden. Yes, the more I think about it, the more certain I am that I wouldn't have made any photos of that night public. Not when there was the chance of something incriminating lurking in the background. And while I hadn't been working in schools that long, I already knew how gossip could spread like wildfire around the hallways. The last thing I wanted was for one of the staffroom busybodies to start asking questions about who was out and what trouble people got into. For reasons beyond the art teacher technically being my superior, we'd wanted to keep our relationship on the downlow. Not that you could even call it a relationship, given how it was over almost as quickly as it started.

'You're right. No sign of it here,' Sasha says, when she's gone through every profile picture I've used in the last two decades.

'So what does that mean?' A hollowness is forming in my gut. Once we'd sat down together, I'd assumed Sasha would get to the bottom of it. That ten minutes with her and I could go to the governors and tell them exactly who was to blame for trying to make a fool out of me. Now I can see it's not going to be that simple. Still, rather than looking dismayed at the failure, a small smile curls up on the corners of Sasha's lips.

'It means we are going to have to dig a little deeper,' she says.

17

I consider myself more tech savvy than the average person my age. I have to be in my job; we are constantly introducing new systems for everything from budgeting to lesson planning and, even though I'm not in the classroom using most of them, I have to have a vague idea what they all do. But this reverse image search is something new to me.

'Okay, how does it work?' I ask.

My question elicits yet another eye roll from Sasha.

'It's really not that special,' she says. 'You just take the photo. Copy it. And paste it into the search bar. Give it a second and... there you go.'

Just like she says, it really is that simple. Within a couple of seconds, the entire screen has filled with pictures, all of which are connected to the original. Mostly they are of women. Quite a few are clearly adverts from fancy dress shops, and there are one or two perfectly posed celebrity shots too, but others are more candid like mine. For a second, I get distracted by the ones that don't seem to fit in with the rest. Images not of women, but of rooms. That's when I realise this search has even picked up on the club. It's a tool for sure, but for some reason, it makes me feel nervous.

'Doesn't look like there are any exact matches,' Sasha says, before scrolling down a little further. 'Scrap that. Hold on, I think we have a winner.'

My stomach lurches as Sasha clicks on the photo before I've found it.

Within a heartbeat, it takes up every inch of room on the screen and I can't draw my eyes away.

There I am on the internet, in all my eighties get-up glory for the entire world to see. I don't know why it makes me feel so sick. I've never been under any illusion as to the type of world we live in now. The type of world where what you do is tracked and monitored and stored forever, so if people want to hunt things down about you badly enough, they can. The thing is, I've never thought anyone would want to. If you're going to track someone, there are billions of more interesting people to choose from. I shake the thought away. No one is tracking me or hunting me down. This is just some silly prank.

'It's almost identical, just cropped down, that's all,' Sasha says, but I'm still only half listening to her. My gaze is still locked on the laptop, and it's like I'm in the assembly hall again, with all the children staring at me and laughing. I think of all the emails I still haven't responded to. They'll have doubled by now, if not more. It's the type of smouldering fire I should have put out before it could spread, but I didn't know what to say. I will in a minute, though. In a minute, I'll know exactly who's to blame.

I take a deep breath in and find my voice again.

'Okay,' I say. 'Can you find out where it's from? Who posted it?'

'It should be easy enough.'

She taps on the screen a couple of times before letting out a slight tut that I know is her sign of frustration, although it's normally used when she's struggling to learn the line of some concerto, rather than helping me out.

'What is it?' I ask, my gut corkscrewing.

'It's from a MySpace account,' Sasha says.

'MySpace?'

'Yeah, you know. Old people used it before Facebook, to chat and share music and stuff.'

'I know what MySpace is,' I say, too focused on the task in hand to chastise Sasha for the use of the word *old*. 'Well, whose profile is it on?'

This time, I know it isn't mine. I was pretty slow to the whole social media uptake and people were already flocking to Facebook by the time I caught on. The page I have now is the only profile I've ever had. Unfortunately, rather than respond to me, Sasha makes that same tutting noise again.

'What is it? What's wrong?'

She draws a long breath in.

'It's just trickier, that's all. MySpace tends to archive a lot of info and then there was this whole big thing a few years ago. Loads of data was deleted and—'

'Sasha, can you find out who the picture belongs to or not?'

'Assuming the account is still active, and the user is still logging on, I should be able to. Just give me one more minute... and... bingo.'

She clicks on the screen. A moment later, the image is small again, part of a much bigger page with other photos and text around it. Though my eyes have gone to the top. To the name.

'You say this page is still active?' I ask.

Once again, Sasha doesn't reply immediately. Instead, she recommences her tapping.

'Yup. She logged on two days ago.' The sickness that was already swirling through me surges in waves.

'That can't be right,' I say, shaking my head. But Sasha sees it just as clear as I can. The photo came from the page of one Alice Fortune. My Alice.

18

My throat has closed shut. It doesn't make sense. Alice couldn't have shared the photo. She couldn't. She's my best friend. A heat floods through me and I grapple at reasons as to why I would find the photo there on a MySpace account that she is still using, but I know nothing about. I scroll up and down the page, wondering if perhaps it's a fake profile, but there are recent pictures of Alice on it too. Pictures taken of her in the summer, travelling. Pictures of her at home, posing with a cup of tea and a book. Pictures I've never seen.

With my heart pounding against my ribs, I stop. Wordlessly, I go back to the photo of me. A flicker of hope ignites as I note something.

'They're not exactly the same,' I say, pointing at the picture. 'This one is far more zoomed in. Right, you can see that? It's only got a small amount in the background. The photo on the screen had more. Much more.'

I take Sasha's phone, wanting to see the original image so I can compare, but I don't know her password. Thankfully, she already knows what I want, and takes it from me. A moment later, I'm looking at the two images side by side.

It's not a massive difference; I'm in the same pose in both, but the one from assembly panned out a little further so that you can see the table. I'm resting my elbow on a table next to me. That's not in Alice's photo.

'So, is it the same?' I say to Sasha. I trust my daughter. All I need her to say is that Alice's picture definitely isn't the one used to humiliate me and I'll start looking for alternatives.

She pulls the laptop back across to her. A pause lingers in the air before she speaks.

'Well, someone could have used AI to expand the background,' Sasha says. 'It's pretty easy to do now.'

'So, what does that mean?'

'That means that anyone who had this image could have made the background a bit bigger? Or that the one we are seeing here is a cropped version, which is probably a more likely reason.'

'So, anyone who downloaded it from her page?' I voice my thoughts as I piece it all together. 'Any of her friends who had access to it, right? I assume it's the same on MySpace as it would be on Facebook.'

'Right, it would depend on the privacy settings she's chosen.'

'And you can check those?'

'I'm already doing it now,' Sasha says, not looking away from the screen. It's another minute before she speaks again. 'Okay, so she's got it set to friends only. Same as you normally do on Facebook.'

Relief should fill me. After all, just because it's on Alice's page, it doesn't mean that she's the one who's guilty. It wasn't like I was going to blame myself if I found the original image on my social media. The same rules apply here. And yet I can hear the 'but' hanging on Sasha's lips. There's more she wants to say, and she doesn't want me to hear it.

'What is it? What are you thinking?' I ask.

Sasha takes a deep breath in and my nerves kick up another notch as her attention moves away from me to the computer. It's not because she needs to look at the photo, but because she doesn't want to look me in the eye. I can already feel it.

'Well, like we said earlier, the most reasonable explanation for the difference between them is that Aunty Alice cropped it before she put in online.'

'Cropped?'

'Yes, so the one that went up in the assembly is the original.'

'The original? You mean the one that Aunty Alice took?'

She nods, offering a quick shrug at the same time.

'It's just one possibility, that's all,' she says.

'But if that's the case, then Alice is the only one who has access to it?' I say.

There's no denying the way Sasha's eyes are avoiding me now. Or the nausea that is so strong, it's making me dizzy.

'Like I said,' Sasha says. 'It's just a possibility.'

19

I wait for Jamie to have dished up the food before I tell him what we've found out. His response is immediate.

'No. No way. You can't possibly believe that Alice did it.'

'No... No, I don't,' I say, confident in the matter. The more I've mulled it over, the more sure I am that Alice had nothing to do with it. She's an entirely innocent victim, like me. Someone just used her photo, that was all. 'Whoever did it felt they had something to gain by humiliating me. That can't be her.'

'Well, have you spoken to her about it?' Jamie asks. 'Told her where you think the photo came from? At least that way she can take down any other embarrassing images from your past.'

I take a mouthful of butter chicken and chew it extra slowly as I work out how to explain my thoughts.

'I don't want to yet. I want to get to the bottom of it first. Sasha said there's a good chance it's someone on Alice's friends list. We were about to start looking through it when you came back. Once I've done that, I should have something more concrete to tell her.'

'So you're going to accuse Alice's friends instead of Alice herself.'

'I'm going to get a list of suspects together. That's all,' I say, not sure if that sounds any better. 'I need to have something to give the governors when I meet with Florence on Monday.'

'Something that doesn't involve throwing Alice under the bus?' Jamie asks.

His doubt stings a little. The fact that he could even think that makes me wonder how he actually views me as a person. Not to mention I'm the one he should be the most concerned about. I'm the real victim in all this, and yet it seems like he doesn't even remember that. Anger at the memory of his previous comments rise within me, but knowing I'm both hungry and tired, I shake them away before they can settle.

'Come on, we should eat up,' I say. 'I've still got work to do tonight.'

'Actual work, or investigative?'

'Both,' I reply.

* * *

An hour and a bottle of wine later, and I'm going through Alice's contact list.

'This is getting a little sinister,' Jamie says, topping up my glass of wine, even though I probably don't need anymore. 'I thought you said it was a prank. One of the kids.'

'I assumed it was. But how would a kid even think to look on MySpace for an incriminating photo of me? Ninety-nine per cent of them don't even know it exists. Not to mention, I don't see how they could have got past all the security stuff on the school computer to put the photo as the lock screen and everything. Sasha doesn't think she would be able to, so I find it hard to believe any other kids there could.'

'Then maybe the school computer is where you should focus your attention, rather than your best friend,' Jamie says.

I don't respond because I've just noticed something on Alice's page. Something I didn't expect to see.

'Okay, that's weird. Seriously weird. Alice is friends with Nathan and Nathan's kid.'

'Nathan as in assistant head Nathan?' Jamie asks.

I nod. 'And Leo. He only left last year. She'd never be friends with an ex-student. It's against all the rules.' Not to mention utterly bizarre. Most of the friends on her page, I don't recognise, at least not well. There are a few names that are familiar. A couple of people that I probably met at her wedding and hen do. But there's no one there from her current life. I mean, I'm her best friend, and I'm not even on the list.

'Why would she be friends with Leo?' I say, more to myself than Jamie.

It was the talk of the school when they first arrived – how Nathan could be so young and have a child Leo's age. I never pried, but it was clear he got a girl knocked up when he was only seventeen. It's actually one of the things I respect about him – not getting a girl pregnant so young, that would be ridiculous – but how he is as an active dad. Always hands on. Never shirking any responsibilities. Basically, he's a decent parent.

Like Sasha, Leo's primary love in life is music, although their tastes are dramatically different. Leo was into the whole music production thing. He played in a school band, and from what I remember was an impressive guitarist and drummer, but he was also mixing, or remixing, or doing whatever it is people do to make songs.

Leo wasn't a bad kid or, at least, I didn't think so, until I got the job instead of Nathan. At that point, Leo showed a different side to his personality. One I didn't like one bit. He started telling students I shouldn't have got the job. Saying things like I only got it because I was a woman. That it was reverse sexism and the school would suffer because of it.

As I sit there with the memories filling me, it all starts to make sense.

Alice could easily have added him by mistake. We get constant friend requests from kids, despite them being told it's completely inappropriate. Even when the teachers use false names or turn on every privacy setting there is, the students still manage to find them. If Alice clicked accept, he would have jumped on the opportunity to find incriminating photos and humiliate me.

'He has friends who are still in the sixth form.' I speak my thoughts aloud. Trying to make sense of the words as they spill from my lips, but, the more I talk, the more it seems to make sense. 'I bet he did it for his dad. I bet Nathan spends all his time whingeing about how I shouldn't be Head. And Leo was such a daddy's boy. You know he only went on and studied maths because that's what Nathan wanted him to do. And he's not even got to uni yet. They start at the end of the month. He'll still be hanging around with his friends here.'

'Okay...' Jamie says slowly. 'So, assuming that's true, that's a pretty crazy accusation to make. And what about the computer issue? About making a photo the lock screen and everything?'

'I bet it's far easier to do if you have staff access, and I bet he knows every one of Nathan's passwords.' My heart is drumming hard again, but it's a steady, confident beat. I've got him. I know I have. 'So what do I do?' I ask Jamie, surprised by the amount of adrenaline flooding through me. 'Do I speak to Nathan in private, before I meet with the governors?'

'Without any actual evidence? That doesn't sound like a great idea. Surely you need to speak to the tech department again?

They must have some way of finding out who put the computer out there, at least. You need absolutely everything to be airtight. You can't go making accusations like this otherwise.'

'Of course. Of course it will be,' I say, unable to hide the flutter of excitement that's filling me. This might be just the thing I need to get Nathan Coles out of my life for good.

20

Given how many messages and emails I have waiting from parents distressed about my photograph, this is my first task on Friday. I send a generic email explaining that it was a learning exercise about the safety of technology and that awareness of such things is important to prepare for the future. It's all bullshit and I wonder if the parents can tell, but experience tells me they won't. Sometimes, I feel like half the emails I send out are bullshit.

Outside, it's raining and grey. It's a stark contrast to this time last year when the summer started in September. This year, summer looks well and truly over, as grey clouds fill the sky and a constant stream of drizzle runs down my window.

Weather affects the kids, and the staff, just like it affects animals. Nobody wants to work when it's grey outside. Nobody wants to embrace a day that is cloudy and cold. You want to sit curled up on the sofa watching TV – in my case, with a large glass of wine. Which is why, before I do anything else, I call Sandra into my office.

'Morning, Sandra. Did you have a good evening?' There it is again, my overly chirpy voice. And I know it grates on her. Which is why I try my hardest never to let it drop. 'Didn't you say you had the grandkids?'

She huffs, but I see her eye twitch. She's impressed by this. These are the kind of comments the old head would have made to her, probably before spending the next fifteen minutes scrolling through photos on her phone, rather than doing his actual job. That won't happen with me.

'She's going to be a stubborn little minx, this one,' Sandra says, I assume about the new grandchild. 'My son had it easy with the first one. Slept through the night. Barely cried. This one's not going to be like that at all. No, she's a right madam, proper tantrums and everything. I can tell that already.'

'Really? How old did you say she was?'

'Eight weeks.'

My back molars grind together. What sort of grandmother makes assumptions about a child when she's nothing more than a baby? Perhaps the poor thing was just screaming because she wanted to get out of Sandra's arms. I can't blame her for that. Still, I put my smile back in place.

'Oh, I'm sure she'll settle down soon enough,' I say. 'Now, I was hoping you could go into town for me? I thought we could do with a bit of a treat in the staffroom today. Doughnuts?'

She looks at me, her lips slightly parted and eyes wide, as if I've said the most ridiculous thing she's ever heard.

'On the first Friday? We haven't even done a full week.'

'You know, a bit of a pick-me-up. Everybody feels a bit grey about being back at work. Nothing major. I thought you could go to the doughnut shop. I think eight dozen should be enough, just the normal plain ones. You know, with the sugar glaze on them.'

Sandra is still looking at me like I'm insane.

'You want me to go get doughnuts for break time? They'd be better at lunch. People have got more time to come and eat then.'

'Maybe, but break is what I've said I want. I wasn't after an opinion, Sandra. Please, go and get them now.'

There is a change in my tone, and I hate myself for it, particularly as I see her eyes narrow and flicker with just a hint of satisfaction.

'There shouldn't be any problem with traffic as long as you go now. Eight boxes should do it,' I say, trying to smile again, although I know it's pointless. Finally, she gets the hint, and with a short scoff, turns around and leaves.

Eight dozen doughnuts sounds crazy, but we've got over fifty members of staff, and I know that plenty of them aren't going to stick to the one doughnut per person rule. I'd bet money that when the head of PE sees a box, he's going to pick up the whole thing and take it straight through to his department, despite the fact there are only six of them.

Then you get the people who have lunch and break in their classroom, rather than braving the canteen or the staffroom, marking children's assessments if they're the studious type, or just playing on their phones and avoiding company, if they're sensible. Either way, they won't hear about the doughnuts until the very end of break, and they won't be able to get to the staffroom until lunch.

Then there are the ones who think this is a complete free-for-all, not just for them, but for their family too. They'll think we won't notice as they wash out the Tupperware they brought their lunch in, and cram as many doughnuts as possible into it, to take home for their children or spouses.

I know it costs money. I'm aware of that. Which is why I

donate five hundred pounds to the staff funds out of my own pocket every single term. Is it buying people's affections? Probably not. They assume things like this come out of the school's pot, but, once last year, when people were really struggling, I tried it and it gave people a little pick-me-up. So I'm going to keep doing it for as long as it works. Or until Jamie asks where fifteen hundred pounds a year out of my account is going.

As much as I'd like to sit in my office and wait for Sandra to return with the doughnuts, I have places to be. Namely, my first lesson observations of the year.

The first Friday of term has to be the worst fucking day for the headteacher to come and observe you. Not that observations are ever fun if you're the teacher being observed. No, having other members of staff go in and nit-pick your lessons apart for the most minuscule details is a cause of maximum stress for most teachers, but it has to be done. But the first Friday of term? Well, it wouldn't be my choice, that's for sure. You don't know the class dynamics; the school is still in chaos and you have a thousand other jobs to get on with. So why am I doing it today?

One word. June.

Part of her job is putting together the observation timetable for all the newly employed – and, particularly, the newly qualified – teachers and she's scheduled them in to start now. I don't think it's malicious – the way it would be if Nathan had arranged it – I just don't think she sees things like everyone else. I know she spends at least half her holiday refining schemes of work and reflecting on all her lesson plans from the previous year, and she just doesn't get that not everyone does that. Some people have families and lives. Still, there's nothing I can do to change it now. Besides, it's good to know early if any of the new staff are going to need support. Most people can pull out one good lesson for an interview, but, if they manage it now, at this time of year, with all the pressures that come with a new working environment, then I know I picked right.

This time, it's Lucy Gadwell, the new Head of Art, and I hope it's not going to be shit. There's so much more paperwork involved when a lesson is shit.

21

The lesson is superb. Thank God. Despite having known the students less than a week, Lucy made a game of it, and the art they produced was seriously impressive given that they only had an hour. I can already tell she's the type of teacher who's going to inspire these children. Every year, we hold an art exhibition in the main hall. We pull out these fancy gilt frames that match the general aesthetic of the building and sometimes, the work the students produce is so good, I wish it could stay there permanently. Of course, sometimes it's pretty shit too.

'I'll get those observations written up and sent to you as soon as I can,' I say, smiling broadly and genuinely as I head back into the main building and upstairs to the staff room. Just as expected, Sandra has already placed the doughnuts out and one box has already gone. I'd bet my entire year's salary it's one of the PE staff, but I don't care. I have somewhere else to be. The real reason I ordered the doughnuts.

Grabbing a plate, I stack half a dozen as securely as I can, ready to carry halfway across the school. It's time to find out who took that computer.

'Morning, gentlemen,' I say, as I let myself into the tech office. Kevin – who is almost never in the room – is actually there for once. He looks up and is probably about to offer me some curt response when he sees that I've got a plate of doughnuts in my hand.

'Brought these down for you guys,' I say, trying to sound casual. 'I didn't know if you'd get a chance to go into the staffroom today. I know how busy you guys get down here.'

My words are a perfect contrast to my internal monologue. Of all the members of staff in the school, these are the ones that have the freedom to go to the staffroom whenever they want to, and take as many doughnuts as they like. They're not stuck on a schedule of lesson plans and break times and lunch duties like we all are. But they won't go to the staffroom anyway because they don't mix with anyone outside of this room.

'Thanks, Liz,' Kevin says, coming and taking the plate from me. 'I was feeling a bit peckish.' My line of sight involuntarily shifts over to his desk, which is littered with crisp packets and chocolate wrappers. It seems like he's already had a few sweet treats this morning. Then again, Kevin is a three-hundred-pound man; I can imagine he's peckish a lot of the time. He takes the plate over to his colleagues, at which point, George and Carl take one each, before Kevin takes the remaining four doughnuts on the plate, and sits down at his desk.

I shudder, not at the food, but at the selfishness, though I suspect the others are used to it. And it's not like it's something I'm going to call him out for.

Besides, I have another reason for being here.

Ignoring Kevin and his greediness, I switch my attention to the person I came to see.

'George, I just wondered if you had worked out anything

about that photograph yet? You know, where it came from or who put the computer there?'

His face pales to near translucent, and for a second I think he's going to tell me something horrendous, but, when he starts to speak, it comes out in a series of stutters.

'I... I... to, to, today. We, we... C, Carl...'

I have no idea what he's trying to tell me. But I don't need to. I turn to look at Carl, who is already on his feet, scowling straight at me.

'What he's saying is that today, when we've got to update the entire bloody system, we don't have time to be dealing with personal requests.'

'A personal request?' I say, stunned that he has the audacity to speak to me in such a way. 'This is a safeguarding issue within the school that requires urgent attention.'

'More urgent than what we're trying to do, I suppose?'

'I don't know what it is you're trying to do, exactly—' I start, but Carl pounces straight on it.

'You're right. You don't. George will get to your little task when he's got time, next week. Now, if you don't mind, we've got a lot to get on with.'

22

'It's like he doesn't want me to find out,' I say to Jamie that night as we sit down in the living room. 'I think he's involved somehow.'

'This is Carl? The miserable tech guy, who you've complained about being grumpy since you first started at the school? Who you have repeatedly called the most unhelpful man in all existence?'

I draw in a long breath, which I release as a sigh. 'I know he's always been an arse, but it's like he actively doesn't want George looking into this. Like he's worried he's somehow going to get found out.'

'So now you think Carl is responsible, not Nathan?'

The question is said half in earnest, half facetiously. After contemplating it for barely a second, I let out a long groan.

'No, maybe. I don't know. All I know is that, while this is hanging over me, I can't focus on my job and, when I can't focus, I'm going to screw things up, which is exactly what whoever this is wants me to do.'

'Then don't give them the satisfaction. And just forget about it,' Jamie says, as if it's the easiest thing in the world to do. As I sit back in the chair, my mind still mulling over Carl and Nathan and Leo, Jamie speaks again. 'Have you talked to Sasha this evening? You know she's out all weekend for this orchestral thing.'

'That's this weekend?' I say, not sure where the time is going or why I'm having such a hard time keeping track of it.

'It is. She wants to get the train, but it's over an hour. I said I'd have to speak to you about it first, but I thought maybe you'd want to talk to her. You know, after everything that happened this week?'

I nod before taking another sip of my drink. He's right. With everything that happened with the photo and Sasha helping me, we completely glossed over how badly I let her down and that's not the type of parents Jamie and I are. We don't gloss over things. It doesn't work. In the long term, it only ever makes things worse. Unfortunately, that means facing up to what I've done.

Sasha is practising her oboe as I stand outside her room. She is so incredibly talented. The way she controls the accents on the notes makes it sound like intonation. Like each bar is part of a story that she's telling. I could listen to her play forever and, for a few minutes I stand there, absorbing the sounds. But I know part of me is just avoiding the issue.

Taking a deep breath in, I knock loud enough for her to hear. A second later, the music stops.

'Can I come in?' I say, pushing the door open a fraction. 'I'm sorry, I didn't want to interrupt, but I didn't know how long the piece was.'

'It's fine,' she says, placing the instrument down on its stand. 'I was going to stop in a minute, anyway. You want something?'

Nodding, I head in and take a seat on the edge of her bed.

'Your dad said you want to take the train tomorrow?'

'And you've come to tell me why you don't think that's a good idea?' Her tone isn't sharp. It's weary.

'No, first I've come to say how sorry I am again. About how badly I messed up.'

'We don't need to do this, Mum,' she says, going to her music stand and closing the book.

'Yes, we do. I do. I need to apologise. And I'm not going to give excuses, because there aren't any, but, honestly, I think over the summer everything was so good, I almost forgot about it. No, that's not right. I'll never forget about it. But when I think back to you telling us about the pregnancy, and everything you had to go through with Christopher while you were waiting for the abortion, it feels like it happened such a long time ago. Not just a year. I think that's why the date wasn't on my radar.'

With a heavy sigh, Sasha drops onto the bed next to me.

'I know what you mean. Honestly,' she says, 'sometimes, when I think back on it, it feels like it was someone else's life. I don't even feel like that person was me anymore. And when I have the sessions with the counsellor, and she makes me go through it again, tell her about it, I feel like I'm talking about somebody else.'

'Is that good?' I ask.

'I think so. The therapist seems to think it is. I mean, we're talking about other things too now. Not just that, and that's got to be a good sign.'

I want to ask what other things they talk about. Like whether her useless mother, who always appears to be prioritising her job over her family, is one of their discussion points, but I wouldn't be asking for Sasha. I'd be asking for myself, and that's not okay. So I don't.

'I'm okay with you taking the train,' I say instead, not entirely sure I mean it. Judging from the way Sasha's eyes widen, she doesn't believe it either.

'You are?'

'I am, but there are going to be some conditions.'

She nods slowly. 'They're not that you and Dad are coming on the train too, are they?'

I let out a light chuckle. 'No, but I want check-ins every half hour until you get there.'

'Every half hour?'

'Yup. Just send a selfie so I know where you are. And you can get the train there both days, but we are picking you up afterwards. These things finish late and I don't want you on the train with a load of opportunistic, drunk creeps, understand?'

She hesitates and for a second, I think she's going to put up a fight about it and tell me how other people in the orchestra have been getting the trains across London since before puberty, but she doesn't. Instead, she smiles.

'Okay, that sounds like a deal,' she says.

23

The weekend goes by smoothly enough. I have work to do. A lot of it, given all the hours I've lost this week because of this bloody photograph. Work at the weekend is a given in my job, but Jamie doesn't mind. He took to playing golf when Sasha was a baby, but it's only since I became Head, and need to spend so much of the weekends shut in my office, that he's had time to get any good at it. A little after he leaves on Saturday morning, Alice messages to see if I want to meet for brunch, but I decline the offer, and not just because of work. Jamie and I planned to go out before picking Sasha up from orchestra and, since she became single again, brunches with Alice means several mimosas, before moving onto wine and cocktails, which isn't something I feel like I can cope with. But there's another reason for me not wanting to meet her and that's because I'm still not sure what I want to say about the photograph. I know she'll feel guilty about it. Blame herself, which is not what I want. I want to have someone I can justifiably point my finger at before I drag my best friend into it.

When Monday morning comes around, I want nothing more than to head straight down to the tech room and stay there until I have some answers. But I can't. I have other things to do. Including the weekly staff briefing.

The staff are settled down, sitting in the chesterfield arm chairs, or standing by the fireplace with their cups of coffee. For once, it doesn't take them long to stop talking when I walk into the room.

I go through the usual list of things – parents' evenings, exam dates, turning up for lunch and break duties on time – but as I make my way down the list, I know I've got to broach the photo. I find myself slowing down, dragging out points far more than I need to, but eventually I run out of notices. There's only one thing left to say.

'Lastly, before we take notifications from the rest of the staff, I want to mention an incident that happened on Friday morning that I'm sure lots of you – all of you – have already heard about.'

The room is entirely silent, as I have everyone's complete attention. This was obviously the piece of information they'd been waiting for. Given that these are people in a compassionate line of work who place human wellbeing at the forefront of everything they do, there are some fucking vultures amongst them. People who'd love to see me fail, not because they want my job, or think someone else can do it better, but because they just like the drama. But they're not going to get drama from me. Jamie was right. I won't give them the satisfaction.

'There was a photo of myself, from my younger years, on the main screen in the hall when the sixth form was coming into their assembly,' I continue. 'As I'm sure you've heard, I tried to make light of it with the students so the situation did not escalate, but we need to be taking things like this very seriously. Along with an obvious violation of school rules in using the computers inappropriately, it is an invasion of privacy. Cyber-crime is a real thing, with real consequences. I can tell you now that I have started an investigation into how this happened, and matters will go to the police if necessary. I would, of course, like to keep that between these four walls until we have a little more information. Lastly, in relation to this, can you please make sure that you use work computers purely for schoolwork? It is entirely possible that one of the students got access to these images through his or her parents.' I am scanning the room as I say this, but as I reach Nathan, I can't help but let my gaze linger there a bit longer. 'We operate on a system of trust at St Anne's, and I hope we can continue to do so without me having to put further measures in place.' With that, I take a breath in and smile, indicating the morning chastisement is over. 'Okay, sorry for such a downer on a Monday, guys. Now, has anybody got any more positive notices?'

While the sports team prattles on about their first fixture at the weekend, I glance at Alice. She offers me the tiniest of smiles.

You did well, I think she's saying, *but it wasn't very nice.*

Fair enough, that's an assessment I can take. And, with that done, my first trip of the morning is to George and the tech team.

24

'Morning, gentlemen,' I say, with my brightest, happiest smile, just because I know how much it's going to irritate Carl.

Every school I've ever been in, for training or teaching full time, or even just on a course, has had a tech department full of men. Not once have I seen a woman in the role and I wonder if it's because the men make the environment so damn unpleasant. I used the word 'gentlemen' to acknowledge them, but I promise, outside of this room, it would never be used.

George is wearing jeans and a comic book T-shirt; the outfit is a step up from what he used to wear last year. Last year, he dressed like Kevin and Carl, in tracksuit bottoms and hoodies with pockets full of chocolate bars. As always, their desks are covered with cans of caffeine-loaded fizzy drinks and, from the bags under their eyes, you'd think they were working some high-powered tech job in Silicon Valley, not making sure that twelve-year-olds can log on to their maths homework. Alice tells me they're all gamers; that's why they always look so knackered. They're up all night on their computers, then they drag themselves into work. It's easy to believe.

'George,' I say, making a beeline for him. 'I hope you had a good weekend?'

I don't really care how his weekend was, but no matter how rude this office can be to me, I have no intention of sinking to their level. The way I treat people is one of the reasons I got this job and not Nathan. Nathan is the one who makes demands. Who calls people out for the type of slip ups we all make. Which is why his whole mindfulness thing is such a joke. He's the one who puts pressure on people. Who makes them think they could constantly be doing more. Doing better. I don't do that, or at least I didn't use to. My conversation with Sandra the week before might be a sign that I'm slipping more into Nathan's way of thinking. Or it could just be that she deserved it.

My whole method of managing has always been that people need to be seen. They need to believe you genuinely care about them. That's how you get them to work for you. As such, I'm not surprised that George's smile widens at the question, though I'm surprised by the answer.

'I did, thank you. I went away with my girlfriend.'

A girlfriend? Perhaps it's judgemental of me, but I assumed the men in this room were the eternal bachelor type, and not out of choice. Maybe there is some hope for George after all. It certainly explains the upgrade in his clothing.

'Well, I'm glad you had a good time. I assume you know why I'm here.'

I expect him to give me yet another excuse, like telling me he hasn't had time to look at it yet, but he stands up and moves in closer before he lowers his voice, though it's probably unnecessary. Everyone in the school knows what happened now, and that includes these guys.

'I, I've got something,' he says. 'But I'm not sure how useful it'll be.'

'Trust me, anything is useful,' I reply.

'Well, it was one of the classroom laptops,' he says. 'From one of the trolleys.'

I know exactly what he's talking about. We have an impressive ICT suite at St Anne's. It's built in what was the anti-library looking over the gardens. They had an architect along with a person from British Heritage to help design it, to ensure that it didn't take away from the aesthetic of the room with its floor-to-ceiling bookshelves and rolling ladders. What we ended up with is nothing short of beautiful. But, given the size of the school, and how the space is used for computing lessons, it's very rarely free. So we have four trolleys around the school that are filled with laptops, and the teachers can book them out to use in their lessons if they want the kids to make presentations, things like that. Nathan was pushing for all students to bring in their own computers. If he got the position of Head, it was one of the first things he wanted to introduce. I think that's another big reason he didn't get the job. I made no qualms in my interview about saying I thought this was such a bad idea. Not all kids can afford computers. And the computers they bring offer a clear indication of wealth. I don't want a kid with a beat-up, ten-year-old laptop that barely works sitting next to one of his classmates with a brand-new, top-of-the-range MacBook Pro. I don't want parents to go into debt, just so that their children can have the latest technology. In my school, all the kids are equal, and I intend on keeping it that way for as long as possible.

'So, one of the trolleys? Which one?' I ask. 'Can you tell that?'

They're separated out in different departments, based purely on geographical location. Music and maths are together, so are languages, art and drama. Science has their own set, as do English, because they have so many children doing A-Level and want to use them for research. I can't remember who the other group is, but, at this moment, it doesn't matter anyway, as George replies.

'It was one of the languages ones,' he tells me. 'I checked the code on the laptop and it matched a missing one in that trolley. I was going to put it back, but I thought you might want to look at it, not that there's anything to see. I cleared the photo off straight away. It felt like the best thing to do.'

'Thank you, George,' I say, not sure if I'm pleased he cleared it off or not. I'm grateful no one else can get to it, but there might have been some sort of evidence on it. Not that I can't get a copy if I want. I'm sure Sasha has had it send to her plenty of times. 'So what did you find out? How did they load it on?'

He shrugs. 'Could've been USB, could've been downloaded. I can't tell, but they set it as the lock screen, the screensaver and the backdrop. That's why I couldn't close it when I was trying. I'm sorry, if I'd thought of that, I'd have done what you did and just pulled it out.'

'It's fine, George, thank you. Thank you for this.'

'I hope it's helpful,' he says.

'I'm sure it will be,' I reply, and then offer a last smile. He's given me a place to start, and it's put me right where I knew it would.

25

As I turn to leave, another thought strikes. Every member of staff can log on to a document with the codes that allow them to unlock the various laptop trolleys. Though the students aren't meant to know what the codes are, any of them with a half-decent memory has them locked down by the end of the first half-term. I know there are several teachers who normally just ask the children what they are, because it's quicker than searching through their computers to find them. It's not something you'd want to do in the average school, but, at a place like St Anne's, I've never seen a problem with it. Particularly when you're covering another class.

'Is it still the old codes from last year on the trolleys?' I ask George, knowing that very few classes will have even used the computers so early in the term.

'No, we changed all the codes in the holidays. I emailed around. It was in the third or fourth week. You definitely got an email about it in your inbox. It went to all staff.'

'Right, sorry, of course it did,' I say.

'It's hard to remember things like that when you get six

weeks' holiday, I suppose,' Carl grunts from the back of the room. I ignore him. This holiday, I had exactly three weeks where I didn't think about work. Three weeks and even then I was still doing schoolwork on the flight there and back. Though, even if I'd checked my computer every day, I still wouldn't have known about the codes. I don't pay attention to messages sent to all staff. Either I'm the one that's sending them, or one of my assistants or heads of year is, based on a meeting that I've had with them. I already know the gist of the information being disseminated. This one, I wouldn't have even bothered opening. I so rarely teach classes that there's just no need for me to read stuff like that. But, still, this is an interesting development.

'So only the teachers know the new codes? Have any other classes used those laptops since we've been back? It would only be from Tuesday to Thursday.'

'We've got a system you can look at all that information,' Carl grunts again.

'Of course,' I say, annoyed at how he doesn't even try to hide his eavesdropping. Thankfully, George is far more obliging than his colleague.

'I can find them. It will only take me a minute if you want to stay?'

I'm about to say that I will when I change my mind.

'Do you think you could email them to me?' I say, and not just because I want to get out of the office. Having a paper trail of evidence will be far more beneficial in my meeting with Florence than her just having to take my word for things.

'Sure, no problem,' he says. 'By the time you get back to your office, it should be in your inbox.'

After walking across the grounds, I barely glance at Sandra as I slip into my office and sit down at my computer, where I ignore the dozen other emails that have been sent to me in the half hour

I was away from my desk. Instead, I go straight to the one from George. I don't know why my heart is beating so fast. Probably because I can tell there's going to be something in there. Something that's going to get me closer to understanding what's going on.

When I open the mail, four names appear on the screen, but only one of them has borrowed the computers more than once. In fact, they've borrowed them a massive six times already. And that person is Nathan Coles.

26

While the meeting with Florence is set in the books for eleven, she doesn't turn up until twenty past. It's obviously deliberate and I'm not exactly surprised. What does surprise me, however, is that she doesn't turn up alone. There are two other governors with her. Two who I thought would have enough respect to at least inform me they were going to be present at my interrogation.

I can't help but wonder if this is what my students feel like when they're forced to sit through a meeting with me.

It's my office, of course. My sofa that we're sitting on – loosely speaking – but it doesn't feel like it. No, the way they've arranged themselves feels very much like it's three against one.

'We have all seen the image, and I think we can all agree that it was inappropriate. I have to say I'm surprised, Liz. I hear it was part of your presentation?'

'No,' I say flatly and with notable annoyance. 'It was nothing to do with my presentation. It wasn't even on my computer. It was on the screen when I came into the hall. Someone had placed it there, using one of the school computers.'

'But that's not what I heard,' Florence says, frowning. 'You're quite sure about this? The email you sent to parents says otherwise. Is there a reason you're changing your story?'

'I'm not changing my story,' I say through gritted teeth. 'I thought that telling the students and parents it was part of a presentation was a more fitting approach than drawing further attention to the fact that someone had deliberately taken an image from social media and tried to humiliate me. And although it was a less than ideal situation, it did actually fit in with the theme of the assembly. Thankfully. The ICT staff and several other teachers I spoke to immediately after the event can back this up. I have the emails too, if you'd like to see.'

Florence's confidence wavers visibly as for a moment she looks perturbed, though I feel it's being made to look like a fool that's annoyed her, rather than the invasion of my privacy. She glances either side of her, to the two governors who have yet to say much at all.

One of them is on his phone, blatantly not paying attention, and it's difficult to know why he's here at all. The other has a notebook out and has made at least a dozen 'ahh' and 'uhm' noises as he scribbles away like he's a detective on a TV show. Prick.

'So, you say the image came from your social media page.' Florence is talking again. 'I'm surprised somebody in your position still has social media in such a prominent manner. And wishes to share such brazen photos.'

My jaw is clenched so tightly, I wonder if she can hear the bones grinding together, yet, somehow, I keep my false smile in place.

'I said it came from social media. Not from mine. It is not a photo of mine.'

'But it's of you?' She frowns.

Jesus fucking Christ. It's like the woman doesn't even know how a camera works.

'Yes, it is a photo of me, but it was taken by someone else a very long time ago.'

I am waiting for the next question. The question where she asks who took the photo and for the first time, I'm nervous. There's no way I can lie and I've not got any reason to, but that means throwing my best friend under the bus for something she didn't do. A moment ticks by. Florence chews down on her bottom lip, but she doesn't ask where the photo came from. Neither do the others. They don't ask any more questions at all.

'Still, there is no way to deny that your social media presence is an issue here. Considering your position, I think it's time you consider removing yourself from it altogether.'

Honestly? What the fuck? It's like she hasn't listened to a word I've said.

'Social media was not the problem here,' I say, with more than a hint of force. 'Someone trying to humiliate me and share private information was. And I don't know if it's spite or incompetence, but, quite frankly, I am extremely concerned that you don't see the real issue.'

'I think that's a bit unfair.' The notepad scribbler finally says something. 'I think Florence is merely trying to ensure issues like this don't occur again.'

For another ten minutes, she and the scribbler continue to circle over the same points again and again: security, child welfare, child protection. They speak to me as if I don't know, as if the buck doesn't stop with me and the whole time they are shirking the actual issue here. The fact that I'm the one who is the victim. When Florence tries to bring up 'my responsibilities' again, I snap.

'I'm sorry,' I say, not sounding sorry at all. 'But I thought you were coming here to help find a way through these issues, not drag me over the coals for something I did not do.'

'I believe that's what we've been trying to do,' Florence says, and I don't know if she's being facetious or she actually believes it. Either way, they've wasted enough of my time.

'If that is the case, then you need to find out who is responsible,' I say. 'And as for me shutting down my social media, it won't happen. I've got family living around the country and abroad, and it is the easiest way for us to stay in contact. Not to mention, there are incredible resources on there for teachers. I'm a member of several headteachers' groups, which disseminate information solely via that platform. But, then, if you paid any attention to the learning aspects that go on within a school, you would already know that.'

The only reply I get is a single sniff from Florence. A second later, she stands up, before glancing at the others, silently ordering them to do the same.

'If you want us to look into this, then we need support from you too, and that means closing down your social media,' she says. Her tone tells me the conversation is over, and I'm glad. Any longer and I'd end up saying something I'd regret.

'Of course,' I say, my cheeks burning from the force of my smile, as I stretch out my hand and shake each of theirs. I finish with Florence, whose grip I squeeze just a fraction harder than is polite. It's probably wrong. She's an ageing woman, after all. I don't think it would take that much to accidentally fracture or dislocate something, but I release the grip before that can happen. I need her to know I'm not rolling over anymore. I've played the governors' game so far, and I'll pretend to do it now, but I'm playing it my way. Over the last few years, I've discovered that's what management is: a game. And it's time I finally stopped playing by the rules.

27

I walk them out of my office, but that's as far as I go. The minute Florence steps into the hallway and turns back to look at me, I disappear back inside and close the door with a click. Petty? Maybe, but I don't care. It's not even Monday lunchtime and I'm absolutely exhausted. The thought of half a dozen more meetings is almost enough to bring me to tears, but crying won't help me and neither will cancelling them. I'll still have to deal with it all, eventually. Better to get it over and done with.

For the rest of the day, there's a stream of people walking in and out of my door. Some are parents – both ones we've called in and ones who have called a meeting with me – but most are staff. Heads of year, heads of department, the school counsellor and support lead. There's barely five minutes between each meeting, yet I have to know exactly what we're going to talk about before the member of staff walks in through the door. Somehow, I stay on top of it all, but I don't know how.

On days like today, leaving the office simply isn't an option. The moment I head anywhere else, I end up being dragged into conversations that I don't have the energy to deal with. As such, I send Sandra to the canteen to get me lunch. Food at St Anne's is pretty good. There's an industrial kitchen attached to the old dining hall, which has the same large bay windows and high ceilings as everywhere else in the building. I've often thought that we could rent out the space during holidays for weddings, to bring in a bit of extra money to the school, but that would require the governors' approval, and this doesn't feel like a good time to broach the idea.

As I continue to tap away, readying various reports, Sandra brings a plate of cottage pie and veg, but, by the time I get to it, it's stone cold. Next time Jamie goes food shopping, I'm going to get him to buy some of those Cup a Soup things, just so I get to eat.

* * *

The school bell has long since marked the end of the day and Sandra has already left. I finally consider packing up and heading home to get some food, but, before I can even close my laptop, there's a knock on the door. I'm tempted to just stay silent and pretend I've already gone home, but my lights are on, and people would know. Besides, I make such a big deal about my door always being open, it would be a pretty shitty thing to do.

'Yes,' I say with the longest possible sigh.

The door opens, and Alice's head peers around it.

'Thought I ought to knock,' she says. 'Just in case you had company. How's it going?'

I groan and drop my head to the table. 'Oh, brilliant.'

'That good, huh?' she says. 'Would you rather I let you work?'

'No. Stay, please. I was about to stop, anyway.'

Rather than taking a seat opposite my desk, Alice drops into the sofa that I used for my meeting with the governors. She moves to curl her feet under her, the way she normally does when she comes in here and knows we won't be interrupted, but, before she can settle, she's already on her feet again.

'I got a text from Katie over the weekend,' she says, ambling towards the fireplace and staring up at the painting above it.

'How is she?' I ask. 'When does term start again? Does she know she's going to have to spend a bit more time studying and less partying now she's in her second year?'

I chuckle at my own comment. Katie was the last girl you would have imagined being a partier when she was at school. She wasn't the brightest girl in the year, but what she lacked in talent she made up for in pure determination. Her final grades were way above what any of her teachers or data predicted her and, the day she got her results, she was practically dancing. She was so happy. Unfortunately, it didn't last. Two days later, her dad, Philip, walked out on Alice. He got a flat in Leeds, where Katie had accepted a place at university and suddenly, Alice was on her own.

It was a strange time. Philip cut out everyone from his old life, including Jamie and me, and I won't lie, it hurt. We'd been friends for so long, I felt this fractured loyalty. A need to ring and check in on him, I decide. See how he's doing. But he's the one who left. He's the one who hasn't even bothered trying to put his side of the story across, probably because he knows there's no way we could side with him. Or even sympathise. Besides, Alice is my best friend. She's the one I need to be there for. Not that she needs me.

I don't know how I'd respond if Jamie did the same to me. I'd probably have some sort of nervous breakdown. But Alice didn't. She said goodbye from the doorstep as he packed up the car and left, and she got on with rebuilding her life.

Katie's always been a daddy's girl, and the fact he moved to be close to her seems to be enough to negate any anger she feels at him walking out on her mother. But Alice didn't bat an eyelid. 'It was time.' That's all she says about the matter. If she says anything about it at all.

I realise a pause has expanded between us, as Alice continues to study the painting, like she's drifted off somewhere else entirely. I sit back in my seat and repeat my question.

'So, what did my favourite goddaughter have to say?' I ask again. Katie's my only goddaughter, but I still refer to her as my favourite, anyway.

Rather than replying straight away, Alice turns slowly to face me.

'She's saying she saw the photo. Some of the sixth form sent it to their older siblings, you know...'

'I know...' I say, though a weight falls on my chest. It would be naïve of me to think I'd kept it within the walls of St Anne's, but it's hard knowing that Katie, who I love like a daughter, is hearing about it. Particularly as I can only imagine the messages it is being sent with.

'I don't know how to tell you this...' Alice finally looks away from the painting and faces me. 'It was why I wanted to meet for brunch. But then you were busy. And I came in first thing this morning, after briefing, but you weren't here and Sandra said you had meetings all day...'

I already know what she's going to say, but a surprising warmth is flooding through me. One thing I've known since the very start of our friendship is that there are two Alices. The one everyone else gets to see. The one who can speak in front of hundreds without breaking a sweat and who is at home on a stage in front of an audience of a thousand as she is in front of her GCSE class. Who has so much confidence, it seems utterly unfair. But then there's this one. The genuine Alice. The Alice who's terrified of getting things wrong, of messing things up or, worse still, of hurting people and that's what she thinks she's about to do to me. Which is why I need to put her out of her misery as soon as I can.

'I know about your MySpace account.'

'You do?' Her expression is one of pure shock. Not relief, not fear. Just shock. 'How?'

'Sasha did a bit of digging around.'

'She did? Of course she's seen it too. Why didn't you say anything then?'

She finally takes a seat, and this time it's opposite me. The look of disbelief is gone, and instead she stares at me with an expression of confusion.

'Did you have anything to do with putting it up there, in the assembly?' I ask.

'No, of course I didn't. I would never do something like that to anyone.'

'Exactly. So there wasn't any point. Not 'til I had some idea of what happened.'

'And do you? Do you know who did it?' she asks.

I draw a breath inward. Nathan's name on the list of teachers who used those computers last week is far from definitive evidence, but it is incriminating, in my mind at least. And then there's the fact that Alice is friends with Leo on MySpace, which doesn't make any sense. I press my lips together, preparing to ask her about it, when there's a knock at the door.

'Another meeting? This late?' Alice questions, but I shake my head.

'No, I'm done. You don't mind, do you? I should just see who it is.'

'Go ahead.'

I clear my throat, before calling loudly across to the room, 'Come in.'

A second later, the large, wooden door creaks open and, with a broad smirk on his face, Nathan steps into my office.

'Sorry,' he says. 'I'm not interrupting, am I?'

28

I don't believe my office is bugged. Just like I don't believe that Nathan Coles has psychic abilities that meant he appeared in my office just a split second before I was about to tell Alice how I think he was behind the photo of me, but, at that moment in time, they both feel like definite possibilities.

'Nathan, can I help you?' I say, feeling my lips tightening into an all too familiar smile.

'Liz, yes, actually no. I was looking for Alice. I figured she might be here.'

'You want me?' Alice says, with a look of surprise.

'Yes, I'm just sorting out the hall for the exams on Friday. I wanted to know what set pieces and things you need storing away and what I can just move to the back of the stage. I was hoping you might be able to do it now. So it gives us the rest of the week to get everything else sorted.'

'It's nearly five o'clock, Nathan,' I say curtly. 'This can wait until tomorrow.'

Alice gets in just after me at seven fifteen each day, meaning she's already worked nearly ten hours, but Nathan wouldn't care about a thing like that. It's just what I always say about him and the way he pushes people past what's reasonable. He would never make a good head.

'It's fine,' Alice says, looking between the pair of us. 'I was thinking about it earlier, anyway. I'll meet you down in the hall in five?'

Nathan's not usually good at taking a hint or, rather, he normally chooses to ignore them, which is why I'm surprised when he smiles.

'Sounds good. And don't work too late, Liz. I'll see you tomorrow.'

The moment the door closes, I shudder.

'God I despise him,' I say. Only then do I remember that I was about to tell Alice about his role in the photo, but, before I can, she's speaking again.

'I better go, but we're doing dinner on Friday still, right? It feels like you and I have barely had any time together for months. I can't believe I only saw you once over the summer holidays. That's not natural.'

'I know. I feel the same.'

She's right, it's not normal for us to go that long without seeing each other. There was a time when Alice and Philip were still together, and Katie lived at home, that we would spend almost every holiday together, two families of three. Sasha and Katie practically grew up as sisters. I know they're still in contact. They still message and call each other occasionally, but it's not the same as it would have been if Philip hadn't left. Somehow, I only saw Alice once in the summer and that was for a quick coffee during the first week. Coffee isn't our normal get together. Normally it's wine, but I'd got these damn migraines, so drinking wasn't a sensible option. A proper night out feels like exactly what I need.

'Do you want me to wait for you?' I ask, glancing at the clock and wondering how much more work I can get done in the time it takes Alice and Nathan to sort out the hall. I'd offer to help, but I find it hard enough to be in enclosed spaces with Nathan as it is. There's no way I can manage it this late in the day. Especially after the day I've had.

'It's fine. I want to set up the classroom for tomorrow morning. My A-Level class is doing all this improvisation with props, and I haven't sorted any of them out. You don't want to hang around until then.'

'I really don't mind,' I say, but she shakes her head again.

'Honestly, I'll see you tomorrow, all right? And please don't forget Friday.'

'It's in the diary,' I say.

A minute later, Alice is blowing me a kiss from the doorway. There's no point pretending I'm going to get any other work done now. Not while I'm this hungry, which means it's going to be another late night in the home office again.

29

During the next couple of days, school is more of the same. Meetings, meetings and more meetings. On Tuesday and Wednesday, I don't feel like I've even left my office. At one point, I try to grab a toilet break, only to be accosted in the corridor, then in the toilets when I'm washing my hands. I get it, everyone's got their own issues, and there really are some that only I can deal with, but at least let me grab a hand towel first.

Several members of staff are after compassionate leave and are trying to get their request in at the start of term, for dates all the way in the summer. As if I'm able to think that far ahead. I must, though, for a lot of things I'm expected to think several years in advance and, if that isn't enough to make your head hurt, I don't know what will be.

By the time Thursday comes around, I don't think I've even seen a student, other than in meetings. I'm hoping that this will be a day to get up to date on the budget and funding paperwork and maybe show my face in a couple of classrooms, just so people know I care about what goes on in them. But, when

Sandra knocks on my door at seven-thirty with an even wider scowl on her face than normal, I know that won't happen.

'We've had to send Lucy Gadwell home. She nearly fainted in the car park, apparently. I don't even know why she came in. Girl looks a mess. Spreading her germs around all of us.'

I bite my tongue. You're damned if you do, damned if you don't when it comes to taking sick leave, and I don't think that's exclusive to teaching. If you don't come into work, people assume you're faking and slacking off. If you do, then people like Sandra will be cross with you for spreading germs. Poor Lucy probably didn't want to put pressure on the rest of her department, given how half the staff seem to be coming down with some sort of early seasonal flu. Which is why, I discover, Sandra has come to me.

'We haven't got enough staff to cover her lessons today,' Sandra says flatly. 'We're missing a teacher for three of them.'

'Three of them?' I say in surprise. It's not unusual to have one or two periods that are tricky to cover, particularly when there are lots of small A-Level classes going on, but we have a good support network of supply teachers and our timetables are pretty generous compared to other schools. Normally, Sandra can piece something together. 'Are you sure?'

I regret the question the moment I say it. Sandra's face turns thunderous.

'Yes, thank you. It's the geography field trip, remember? They've had to take Tucker from science, so they have a man on the trip. The maths department is off timetable too, for the training on the new syllabus. Two of the PE staff have called in sick as well, along with Layla from maths and Mark from drama. Naomi is on compassionate after her mum was taken ill last night.'

'Jesus.' I let out a long blow of air. Normally, days like this don't happen until the end of term when everyone is exhausted and picks up viruses like they're discount coupons. Still, how the hell I approved two departments to be off timetable at the same time, I have no idea. I feel like it's got Nathan written all over it. Not that it makes any difference. I still have to be the one to come up with a solution. 'So, everything else is covered?'

'Just these three art ones left.'

I know what's coming, but I really want to avoid it if I can.

'Have you asked the assistant principals?' I say, only to remember June is on the field trip. 'Nathan's still here, and I'm pretty sure he's got a free timetable today.'

'He's already covering PE. He's going to double up the classes and take them all, so we don't need to use any extra teachers there. I've already spoken to him about this.'

'Of course, he's going to double up classes,' I mutter, sure he offered just to make me look bad. 'So three lessons of art,' I say, more to myself than Sandra. It's not that bad; they can draw or paint or do whatever it is quietly while I try to get some work done on my computer. Honestly, I need to stretch this budget to afford another member of supply staff.

'There's a trainee in there, so you won't have to do anything really,' Sandra says, as if she's reading my thoughts. 'You're just the body in the room.'

'A trainee can't teach full lessons already,' I say, feeling the lightness that formed only a second ago ebbing a way. Trainee teachers need support. Feedback. If anyone is a body in the room, it's most likely going to be them, not me.

'According to Lucy, she can. She's more than happy for the trainee to take them all.'

I'm not sure how to respond to that. We're not even two weeks in, and normally the trainee teachers start with little bits. Maybe taking the start or the end of the lesson, or just doing a Q&A

session halfway through. I don't know a time when they've taken the whole lesson. But, then, Jessica trained a lot more recently than me. And, judging by what I saw in her observation, she's perfectly capable of making that decision. Besides, if it's less work for me, then that's what I need.

'Okay, what period am I there?' I ask.

'Two, three and four. I've already emailed you the lesson plan.'

'Great,' I say. Because there is no other response I can give.

I guess I'm going into a classroom today after all. I just hope this trainee is as good as Lucy thinks.

30

Our school is known for its art. It's one of the departments that consistently produces the best results, and the annual exhibition in the main hall is one of the most well-supported events of the year. But, then, they've got an impressive set-up to help. The studio building is just past the tennis courts, and is far more modern than the rest of the school, but somehow it fits in.

The classrooms inside are immense. Along with the standard art equipment, there is a proper kiln. Each year, the Year 7s do a project where they sell their earthenware at the Christmas fair to raise money for charity. Plenty of our students have gone on to study art, and several of them have even made full-time careers of it. Some regularly come back to the school to talk to the students about projects they've been working on. Any teacher who gets St Anne's as one of their training schools is lucky, but particularly those doing art.

Given how early on in the course it is, I assume the trainee teacher is going to be nervous about taking a full lesson by herself, so I turn up five minutes early, just to make sure everything is set up.

'Mrs Croft,' she says, as I step into the room. 'I didn't realise you were going to be sitting in on this lesson.'

'Jessica, isn't it? I assume you heard about Lucy going home?'

'Yes, I hope she's all right.'

'I'm sure she will be. There are a lot of bugs going around this time of year.'

Jessica nods quickly, but even when she stops, she carries on looking at me with an intense gaze. A silence elongates around us, as if she's waiting for me to say more.

'So are you going to be sitting in on this lesson?' she says eventually. 'Observing me?'

'Oh, it won't be a formal observation. I'm just here to cover. No observing at all. I'll just sit in the back. Unless you need my help with anything, that is? I understand this must all be quite daunting for you.'

For a second, her mouth bobs open before she speaks again.

'Well, I was going to have music on this lesson and get the children to paint according to the emotions they hear in the songs, but if that's going to be too loud for you, I don't mind changing it. I'm sure there's something else I can do. You probably don't want loud music if you're trying to work, do you?'

She says this all fairly confidently. The same self-assurance she displayed when she was in my office, as if she was already at ease in the environment. Those same vibes radiate from her now. Like an undercurrent of confidence.

'You don't want to be changing your lesson plan on my account,' I tell her. 'Besides, it will be nice to listen to someone new and enthusiastic teaching.'

'You're not still enthusiastic about teaching?' she asks.

The question takes me by surprise. Perhaps because I can't tell if there's a tone of judgement within it.

'Oh, well, yes, I will always be enthusiastic about teaching. It's my passion. I guess I should have said someone who is focused on the lessons. It's hard. As soon as you're in a full-time position, the teaching seems to come second to everything else. Reports, meetings, marking and assessments. You'll find all that out soon enough. But, look at me, I shouldn't be saying these things. It makes me sound like I don't love the job and I do. Honestly. Teaching is the best job in the world. I wouldn't have been doing it for nearly twenty years if I didn't love it.'

'Twenty years?'

'Near enough,' I say. 'Nineteen, actually, but it's easier to round it up.'

I'm about to ask her a question about the lesson and where it's best for me to sit when I hear the children out in the corridor waiting to come in.

'I'll just sit at the back,' I say, before moving with my computer over to a desk in the corner. It's the same desk I sat at before when I observed Lucy, which reminds me I still haven't sent her any observation feedback yet. There's no point in me sending it to her now when she's sick, though. That's one of my pet hates. Teachers emailing each other at all hours of the day, or when they're off sick and need time at home to rest. Work hour emails only is one policy I put in place last year and most of the staff respect it, though several people don't seem to think that rule applies to me. Nathan sent me more emails during evenings and weekends than during the school day last year. But that was probably just to piss me off more than anything else.

As the students filter in, Jessica stands at the door and greets them, asking them all their names as they enter. I'm surprised by how many of them she knows. I'd say it's at least half, and she offers them a high five when she gets it right. I'm impressed.

There are some of my older teachers who could do with taking a leaf out of her book for building student-teacher relationships.

My plan was to get on and work straight away, but I find myself drawn into the lesson. Like Jessica told me, it's about letting the music dictate what art the students produce. There's no wrong or right, and there's a selection of mediums in front of them to choose from. After each piece of music, she asks the children if any of them want to share what they've done, and I'm impressed by the number that do. By the time she's finished the lesson, I'm pretty sure that every person in the room has contributed.

When the bell rings and the lesson ends, Jessica gets the children to tuck their stools in under the benches before they head out into the corridor. I can't help but go across and talk to her.

'That was a really lovely lesson,' I say. 'Really lovely. The children clearly had a great time.'

'Thank you,' she says, her cheeks beaming with pride.

'And this is your first teaching practice? You didn't work in a school before? As a TA or something?'

She shakes her head. 'No. Not exactly. But I have teachers in my family. I guess I've always been around them. Things rubbed off.'

'Well, I'm glad they did. You're obviously a natural. And I'm sure you're going to have a great time here. Lucy is a wonderful teacher.'

'She really is. I've already learned so much from her.'

I make a mental note to tell Lucy what a great job she's doing with Jessica when she returns to work. Even if the trainee is naturally good with the students, the confidence their mentors give them can make all the difference.

'So, if you weren't in education, what were you doing before you started your training? I assume you're a little old to come straight from university.' It's only as the words come out of my mouth that I hear how blunt they sound. A flush of embarrassment rolls through me. 'Apologies if that came across as rude. That wasn't my intention.'

It's not like she doesn't look young. She really does. But twenty-five, twenty-six young, as opposed to the twenty-one and - two-year-olds we often get here for training.

'No, it's not rude. I understand. You want to know who you've got teaching the children in your school. I think that's a good thing. I did various jobs.'

'Locally? I feel like I've seen you around before.'

'Maybe, I haven't been down here that long, but I've done a few odd jobs. Working in hotel bars, lots of secretarial work and front desk positions. Everything really. The plan was always to go into teaching; I just needed to save up the money for the training. You know how it is.'

I do, and it makes my toes curl. We need teachers in the profession more than ever, but they're leaving in droves, either going to jobs where they get paid far more, with less hassle, or moving abroad. The fact that somebody as obviously talented as Jessica needed to delay her training because she couldn't afford it is an absolute disgrace.

It also explains why I've probably seen her before. Alice and I always opt for hotel bars rather than clubs when we're in the need for a night out. Jamie always laughs at this, what he calls our 'lame attempts at going out', which usually involve sitting on a plush sofa in a swanky hotel bar that feels like we could still be in our living room. Assuming we had a renovation and learned how to make decent cocktails, that is. But that's the age we're at now.

I'm about to ask Jessica which places she's worked in when there's a knock on the door. A second later, Sandra steps into the room and crosses over to me.

For Sandra, being on this side of the school is even more unusual than me being here. She likes the comfort of her own chair and desk. Also, the main building is normally where all the gossip goes on.

'Mrs Harper. Is everything all right?' I say.

Rather than responding immediately, Sandra looks at me, then at Jessica and then back to me, before she takes a step forward. When she speaks, her voice is decidedly quieter than normal.

'I wonder if I can have a word,' she says.

Jessica doesn't need any more of a hint. She offers a fleeting smile before she speaks. 'I should go set up for my next lesson. There were a few things I wanted to check before the class comes in. Thank you again, Mrs Croft.'

I nod and wait for her to have walked several steps away before I turn back to Sandra.

'What is it?' I ask.

'It's Sasha.'

'Sasha? My Sasha?'

Sandra nods. 'She rang the school. She sounded very upset. She wants you to go and pick her up.'

'Sasha wants me to pick her up?' I have to repeat the comment because it's so ridiculous. Sasha knows what I do. Even when she was at the same school as me, she never came into my office, or tried to draw my attention away from work. Now I wish she had. Maybe it would have made a difference to how last year panned out.

'It sounded serious,' Sandra says. Her voice low again.

I nod. Fear rises through me. I thought we were past this. Past the bad things. I feel the colour draining from my cheeks as I look around the classroom. Sandra knows immediately what I'm thinking.

'It's fine. I'll get someone else to cover the class somehow,' she says. 'I'll do it myself if I have to. You go.'

31

I jump into the car and type the school's name into the sat nav. I know the way I'd normally take, but the last thing I want is to be stuck in traffic. This car's system does it all, planning routes and taking in congestion to make sure you're always on the fastest route, then records everything too. Not sure why, probably so the car dealers can charge us an extra grand. As soon as the school address appears, I hit go, then start the engine.

'Call Sasha,' I say, as I accelerate out of the car park. I've tried ringing her so many times I've lost count, but she's not picking up. But that's another thing about the car's system; it'll respond to my voice, meaning I can keep trying for as long as possible.

As I take a left onto the main road, I'm struggling to breathe. For once in my life, I'd be happy if this was Sandra playing a trick on me. Trying to get me in trouble for leaving St Anne's without notice during the middle of the school day, but even she wouldn't do that. Besides, there are all the missed calls on my phone. Whatever happened, Sasha wasn't in a good place, but there's only one thing I can think of that would make her react so badly, she'd want to come home. And there's no way that can happen. It just can't.

After trying Sasha another five or six times, I switch up my voice command.

'Ring Jamie,' I say instead. It takes a couple of tries, but, on the third attempt, he picks up.

'Have you heard from Sasha?' I say, not bothering with a greeting. I don't have time for that.

'Since when?' he replies. 'She got the bus okay, didn't she? She wasn't waiting when I went past the stop this morning. Why, what's happened?'

'I don't know. I have all these missed calls from her. Then she rang the school and was really upset. She said I needed to get her.'

There's a pause.

'I had a couple too, but I was in a meeting. My phone was on silent. Do you want me to go pick her up?'

I shake my head, only to remember he can't see me.

'No, it's fine. I'm on my way there. I just don't know what it can be. You don't think it's... You don't think people found out, do you?'

'No, they can't. How can they? We are the only people that know. No, it must have been something that happened in her class. They were auditioning for the play this week, weren't they? Maybe she got the lead and the other kids were being bitchy.'

'I can't think she'd let something like that upset her. She's pretty tough.'

It's taken a rough journey to get there, but Sasha's now the most self-assured sixteen-year-old I've ever known. Though that's not always a good thing.

'I better go, hon,' I say as I approach a set of traffic lights. 'I'll ring you when I've found out what's going on.'

'Thanks. I've got a meeting this afternoon, but I'll keep my phone on. I can come home if you need me to.'

'Love you.'

'Love you too.'

A moment later, he's hung up and I'm driving down the long, gravel driveway of Sasha's school.

There's no denying her school is a notch above even St Anne's and that's saying something. It's a small private school, with the class size capped at twenty. The lessons run from eight-thirty in the morning to four-thirty in the afternoon, after which there's an array of clubs, from debate team and choirs to hockey teams and even lacrosse. Most of the time, Sasha doesn't get home until gone six, after which she starts on her oboe practice for the evening. For the first term, that worried me. I don't know if it's good for a child to spend so much time working. Particularly as it wasn't the greatest environment for her, and she was still dealing with all the issues from before. But she's told me she likes the long day. The structure stops her thinking too much. And I believed her. Now I wonder if that's a mistake.

I walk straight through to the reception. There are large plaques on the walls, with the names of the head boys and girls from the last century on display, and that's not an exaggeration. This place has a history.

'Hi, I'm here to pick up Sasha Croft,' I say to the woman at reception, whose name I should know by now. After all, I've met her enough times. But something happened to me when I took on the role of head. There are so many names in school to remember – from the staff and teachers and parents and benefactors – that I can't deal with any names outside of it.

'Mrs Croft? You've come to pick up Sasha?' she repeats. A thick frown line appears between her eyebrows.

'Yes, she rang me. She said something was wrong, and I needed to come and get her.'

'Right. Yes. I know that. I know she was upset. But she's left already.'

'Left?' There's a hitch in my pulse, but I try to keep it steady. Has Sasha gone back to class? Is that what the receptionist is trying to say? I'm about to ask for clarification when she carries on talking.

'A car came and picked her up about ten minutes ago. She said they had come to collect her. Could it have been your husband?'

I shake my head. 'No, I spoke to him a couple of minutes ago. He's still at work. I'm the one she rang to come and get her.'

My voice is louder than it should be. Certainly louder than I'd speak to any of the parents at my school. But, then, I'd never lose one of their children.

'Let me ring her classroom,' the receptionist says, offering me one of those smiles I've perfected when I'm trying to appease an angry staff member or parent. 'I'm sure it's just been a misunderstanding.'

She does as she says and rings a number, asking if Sasha is there. I don't get to hear the reply, but her eyes flick over to me quickly as she hangs up. A second later, she picks up the phone again. She repeats this until she's dialled four different numbers. At that point, she looks up at me.

'I'm sorry, she's definitely gone,' she says.

'Gone,' I repeat.

'Yes, about ten, fifteen minutes ago. She's no longer on the school grounds.'

I stand there and stare at this woman, who's casually trying to tell me that my daughter, who should be in her care, is missing. It's safe to say, I snap.

'Where the hell is my child?'

32

The receptionist calls the Head, who comes down immediately, but I'm already heading to the car. It's clear they don't know anything, and any time I spend here is wasted. I need to form a plan, which right now means ringing Jamie before I get the police involved. Unfortunately, the headteacher runs out from the front of the school and catches up to me as I slam the car door shut.

'Mrs Croft. Mrs Croft, please wait.'

She taps a few times on the window, and I know I don't have a choice but to speak to her – other than running over her toes, that is. And that's a pretty tempting option. I check the key in the ignition, and for a split second consider turning it, before I shift my hand and wind down the window.

'I'm so sorry for this, Mrs Croft. There's obviously been a bit of a mix-up. If you could just hold on for a second, I'm sure we can work out what has happened.' She says all of this without taking a breath, while her cheeks are bright red, which highlights just how wide and white her eyes are.

'You want me to hold on?' I say. 'I've just found out that you let my daughter – my sixteen-year-old daughter – get into a car with a complete stranger, when you were well aware she's in a vulnerable state.'

'Well, yes, about that. The thing is, we assumed—'

'I don't care what you assumed,' I say, cutting her off mid-sentence. 'Right now, my priority is finding Sasha. Whatever issues you've got with utterly lax protocols or bullying or whatever caused my daughter to leave campus, I will deal with those later. Right now, I need to find my daughter, and I suggest you totter back into your school and find out exactly who you need to fire for negligence, because, if you don't, you are going to have a lot more issues than we already do.'

At this she pales, her complexion now the same colour as her bulging eyes. Slowly, she backs away.

'Of course. Of course I will.'

As I wind the window back up, I know I should feel sorry for her. After all, she wasn't the one who let my daughter leave school. She was probably typing away emails to overly pushy parents or working out how to spend all the money that they get from the astronomical school fees. But the buck stops with her. Just like with me.

I skid on the gravel, spraying up stones as I speed down the driveway, though I don't even know where I'm going. All I know is that Sasha isn't at the school, so I shouldn't be either.

'Ring Jamie,' I say to the car. A second later, the phone is ringing away through the car's system.

'Hey, did you get to the bottom of it?' he says, with only a hint of concern.

'She's missing,' I reply.

'What?'

'She went. They watched her get into a car. They thought it was you or me picking her up.'

'And the school let her go?'

'They did.'

For a second, he says absolutely nothing, but in the silence between us, I hear his panic rising.

'So where is she?' he says, eventually.

'I don't know. I've tried ringing her. There's no answer.'

Once again, Jamie struggles to reply, and the silence causes my stomach to twist and tighten. Jamie is the calm one. The one who has answers. Who provides pragmatic solutions to whenever I'm getting stressed or panicked about something. But he hasn't got any solutions right now.

'Do you think it could be... She could be with...' He lets the rest of his sentence fade into nothing. I hate him for voicing it aloud, though it's not like I haven't had the same thought. 'What kind of car was it she got into?' he asks, suddenly sounding more like his normal focused self.

'Sorry?'

'The car. Did you ask the school what kind of car it was? That's the first thing we need to check before we go pounding on his front door.'

'Shit, I didn't ask.'

'You didn't ask what type of car she got into?'

Now Jamie's brought it up, asking what type of car Sasha got into seems like the most obvious thing in the world, but at the time of learning she was missing, it didn't even cross my mind. The number of times I've watched films and read books and tutted with annoyance at lead characters making stupidly idiotic choices must be in the hundreds. But I get it now. It's not so easy to think when blind panic has taken over.

'I'll ring the school now,' I say. 'Do you remember what sort of car he had?'

'Something old. Beat-up.'

'That doesn't narrow it down, Jamie.'

'And red. It was definitely red.'

That's a little more to go on.

'What if he hasn't got it still? It's been a year; he could have a new car?'

'On a student musician's wage? That seems unlikely.'

I suspect Jamie's right. I haven't had a new car since this one for close to a decade, and Sasha's former boyfriend was definitely earning a lot less than me.

'Okay, I'll let you know what they say.' I hang up without so much as an 'I love you'. We don't have time for that.

A moment later, I'm dialling the school's number.

The receptionist picks up in one ring, though I don't bother giving my name. My question is more than enough to identify me.

'What colour was the car she got into?' I don't even say Sasha's name. If the woman doesn't know that already, then this school's got more than one serious problem on its hand.

'Mrs Croft?' the woman says, as if there might be someone else ringing in with the same question.

'What colour car did my daughter get in? When you let her leave your care?'

Her throat crackles, and she coughs to clear it.

'Um, I didn't get much of a look, but I think... No, I'm sure... it was a red car. Yes. It was red. An old, red car. I thought it was unusual, you know. The parents here mostly drive—'

I hang up and dial Jamie back immediately.

'It was Christopher,' I say, my heart pounding in my chest so hard, I can hear the blood rushing behind my ears. I don't know if I'm relieved or not. Sasha's not missing, that's something. But she's in the last place I want her to be. 'Christopher is the one who picked her up.'

'You're sure.'

'I'm willing to bet on it.'

Jamie's silence reverberates down the line as I wait for him to speak. I assume he's going to tell me not to go. To wait for him, but he probably knows that would be pointless.

'You know where you're going?' he says instead.

'I think I can remember.'

'You want me to meet you there?'

At this, I let out a brief chuckle. It's the first laugh since hearing about Sasha disappearing, and it's brimming with bitterness.

'That's probably wise,' I say. 'A murder record wouldn't look good on a headteacher.'

33

Boys. Before I was a mother to a daughter, I had never really worried about them. Even when Sasha was little and in her early teens, I never thought they would be an issue for my daughter. She grew up surrounded by people who love her. She was smart, had her head on straight and a good family to fall back on. There was no way I thought she'd fall fool for the immature tricks of boys at school, who were doing anything they could to get their first flash of boobs or snog behind the bicycle shed. And I was right. Sasha was way too mature to fall for the antics of young boys like that.

But what happened was so much worse.

They met at a youth orchestra. Only Christopher wasn't part of the youth section. He was one of the adults, brought in from a local music college to boost the numbers and the standard of performance. They played the same instrument – the oboe – and Sasha would often stay back for half an hour after the sessions for him to help her. Despite being one of the youngest, she wanted the first position, and was a good enough player to get it, too. I wasn't foolish enough not to realise she had a crush on him, but I didn't think he would reciprocate. She was fifteen, after all. He was twenty-one. At that age, it might as well have been half a century difference between them.

Jamie hit the roof when he found out that they were in a relationship. It's probably the only time in my life I've seen him truly lose it. Don't get me wrong, I was equally horrified, but I tried a gentler approach. I'd been like her once. Headstrong and heartfelt. I wasn't approving of it. No, I was as appalled as Jamie, but I was sure it would fizzle out and so I said all the things I thought a supportive, loving mother should. I made sure I was there for her. Made her know she could be open with me. Though perhaps a harder line would have changed what happened next. I can't think about that too deeply, though. Even after a year, the guilt is still too raw.

'Why would she be in contact with him after the way he treated her?' I say to Jamie, still struggling to piece the situation together. I still haven't got to the bottom of why she left school, but, with him on the scene, I'm getting a clearer and clearer idea.

'Who knows, but, when we find her, she is grounded. Forever.'

'Agreed.'

'I'm heading over to Leigh now,' I say.

The town Christopher lives in is securely etched into my memory, not that I was ever planning on visiting him again.

'I'll try ringing him on the way. I'm sure I still have his number. I'll let you know when I get there.'

'Okay,' Jamie says. 'I've got to excuse myself from a meeting now. You'll keep in contact, right?'

'Of course I will.'

I take a deep breath in, trying to steady the tremble that's spread down to my knees. I don't know if Jamie can hear the tension that's wrapping itself around me or if he just knows the state I'm in.

'Liz, it's fine. She'll be okay. She'll be okay.'

'She will?' I say, half as a question. Half as a statement.

'She will. He was an arsehole to her at the end, but he never hurt her physically or anything. You need to remember that. The only thing he actually broke was her heart.'

The state Sasha was in a year ago makes it hard to believe she wasn't physically wounded, but Jamie's right. Not that it's much comfort.

'We'll speak soon, okay?' he says. 'Love you.'

'Love you too.'

A second later, he hangs up.

It's only a twenty-minute drive from the school to the house, but it's an impossibly slow twenty minutes. The traffic is against me, with people waiting at every zebra crossing, every set of traffic lights turning red, and various trucks and lorries reversing into the road, bringing everything to a halt. Just as I said to Jamie, I try to ring Christopher's number, but it goes straight to voicemail.

I leave a message.

'If she's with you. Ring me. Now.' I hang up, then try again a few minutes later. Still no answer. This time, I don't bother with a message. He's not going to pick up, and I need to leave the line open, in case Sasha tries to get hold of me.

'What if they haven't gone to his house?' I say, voicing my thoughts aloud. 'What if they've run away?'

It was only a fleeting thought, not something I considered with any seriousness, but, once it's out there, it refuses to shift. I'll have to go to the police. Tell them all I know. See if they can track Christopher's car.

As my mind goes down a rabbit hole of worst scenarios, I try to focus on what I actually know. I try to remember how Sasha was this morning. She only had her normal school bag waiting by the door. It's big, but she would have needed more if she was running away, wouldn't she? I remind myself that, whatever happened, it didn't take place until she was at school. I'm the one she tried to get hold of first. I'm the one she wanted to come and get her. I was just too busy with my fucking job.

I'm picking at my nails as I wait for the traffic to move off, but I'm so distracted that I don't even notice the light has changed until the other cars start beeping behind me.

As I turn into the estate, my pulse kicks up a notch. As much as I don't want her to be here, I need her to. I need to know that this is where Sasha is. And so, as I see the battered red car, parked outside a block of flats, I close my eyes and say a prayer.

34

As a headteacher, you occasionally visit student homes, and it's never a positive experience. You don't visit parents of students who are doing well. You don't pop in to congratulate them on raising a wonderful child and doing a fantastic job of parenting. No, when you go in, it's as a last resort.

Sometimes, you're worried about the child and their home situation, so you make it look as casual as possible and keep the conversation light while you're secretly trying to take everything in. Other times, it might be a serious issue with attendance, or it could be the parents refusing to come into school to discuss matters and leaving you with no choice.

Whatever the reason, I never go alone. There's normally someone from social care with me to make sure everything is above board and no one is at any risk and, if not, there will always be another member of staff.

But this time, I'm on my own, and the child I'm worried about is my own. But that's not the only reason I'm shaking. I'm shaking because I remember the only other time I came here.

It was only by luck I discovered what Sasha and Christopher

were up to. It started like a normal Saturday. Sasha was attending the orchestra in the morning and then was meeting friends in the afternoon to go bowling. It had become the weekend routine, which finished with her getting the bus home, offering her a level of freedom we were all comfortable with. At least, that was what I thought, but that was the weekend I found out she'd been lying to me for weeks.

I met Alice for brunch after dropping Sasha off. It was meant to be one drink and a natter, but, as was often the case with Alice, it turned into a little more than that, and soon it was gone three. Given that I couldn't drive, I thought I might as well get the bus home with Sasha. I thought it would be fun. After all, she always used to like things like that when she was younger, and the bowling alley was just around the corner from where Alice and I had met.

I know it sounds strange for a mum of a teenager to say, but I really didn't think Sasha would mind me turning up and seeing if she wanted me to wait for her. After all, I'd known all her friends for years, and while I was Mrs Croft in school, I was still Liz, or Sasha's mum, to them outside of it.

The friends were there. Only Sasha wasn't. She'd been moved up to another level of orchestra that went on all day, they told me. That was why she hadn't been able to meet them for weeks.

I shook my head and laughed, and commented on losing my head if it wasn't screwed on. Somehow, I kept my pace steady as I walked out of the bowling alley. Only then did I allow myself the luxury of panic.

I rang the orchestral director first, just to make sure I hadn't got confused and Sasha's friends were telling me the truth, but the orchestra ran from eight until twelve. There were no extended sessions. Any lessons older students might have offered were on their own time in locations that were nothing to do with the orchestra. It was when I rang Jamie that the panic really set in. Of course, he was logical about it. Furious, but logical. Given how I had spoken to Christopher once at drop off and he'd talked about how well Sasha was doing in their private lessons, it didn't take long to put the pieces together. Why she'd lied to us. Where she could be. In the end, it took me half a dozen guesses to work out the password to Sasha's laptop and ten minutes reading through her messages to track down where Christopher lived. Jamie and I went in together, all guns blazing.

But that was over a year ago. When Sasha had fallen pregnant and Christopher had tried to pressure her into keeping the baby, Sasha had been heartbroken, and part of me had been glad. Not to see my daughter in pain. No, no mother wants that. But because I thought it meant she would never fall prey to a man like that again. And yet here I am, standing outside his door.

I take a deep breath, step forward and check on the flat numbers before I press the buzzer. It's not the nicest part of town. But I won't pretend it's not still impressive – a lad of his age already owns a property. That's something young people are finding harder and harder to do. Especially in this part of the country. Jamie and I were lucky.

I push the buzzer, holding it for a second longer than normal, before I release. A few seconds later, I hear the voice on the other end.

'Hello?'

It's a single word, but I know it's him. Nausea sweeps through me.

'Christopher, it's me. I know she's with you. I need to see her. I don't know what's wrong and I'm not mad. I just need to make sure she's okay.'

For a second, there's nothing other than him breathing down the end of the line, and I think he's going to refuse.

'She doesn't want to speak to you.'

Those were the words I didn't want to hear. Because if he won't let me in, then I'll break down his door, and do a whole lot of things that are gonna get me in an awful lot of trouble.

'Christopher, let me see my daughter. Now.'

A moment passes and I'm looking around, wondering how I'm going to get inside, when the door buzzer is pressed.

Relief floods through me, but it's gone within a heartbeat.

I push the door open and walk up the stairs. Now that I know she's here and safe, all I want to know is why? Why she ran out of school when everything has been going so well? What could have been that bad that she couldn't wait for me or her dad to pick her up?

I'm preparing these questions in my head, not to ask Sasha, but Christopher, because I don't expect her to speak to me first.

Which is why my heart surges and aches as I reach his floor and see her standing there in the doorway.

'Sasha!'

I run up to her, let her fall into my arms and pull her so close, I don't think anyone's ever going to be able to prise her off me. I never want to let her go. Ever. I'm still having that thought when she pulls away and looks up at me.

Her face is tear-stained, red and blotchy like she's been crying for hours. There's not a hint of colour to her cheeks. Her whole body looks drained in a way I've only ever seen once before.

'They know, Mum. Everyone knows.'

35

I stand there in the doorway, my head shaking.

'What do you mean?' I say.

'*They know*, Mum. Everybody knows.' The tears are back, but this time they're angry tears, and I can't help but feel the anger is aimed at me. A fact that's confirmed as she turns around and storms back into the flat. For a split second, I think she's going to slam the door in my face but she leaves it open. Given that I have no intention of leaving here without her, I take it as an invitation to follow her inside.

I close the door behind me and, within two steps, I'm standing in the main living area of the flat. Tucked away to one side, Christopher is in the corner of the kitchenette by the kettle, trying to look inconspicuous. It doesn't work. Just the sight of him is enough to make me want to hurl something across the room. It might sound ridiculous, but maybe I'd have understood if he was less attractive. If he would have had difficulty finding a girl his own age. But he's not. He's a stereotypically good-looking lad. Tall, floppy-haired, slightly brooding eyes. Though I know he's shy. Sasha told me that. He struggles to talk to people he doesn't know well, unless it's about music. That's why they hit it off. But there are plenty of women his own age who play in orchestras.

I feel my fingers flexing, like I have a physical allergy to being near him. But, despite the urge to wrap my hands around his neck, I manage to ignore him. I'm not here for Christopher. I'm here for my daughter.

Sasha sits down on the sofa with a thud, and I move across to her, but, rather than taking a seat, I kneel on the ground and take her hands in mine. Tears are streaming down her cheeks.

'Honey, I need you to back up a bit. Tell me what happened.'

She scoffs. 'I just told you what happened. I went to school. We had assembly. Break, and everything was normal, and then a girl came up to me. I barely even know her, but she just came right out and said it. "You're the one who had to move from Saint Anne's because you had an abortion, right? You were the one that got pregnant by the music guy."'

I drop from where I'm perched on my feet and can feel my jaw hang open in disbelief.

'No, how... They can't have been serious. They can't know. It must've been something they said. Just to get a rise out of you. You know girls do that. You know they say mean things.'

Tears are still filling Sasha's eyes as she shakes her head. 'And they just guessed my exact situation? No. No, they knew. By the time I went back to my lesson, everyone knew. I tried to get hold of you, but you weren't replying. And I've been messaging Christopher for the last couple of weeks and—'

'You and Christopher have been messaging?'

For the first time since I've entered the room, my head snaps to where Christopher is now busy with the kettle. It's clear he's trying not to look at me.

'He messaged to apologise, Mum. A couple of weeks back...

We were in Singapore. He saw all of my photos on Instagram and liked them. He's just been through a break-up. Had his heart broken. He understands what he put me through. He realised he was wrong. He wanted to apologise.'

'He will *never* understand what he put you through. What he did to you. The way he tried to pressure you.' My jaw is locked now and tension is the only thing that's stopping me from flying across the room. And judging from the way Christopher edges towards me, he knows that.

'You're right, Mrs Croft, I get it. I mean, I know I can't ever fully understand, but I get that.' It's not unusual having a twenty-two-year-old man calling me Mrs Croft. I've taught enough students who are now full-grown adults, with families of their own. But I didn't teach Christopher. He's just calling me Mrs Croft because he's terrified of me. 'But last weekend was the first time I've seen Sasha all year.'

'Last weekend?' I say, then it twigs. The train journey. She probably didn't even get on it. Christopher probably picked her up and drove her there. I pull in a lungful of air and hold it in my chest for a second before letting it out with a long sigh. There are discussions we need to have as a family. Lying, sneaking around, being back in touch with Christopher and not letting us know about it. But not now. Now there are more immediate issues.

'Darling, I don't know what to say. But people have no evidence of this. It's a rumour. It doesn't matter what the truth is; only we know that. You could just go back to school. Go back to school like nothing happened, and I'll get these girls hauled in front of the head for spreading vicious rumours.'

She shakes her head, flicking the tears from her cheeks as she does so.

'No, no, I can't. I can't go back there. It's not just them. I've had messages from other people, too. From Cali, Naomi...' The names she's telling me are all the people she was friends with at St Anne's. The ones she used to cover what she was doing when she used to meet up with Christopher. Girls who are still under my care in my school. 'They know too. Everyone knows everywhere.'

I shake my head. 'I'm so sorry, darling. I'm so sorry.'

As I wrap my arms around her, I hear my phone buzzing in my pocket. Most likely it's Jamie, telling me he's on his way, or wanting to know if I've found Sasha already. I need to message him. I need to tell him she's okay. But I won't do it until I have her in the car. Until I know she's safe with me.

'Come on, baby girl. I'll take you home now. We'll work it out together, okay? We can work out what we need to do. But I need you to come home with me now.'

For a moment, I think she's going to stand up, but her eyes narrow on me.

'You didn't tell anyone about it, did you?' she says. 'You promised you wouldn't. Not even Alice. You said you wouldn't tell anyone.'

A twist of guilt corkscrews behind my sternum, and my heart rate flickers up by just a notch. We swore. Jamie and I swore to her that no one outside the three of us would ever know about the abortion. Promised her on all our lives that we would never tell another soul. Which is why, as I look at her, I say in the most truthful voice I can muster, 'No, darling, of course I didn't.'

36

Jamie is waiting for us when we get home. I messaged to say that I'd got her. She was okay. And to meet us at home. I was quite forceful on that point, knowing how, just like me, he'd like to show Christopher exactly what he's had coming since he first laid hands on Sasha. But Christopher can wait. Sasha can't.

The moment the front door opens, she bounds up the stairs and slams her door shut.

'Is it too early for wine?' I say to Jamie, moving into the kitchen.

'It's half one,' he tells me.

'I'll take that as a no.'

As I pour a glass of rosé, I fill him in on everything, from the fact that Christopher and Sasha are talking again to the rumours at the school. By the time I've finished, the glass is empty again and I'm already going for a top up.

'I take it you're going to stay home today?' Jamie says. 'You're not going back into work.'

I shake my head. 'Sandra emailed to say she'd cancelled al

my meetings. No questions asked. Though I'm sure she'll be stirring that gossip pot again tomorrow.'

Jamie nods thoughtfully.

'And what about tomorrow? Are you going to take that off work too?'

'Why would I do that?' I reply, confused.

'To be with Sasha. You can't expect her to go into school tomorrow. And I don't think it's wise for her to stay home on her own. I would stay, but I've got meetings I can't miss.'

'Sasha going back to school is the best thing for her,' I say. I pinch the stem of my glass between my fingers as I speak. 'If she stays away, people will think the rumours are true.'

'But they are true,' he states.

'Nobody knows that. Nobody but us.' This time, I pick up my glass and take a long draw before placing it back down on the table with a sigh. 'We should have gone to the police back then,' I say. 'I should have just done it.'

This time last year, every part of me wanted to see Christopher behind bars for statutory rape. Do I think he's a predator who will do the same thing again, to other teenagers? I don't know. I honestly don't. Sasha tried to convince me that she was pushing the physical side just as much as he was. But she was a child. She didn't know what she was pushing for. He was the adult. He should have known it was wrong. If he loved her, he should have protected her. Instead, he got her pregnant, tried to convince her that, if she really loved him, she would keep it and broke her heart when she didn't.

I press my lips together tightly as my mind remains lost in the past. The only reason I didn't report him to the police was because, if I did, I knew I'd lose her. The number of screaming matches we had that year still makes me light-headed to think of. So many times, I thought she might walk out the door and not come back. But that was before the pregnancy. When Christopher made it clear what type of man he was, Sasha came right back to us, begging for help.

'I can't raise a baby,' she says. 'With him, or without him. I can't do it. I can't and I don't want to. I want to go to music college. I want to travel around the world on stage. I can't do that if I have a baby, can I?'

I took a full week off work after her appointment, which I said was because of my mother being ill – although that could be true; I haven't spoken to her in the best part of two decades, after a remarkably similar experience to the one that Sasha went through. That was when I finally told Sasha the truth about why she didn't see her grandmother.

After it happened, Sasha started over at the new school. And that came with enough issues of its own. So it was like those months had never happened. It was a relief, in some ways.

Silence has cloaked the table, and I know exactly what I have to say to break it. But it's easier said than done. My hands are back around my glass, cupping it this time as I finally speak.

'I told Alice,' I say to Jamie, as I stare at the table.

'What?'

'I told Alice about the abortion.'

I finally lift my eyes to look at him, only to find his face crinkled in confusion. Like he doesn't believe what I'm saying.

'You did? When?'

'About a week after it happened. You were working late. Sasha had gone for an oboe lesson and Alice came round for a drink. I broke down and told her. She'd been there for me when I went through the same. I knew she'd get it. You don't think she would've told anyone, do you?'

'You mean like Katie?'

In one word, he's confirmed all my worst fears. Katie is at an age where her and Alice's relationship is different from mine and Sasha's. They don't see each other that much, but, when they do, it's more like they're friends than mother and daughter, going out together, drinking cocktails, dancing 'til the early morning. What if, after one of those drinks, Katie asked how Sasha was doing, and Alice let it slip? It's certainly feasible. But why would Katie want people to know? I always thought she considered Sasha a younger sister of sorts. I could never imagine her wanting to hurt her that way. But then relationships change, and I'd be naïve to think that Sasha hasn't hidden more from me than just speaking to Christopher again. Perhaps she and Katie had a falling out, and Katie used this as a way to get back at her. It doesn't seem very in character for my goddaughter who I used to spend so much time with, but those days are a long way in the past. Who's to say she hasn't changed.

I scrunch my eyes closed, trying to block out the whirl of questions spinning through my mind, and pick up my glass, only to find it empty.

'I have to go in tomorrow,' I say, pushing back the hurricane of thoughts to focus on Jamie's previous question. 'If I don't go in, it'll look like I need to comfort Sasha.'

'Better for Sasha, or better for you and the school?'

The harshness in Jamie's voice takes me by surprise.

'Better for her, of course,' I say. 'If I don't go in, people will assume it's true and I won't be able to put a stop to any of the rumours. I think she should go in too.'

'You can't be serious.'

'What other option do we have, Jamie? Wait for it to die down? That will never happen if she doesn't go back. There are going to be a couple of tough days, I'm not denying that. But they'll happen whenever she goes back. Better she gets its over and done with if you ask me.'

Jamie tuts as he stares at the table. I don't know if the noise is aimed at me, or the situation, but, when he speaks again, his voice is far quieter.

'There has to be a way of making this go away for her.'

'You mean like moving school again? We're already paying the fees there. Besides, this is an exam year. It's one of the most important years for her.'

At this, Jamie scoffs.

'Please, I'm not one of your parents that you have to convince about getting grades to hit your school's residual targets. I know how it works, remember? My daughter is a good kid. She will do well wherever she goes.'

'Our daughter,' I reinforce, not sure why he said it in such a manner.

A tension is wrapping itself back around the room as Jamie lets out a long sigh. 'It's only her GCSEs, right? She only needs enough to get through to her A-Levels, anyway. And she could do that with her eyes closed. Didn't she already pass one last year?'

Two, I want to say, but I don't. I keep that to myself. It doesn't help the argument. Jamie carries on regardless.

'So she only has to pass four more, right? To do her A-Levels, which don't really matter because she's going to go to music college, anyway. Why don't we just home-school her?'

'While we both work full time?' I say, struggling to believe we are having this conversation. 'Are you going to quit your job to do that, or are you expecting me to?'

'I'm not saying we actually have to teach her. She'll be able to do that herself. Videos and things. Online tutors.'

'And cut her off from all her friends and schoolmates. You think that will make it easier in the long run?' This time, my question is met by silence. Silence that I desperately want to break. After all, us sitting here, bickering about it, isn't going to solve anything.

'We can't think about this right now,' I say. 'There's too much going on. I've got a load of work to do. Stuff I missed from school.'

'Of course you do,' he replies before stepping forward and placing a kiss on my forehead. 'We don't need to be fighting about this. At the end of the day, all we want is what's best for Sasha.'

'I know you do. And I know that is.'

It's not Jamie who speaks. He and I turn our heads simultaneously and look at the doorway. Sasha is standing there, staring straight at us, and for the first time since I picked her up, her breathing is steady and her eyes are focused as she looks at us.

'I'm so sorry I've caused all this stress. I know you only want the best for me. I get that. But I've thought about this a lot, and I know how we solve it.'

'Sasha?' I move to stand, but something about her makes me stop.

'I want to move. I want to move and live with Uncle Tony. I want to move to Singapore.'

37

I don't speak. Jamie doesn't speak. Instead, we both stare at Sasha, who takes a tentative step into the room.

'I think it's the best thing I can do,' she says. 'I'll go to his school. Start afresh. Completely afresh.'

All of a sudden, it's like the blood has returned to my limbs. I jump to my feet, dash over to her, then clasp my hands on her arms, holding her square on.

'My darling, I know it feels like running away is the only thing you can do at the moment, but it's not. I promise we can sort this out. We can find a way around it. A way that doesn't involve you moving halfway across the world.'

Sasha shakes her head and looks behind me to Jamie. There are no tears in her eyes, no fear or doubt in her voice as she carries on talking.

'There's not, Mum. I need to get away from it all.'

'But you're doing so well. Just give it a bit of time to settle down.'

'I haven't been doing well, Mum. I'm a mess. A complete mess.'

Her eyes are welling now, and the last thing I want is for her to be in tears, but I just don't understand.

'But you're doing well at school. And your counsellor, you said the counsellor—'

'I've been telling her exactly the things she needs to hear. That's all. I need to get my head clear, Mum. It won't happen if I stay here. I know it won't.'

'Darling... yes, it will.'

I press my lips together and shoot a glance at Jamie, but I see the same look of confusion and fear on his face, too.

'Sasha, you need to think about this practically,' I say, trying a different approach. Whatever she says about not coping, she's a straight-A student and that hasn't slipped, even with everything going on. 'They don't even do the same exam boards as we do. It would be a massive adjustment. You might not be able to carry on with some of your subjects.'

'I thought about that,' she replies. 'I'll go back a year, into year ten for the first year to settle in, then I'll know what I'm doing, and I can really make the best of my GCSEs.'

'You'd want to be in classes with children who are younger than you?'

'I had a boyfriend six years older than me, Mum. I can deal with a bit of an age gap.'

I don't know what I'm supposed to say to that. I look at Jamie again, but this time I hold his gaze. I need him to have some sort of input in this conversation. To stop me from being the lone bad guy, pointing out all the reasons she can't go. I need him to own this, too.

Finally, he clears his throat and looks at Sasha.

'This isn't something we can decide on now. We don't even know if it'll be possible for you to transfer. These places are expensive. We'd have an awful lot to think about.'

'I know, but I'm sure Tony could get me in. He joked about it when we were there enough times. Saying I would have a place in the orchestra waiting for me. I've already messaged him.'

'Sasha, you can't do things like that,' I say, feeling exasperated, but I catch myself. 'It's the middle of the night there at the moment. Let me write something to your uncle and I'll send it in the morning, okay? Maybe we can have a conversation. But, darling, you might find that after you've had some sleep, this isn't as bad as you think it is.'

'Really?' she says. 'Do you really think that?'

I want to say I do. I want to say that by the time she wakes up in the morning, it will all have blown over, but I love my daughter too much to lie. So, instead, I just hold her close. 'We will find a solution,' I tell her. 'I promise you that.'

I fire off something to Tony before I go to sleep and the next morning when I wake up, Sasha is still in bed, but Tony has already replied to me.

> What happened? Is everything okay? Of course, she can stay with me if that's what you need. But ring me, okay? I'm worried.

I type a quick reply.

> Thank you, I'm going to work, and I'll try to ring you later.

The truth is, I want to speak to Sasha first. I'm hoping that after a good night's sleep, she's reconsidered her stance. Moving to Singapore is just running away from her problems and she's smart enough to know that. I just hope she hasn't got to the point where she doesn't care.

Before I leave for work, I make a cup of tea just the way she likes it, with far too much sugar and milk. I expect her to still be asleep, so it's a surprise to find her sitting up in bed.

'How are you feeling?' I ask, placing the tea down on the bedside table.

'Like my skull is having nails hammered into the back of it, and I feel like I've been hit by a truck.'

'Yes, crying can do that to you,' I say. 'Have you drunk plenty of water? I left you some last night.'

I gesture to the glass that I placed on the table when she was sobbing herself to sleep. It looks completely untouched. Without another word, Sasha reaches across, downs half the glass, then puts it back.

'What you mentioned last night,' I say. 'About moving? We'll talk about it properly over the weekend, okay? But, darling, like I told you before when it happened, I know it feels like the end of the world, but it will pass. I felt the same. I did. And it will always be a part of who you are, but it will pass.'

At this, Sasha shakes her head and scoffs. 'Please, Mum, don't.'

'Don't what?' I say, confused.

'Don't go there again. Don't try telling me how we're the same, just because you had an abortion too when you were younger. You were in your twenties and got pregnant with a guy you barely even knew or liked. You had a career, or at least were going to. We're not in the same situation. Christopher and I—'

'You're not thinking of getting back together with him, are you?' The words slip out of my mouth before I can stop them.

Sasha's face hardens.

'No, I'm not. It would be nice if you'd actually trust me and let me finish what I was going to say. And that's part of the problem. You're never going to trust me completely while he's living so close. Christopher and I loved each other, genuinely. And before you start on how young I am, I know, okay? But that doesn't mean it can't be real love. It doesn't mean that we couldn't have been something in the future. Had things turned out differently.'

She falls into silence, and I find my heart pounding unusually hard against my rib cage. I don't want silence. I want to keep her talking and make her see that everything is going to be okay, even if she can't see that now.

'Are you saying you regret it, sweetheart? Because that's normal too. I promise. And you're right, my situation wasn't the same. I'm sorry, I was just trying to make you see there are parts I understand. Not all of it. Just parts.'

Her lips disappear as she presses them tightly together, before releasing a long sigh.

'You should get to work, Mum,' she says. 'You don't want to miss any more time at school, not after yesterday.'

And just like that, I know I've been dismissed.

38

The morning conversation with Sasha means I'm later getting to school than I want to be. As I head down the corridors across the creaking floorboards, most of the staff are already in their classroom, while Sandra is there, sitting at the desk outside my office.

'I didn't know if you were going to come in today,' she says, standing up the second she sees me. 'Is everything all right with Sasha?'

'Everything's completely fine,' I say.

'Really? Because I've heard some rumours about—'

'You're not really going to spread schoolyard rumours about my daughter, are you?' I snap.

She pales. 'No, no, I just wanted to check she was all right, that's all.'

'Yes, you did, and I've told you she's fine. Now, can you send me through the meeting schedule for today? I've got half a dozen policies that need to be rewritten and go to the board by the end of the day.'

'Of course, of course, but you're going straight to the main hall first, aren't you?'

I tilt my head as I try to work out what she's talking about. Fridays are normally assembly day, but there's a niggle of doubt twisting in me. I know there's something I'm meant to be doing, but my head is still too full of thoughts of Sasha to think clearly.

'It's the first mock exam for the Year 11,' Sandra clarifies. 'You were going to start it off. Give the students the lay of the land with respectable behaviour and so on. I know you did it last year. But if you don't feel capable, I'm sure I can—'

'Thank you. I'm perfectly capable,' I say, irked by her choice of words. There were a lot more diplomatic approaches she could have chosen. She could've asked if I was too busy, for example. But no, she chose the word 'capable' just to get under my skin. And I'm annoyed that it does.

'Where are the exam papers?' I should have already been on top of it. But there's nothing I can do. I just have to make the best of a bad situation.

'Nathan already took them down,' Sandra says.

'And what about the hall? Is it ready?' I hate myself so much for being so incompetent so early in the term.

'Yes, I think he sorted it out earlier in the week.'

'Right, that's right. I remember.' That was when he came into my office demanding Alice help him, although it was well past a reasonable time to ask a member of staff to work.

'Nathan is down there,' Sandra continues. 'I'm sure he's got everything sorted the way it should be.'

'I'm sure he has, but it's my job.'

I can't even force one of my overly grateful, completely fake smiles. Instead, I dump my computer in my office and head across the school.

In the main hall, Alice and Nathan are talking together in the corner of the room; by the looks of things, everything is good to go.

always feel bad for Alice during exam time. She has to uproot all her lessons into whatever space is free. But she gets an amazing classroom the rest of the time. This hall has dozens of original features, from the floor-to-ceiling wooden windows to ornate coving.

'Elizabeth,' Nathan says, leaving Alice. 'We were wondering if you were going to be in today.'

'Why was that exactly?' I look him in the eye, daring him to make the same mistake as Sandra in bringing up Sasha. But he's smarter than that.

'Well, I'm glad to see you here. I'm just going to make a quick dash to the little boys' room, and I'll be back to help you start the exam off.'

'You don't need to do that. I'm perfectly capable of doing it myself,' I say.

'I know, but it's French, my subject. And I'm down for invigilation for the first hour.' He turns to Alice, directing his full charm at her; it's enough to make my toes curl. 'Good job setting all this up. I have a feeling this exam is going to run incredibly smoothly.'

Only when he's gone does Alice approach me.

'You all right? You look like shit.'

At least I know I can rely on my best friend to be honest.

'I am feeling pretty shit, actually. Sasha has decided she wants to live in Singapore with Tony.'

Alice's mouth hangs open.

'What, why? Has something happened? Is it to do with Christopher? You should know the rumours about what happened are all over St Anne's. The kids in her year and the years above were all talking about it yesterday.'

I draw in a long breath. I'd made a big deal to Sasha about how it would be easier to face this sooner rather than later, but I had been thinking solely about her. I hadn't considered the fact that I would have to face it too.

'I'll chat to you about it when we have more time,' I say, wondering how I'm going to broach the subject of Katie.

A second later, Nathan strides back into the hall.

'The kids are lining up outside,' he says with an overly authoritarian tone he should not be using with me. 'Let me know when you're ready for me to bring them in.'

There's so much to deal with for examinations: signs on the walls, reading the riot act, different timings according to the different levels of examination and personal criteria of the students, constant monitoring, walking up and down the aisles making sure there's no cheating. This is only a mock, but it sets expectations for how they do in the actual exam, so we set it up like it's the real thing. Although, as this is St Anne's, the chance of there being any issues is highly unlikely.

'I'll leave you two to it then,' Alice says before striding away.

'So, I'll get them in, and you do the papers, or the other way round?' Nathan says.

'I'm easy, whatever's best for you,' I reply. 'Though you know what exam papers the children are doing? It's probably best if I put them in their seats.'

After nodding in agreement, he grabs the papers, ready to place them on the desks while I let the children in.

'Remember, there should be no talking in the examination room,' I say at least ten times as the children walk in. It's not that they're really talking, it's just what I'm meant to say. Nothing like labouring a point.

'There should be no phones in your pockets or in your pencil cases. If you do have a phone on you, I will be forced to confiscate it and ring home to say you've broken exam protocol.'

I repeat myself until all the children are sitting in the allocated places, after which Nathan starts to hand out the papers, while I go through the instructions for the examination itself, including the equipment they can use, how long they've got to do the paper, et cetera et cetera. With the papers all out, Nathan writes the start time on the board, and with a quick look at the clock, he nods to me.

'Okay, ladies and gentlemen,' I say. 'If you would like to turn your paper over, you have an hour and a half starting now.'

There is a rustle of paper as every student simultaneously opens the first sheet of the examination booklet. I've seen the set-up hundreds of times. Some scan down the first pages before turning straight over to the next and reading every word before they even start putting pen to paper, while others grab their pens and start scribbling away, probably not reading half of what is required. But, this time, the situation is different. I feel it before I realise why. Nobody has reached for a pen and paper, and nobody is turning the pages of the booklet over either. Instead, they're glancing sideways, trying to catch each other's eyes. Some are wearing looks of confusion. Some smirks. But, in other cases, it's outright shock.

'Ladies and gentlemen, do I need to remind you it's eyes down on this exam, please? There should be no communication at all now you are in the hall.'

I'm speaking clearly, yet one or two are still whispering. And the number rapidly increases.

'Did you hear what I said?' I raise my voice now. 'You are going to be in breach of examination regulations if you carry on talking.'

I'm at a loss. Never have I known anything like it, and certainly not at St Anne's. I'm the head of the school, and these children are just ignoring me, raising their voices. I take a step back, prepared to bellow if I need to, when Nathan steps forward and grabs one of their exam papers.

'Liz,' he says. 'You need to see this.'

I walk over to where he's holding the paper out to me. Given that it's French – and my knowledge stops at GCSE level from thirty years ago – I'm not expecting to understand it. Yet the first page inside the booklet isn't in French; it's in English. And rather than printed text, there's a handwritten scrawl across the top of the page.

Like mother, like daughter.

Below it is what looks like a medical record. It takes me a second, then my hand flies to my mouth as I realise what it shows.

39

I'm standing there, frozen to the spot, unable to draw my eyes away from the printed piece of paper on the students' examination. It's a medical record, my medical record. And there's everything on there. There are the antidepressants I was prescribed for six months when I was suffering with PPD after Sasha was born and various bouts of antibiotics I've had throughout the years, normally after I've been away on holiday, swimming somewhere. There's information about blood tests and painkillers for migraines, but one thing is highlighted. The abortion I had.

Like mother, like daughter.

The abortion is what they're talking about. The students in this room are Sasha's friends. Or, at least, they used to be. Whoever has done this has hit me and Sasha at the same time. This isn't some prank; this is goddamn evil.

'Ladies and gentlemen, there's obviously been some sort of error. I think there might be a sociology part of the paper mixed up with this one.' Nathan is talking to the students. Addressing them with a chirpy voice. 'If you could just close those booklets, everything needs to stay in place. I'm going to come round and collect those papers back up. Like I said, I think this is part of a sociology A-Level examination paper that has somehow got muddled up with the French GCSE and, obviously, we don't want that. Once I've taken everyone's back in, you're going to be dismissed so we can work out what has happened to your examination papers. You will not have your French exam today, as timetabled. When I've dismissed you, please go quickly and quietly to your tutors in your study rooms, and wait for more instructions.'

Even as Nathan moves through the students, collecting up the incriminating material, I'm locked in the same position of disbelief. It's only when he has a stack of papers in his arms that I realise I need to join in, too. I need to make it look natural. As it is, all the children who aren't still reading my private medical records have their attention on me, reading my response instead. Probably ready to relate this latest piece of gossip to all their friends.

I force myself into action, following Nathan's lead, helping collect up the remaining papers and dismissing the students. When all of them have gone, Nathan turns to look at me.

'Liz, I'm—'

'What the hell was that?' I snap, having no intention of giving him time to defend himself.

'Elizabeth, are you all right?'

'What did you do? Do you think this is funny? Do you think this is a joke? I was willing to let it go when it was just that silly little photo.'

Nathan's brow folds in confusion.

'What are you on about?'

'The photograph of me last week...'

Nathan is still looking at me like he doesn't have a clue, but I can't believe he's playing that ignorant.

'It could only have come from MySpace. From someone who was friends with Alice, to be exact. And, for some unknown reason, that includes you and Leo.'

'Leo? My son, Leo?'

'I don't know many other people by that name, do you?'

His lips twist together. Pursing and pulsing, and for a split second I think he's going to admit to it, but then he speaks again.

'Let me get this right? You think because Leo is friends with Alice on MySpace, he took a photo of you and what? Had me put it up on the main screen in the hall?'

'It was on a laptop the French department uses. One you have used numerous times.'

'They're school laptops, for fuck's sake, Liz! We're meant to use them.' His outburst is followed by silence, after which he lowers his voice substantially. 'You're making some pretty big accusations here, considering you've got no evidence at all.'

'No evidence, apart from how blatantly clear you made it that you thought you should get my job. You and Leo both. But to stoop this low. To involve Sasha.'

'You need to stop right now,' Nathan says. 'Stop what you are accusing both me and my son of. It's libellous. It's entirely out of line. I get that you're upset about what happened here, but it's got nothing to do with me, or my son.'

'Do not tell me how I feel,' I say, shaking my tongue against my teeth as I enunciate each of my words.

Nathan chews on his bottom lip as he steps back a little, and it's impossible not to feel looked down upon. He's six foot three.

'Elizabeth, you need to go home now. You need to go home and let me deal with this.'

'Like I would trust you.'

'Right now, you don't have a choice. This situation needs diffusing. It's about more than you and Sasha. It's about St Anne's.'

I go to refuse, only to glance at the double doors and see a group of children staring at me. Whispering. My words from last night come back to haunt me. How I told Sasha that it was something she just had to face. Face and get over. What a hypocrite I am.

40

I don't tell Sandra that I'm leaving, though she probably works it out for herself. I storm into the office, grab my bag and computer, then march back out of the school. I feel numb. That's the only way to describe it. Like my body and mind have somehow separated from each other. It's probably not the safest state to be behind a wheel in and, when I pull into our driveway, I can't even remember the journey.

Inside, I head straight into the kitchen and don't even bother checking the time as I pull a glass out of the cupboard. It's only when I uncork a bottle of wine and hear footsteps on the staircase that I remember Sasha didn't go to school.

A second later, she's standing there, bleary-eyed, as if she's just woken up.

'Mum, what are you doing? Why are you back? Is everything okay?'

I stare at my baby girl. It doesn't matter how old she gets, she will always be my baby, and every parent will tell you the same thing; they just don't know where the time has gone.

I've tried my best. For sixteen years, I've tried to protect her from the world. Tried to raise her to be confident, and self-assured, but humble at the same time. I've tried to prepare her for disappointments in life, but never actually disappoint her. I've tried to make her empathetic and understand that all people hurt, but convince her to be strong enough to never show it when she's hurting. You want your child to be strong enough to rebel, but cautious enough to toe the line when needed. Brave enough to stand up for what she thinks is right, but never put herself in harm's way. I've tried. Every day since I first held her in my arms, I have tried. But now I'm pretty sure I've failed.

Leaving my glass on the side, I step forward, wrap my arms around her, and bury my head in her shoulder as I cry.

'I'm so sorry, darling. I'm so sorry.'

I don't know how many minutes I stay there. Holding Sasha and sobbing. At some point, she starts crying too, and I wonder if she even knows why. Whether it's for me, or for her. Or just because. More than once, I hear my telephone ringing – probably with someone calling from school to find out what the hell happened to me, and Sasha's phone buzzes too, but we don't move apart. Right now, this is what we need.

When I finally break away, she looks me in the eye and wipes the tears from my cheek the same way I did with her the night before.

'Did something happen?' she says. 'Something to do with me?'

I shake my head. I don't want to tell her the truth, at least not yet. What I want to do is get her on the next plane to Singapore so she's as far away from me as possible. That's not something I ever thought I'd say, but, right now, I don't know what's going on with my life. All I know is someone wants to tear me apart and, if I'm not careful, Sasha is going to get caught in the firing line.

Her phone buzzes again, and this time she glances down. Only to shake her head.

'They're sending me photos now,' she says, in disgust. 'They're sick. Horrible, sick bitches.'

As she moves to open the phone, I take hold of it.

'No, Sasha. Not now. You don't want to open that. You don't want to see that.'

She pauses, her eyes on me. 'You know what it is? You know what they're sending me?'

'Darling, I'm sorry. I'm so, sorry.'

I don't know why I let her take the phone back off me. Perhaps because I don't have enough strength to keep hold of it. Perhaps because I know that she's going to see it soon enough, and I'd rather I was there with her when she sees it for the first time.

My eyes stay solely on her as she swipes it open and looks at the image. Her fingers pinch and pull on the screen to make the photograph bigger. To see all those details. All those details about me and my past. Not to mention the insinuation about her, scrawled in just four words. A minute passes, and no words are spoken. All I can hear is the hammering of my heartbeat, so loud it sounds like I'm underwater. Finally, Sasha puts the phone down. She looks at me and motions her head towards the countertop where the bottle of wine and glass are sitting.

'I don't suppose you're going to let me have one of those too, are you?' she says.

41

It turns out that my sixteen-year-old stating she wants a glass of wine at 10 a.m. is just the thing to put me off the drink. I grab the glass, and pour it down the sink, then put the cork back in the bottle. Together, we sit in silence at the kitchen table. I think about messaging Jamie. I probably should do, but I don't know what I can say to him.

He knows I had an abortion, of course, but I didn't tell him until last year. Not until we were faced with a pregnant fifteen-year-old and a future of uncertainty. He acted as I would have expected him to, respectful of my decision. Understanding that I wouldn't have gone down that route unless I didn't have another choice. And I didn't. The man was supposed to be a fling. An older guy who was bored with married life. Trust me, when I think about it now, it makes me sick to my stomach. From what I remember, he had a kid, too, although I could have got that wrong. Either way, it's not like it makes it any better. He had a wife who trusted him. Like I trust Jamie. The thought of him betraying me makes me nauseous. I could try to shift the blame to the older guy. Say a cheater will always be a cheater and, if i hadn't been me, it would have been someone else, but I know that's just an excuse. I knew there was a wife, and I didn't even care when he said he would leave her. It was fun, that was all.

'You know, looking at your doctor's records, I'm a bit worried about the number of times you've had antibiotics,' Sasha says, breaking the silence. 'You know you can build up resistance to it if you have it too often.'

'Really, antibiotic resistance. That's what you're worried about now?'

I catch her eye and, a split second later, we burst into laughter. It's ridiculous laughter. Stitch-inducing, tear-streaming, breath-stolen laughter.

'Antibiotic resistance,' I say again, still choking through the tears and the gulps of air as I try to gain some control. And then, suddenly, it's silence again. And when I catch Sasha's eye, a smile tries to flicker on her lips, but it's gone before it can form.

'Why's this happening?' she says to me. 'Who's doing this to us?'

'I don't know,' I say truthfully. 'I don't know. But I'm so sorry, my darling. I'm going to do whatever I can to sort it out and stop it.'

She nods. I wish I could know what she's thinking and I'm about to ask her when the doorbell rings.

'Are you expecting anyone?' she says, a look of fear flashing across her face.

'I'm sure it's just a delivery. Why don't you go upstairs? Have a bath. I'll get that.'

She looks like she's about to refuse when she offers a quick nod.

'Okay, but don't leave, will you? Not without telling me.'

'I'm not going anywhere,' I promise.

I wait until I hear her bedroom door open before I go out into the corridor. I know from the silhouette who's standing there and, for less than a heartbeat, I consider not opening the door. I don't want to face anyone at all, especially not someone who I think has a role – however unwilling – in doing this to us. But I told Sasha less than twenty-four hours before that there was no point hiding from things, and it's time I live up to that. Besides, I have questions I need answering.

I open the door and Alice turns around and faces me. A glistening of sweat covers a brow as if she's run to get here. Given how fit Alice is, I wouldn't put it past her. She looks at me and shakes her head in disbelief.

'What the fuck is going on?' she says.

42

I lead Alice into the kitchen, where I flick on the kettle.

'I'm glad you came. There are some things I wanted to talk to you about.'

'Of course. Of course I came. I saw the papers. Nathan showed me. Liz, I'm so sorry.'

'Are you?' I say curtly.

'Sorry?' I turn around to find her face crinkled in confusion.

I want to blurt it all out at her. Scream at her, in fact. But Sasha is still in the house. As such, I move across to the staircase and call up.

'Sash? Do you need anything for your bath?'

She appears on the landing, dressed in only a towel.

'I was just going to get in.'

Good, I think. Sasha's one of those people who keeps the hot tap in the bath running, even when she's in it. It drives Jamie mad, as he's convinced it's going to wreck our boiler, along with being a massive waste of money, but I can hardly criticise her. I do the same. And right now, it will make it pretty much impossible for her to hear what Alice and I are talking about.

'Who was at the door?' she asks, still looking down at me.

'Aunty Alice. Just checking in on us. I'll come up in a bit, okay? Have a nice long soak.'

She offers me a fleeting smile before heading off in the direction of the bathroom.

When I come back into the kitchen, Alice is in the exact place I left her.

'Is Sasha okay?' she asks.

'She's handling it better than she should have to. You should be at school. You must have better things to do.'

'Better than checking in on you? I don't think so. Liz, what is this? What is going on?'

'You know what's going on. That's why you're here, isn't it?'

'I don't mean about school. Maybe I'm wrong, but I feel like you think I'm to blame for this somehow.'

'Do you? Why could that be?' I make no attempt to hide my animosity. 'Could it be because it was your photo of me that's been spread around the entire school, or because you were the one person outside of the family who knew about Sasha? Until yesterday, that is.'

Her eyes widen as she looks at me. Staring in disbelief.

'You can't really believe that,' she says.

'Then swear to me you never told anyone. That you never told Katie.'

She shakes her head, with her jaw still open, creating a strange wobbling effect on her cheeks.

'Liz, I didn't. I swear on Katie's life. I have never mentioned it. Not to anyone. You told me that one time, and that's been it. That's the only time I've ever talked about it with anyone. I swear. I would never do that. I love Sasha, you know I do. And I told you about the photo. I came to tell you about it. Why would I have done that if I'm to blame? I'm so sorry this is happening to you,

Liz. To you and Sasha. But it's got nothing to do with me. I swear. I swear.'

Silent tears trickle down her cheeks. I've seen through a lot of highs and lows. We've been there, through the toughest and most incredible moments of each other's lives, but I've never seen her looking like this before. Looking so absolutely distraught. There's no doubt in my mind that she's telling the truth.

'I promise, I promise, Liz.'

And just like that, I feel like the worst human and friend in the world.

'Screw it,' I say, standing up and marching over to the cupboard. 'I need a glass of wine for this.'

43

Two minutes later, and we're sitting in the living room. I've topped my wine up with lemonade to make a spritzer, which seems like a more reasonable option for day drinking. Alice has got to go back into school, so has opted for a cup of tea instead.

'I'm sorry, but the whole thing has got me so paranoid,' I say. I've got my fingers pressed into my skull by the bridge of my nose. Migraines were something I didn't really experience until I took the job of Head. Some would probably say that's a reason not to keep doing it. Jamie certainly did. After all, any profession that affects your physical health can't be a good thing, can it? But this year was meant to be less stressful.

'You know, he lied straight to my face,' I tell her. 'Said he had nothing to do with it?'

'Who did?' Alice says, once again looking at me like I'm talking in riddles. But I probably am to her.

'Nathan.'

'Nathan? You think Nathan has something to do with it now?'

'I always have,' I say. 'He's the one who has the most to gain from this. From bringing me down.'

Alice shakes her head while looking at me like I've gone crazy.

'Nathan would never do anything like that. He's the one taking my classes now. He wanted me to come and check on you. Make sure you're okay.'

To me, that's just more evidence. 'Of course he does,' I say. 'Because he thinks he's pushed it too far.'

She looks at me, her eyebrows butted up to her forehead.

'You can't seriously think Nathan is behind all this, can you?'

I take a sip of my drink, before allowing myself a long and ponderous breath in.

'Assuming that you didn't tell anyone about Sasha—'

'You don't need to assume,' she says sharply. 'I've already told you I didn't.'

I let out a sigh. 'You're right, I'm sorry. I'm just still working this all out in my head. As you didn't tell anyone about Sasha, then it makes sense, even more now. His wife is a doctor, right? She would have access to the medical records. Mine and Sasha's.'

'His ex-wife,' Alice says.

'Sorry?'

'Ex-wife. They split up, well over a year ago now.'

'Wait, why? How come I don't know about it?'

'He doesn't like people to know his business at all. Probably didn't want you to think it was impacting the way he was doing his job.'

'But he told you.'

'Yeah... about that...'

I am struggling to believe there's something so fundamental about my staff, I don't know. Not that I think Alice is lying. She's got absolutely nothing to gain from doing that. But I'm just surprised that I didn't see some signs. Maybe that's why Nathan wants to do all the early-morning and after-school things.

Because he needs to find some way to block out the loneliness. Alice goes to speak, but I need to keep verbalising my thoughts. Like putting together an audible jigsaw.

'In that case, it makes even more sense about Leo,' I say. 'You know how kids can act up in divorce? It can change them. Make them lash out at people they think are to blame. Maybe he thinks I'm the reason his family broke up. Because his parents wouldn't have got divorced if his dad got the job. Yes, it makes sense why he would do that.'

'You're clutching at straws with this,' Alice says, rising. 'I promise you. Look, I have to head off. Nathan said he could cover me until lunch, but I should get back as soon as I can. He and June need to sort out the exam rescheduling.'

I hadn't even thought about that, but obviously it makes Nathan look good. Jumping in and taking the reins. He's probably got a name plaque already engraved to go on my office door. Well, he's not getting in there.

'Have you heard anything from the governors yet?' Alice adds as she moves to the door.

'The governors?'

'Well, they wanted to have a meeting about the photo, right? They're going to want to talk about this too. Abortions. Catholic school. You know.'

'Shit,' I say, when I realise she's right. One of the parent governors has a child in that French class, too. I bet they already know. I've just put my glass down on the side table when my phone starts ringing and I glance down to see Florence's name flashing boldly. Lifting it up, I turn the screen to Alice so that she can see it.

'Freaky timing,' she says.

'Freaky indeed.'

She pulls me in close and places a light kiss on my cheek.

'I'm here for you, Liz, you know that. Always. I'm always on your side.'

I nod. The knots of guilt inside me tug tighter. I have no idea how I could have ever thought she was to blame. When we break away, the phone is still ringing, and I get the feeling it's not going to stop anytime soon.

'I guess I'd better take this,' I say.

44

Alice doesn't need showing out. Instead, she offers me one more look of sympathy, then leaves me to pick up the phone.

'Florence,' I say. 'I take it this isn't a social call.'

There's no point beating around the bush, and I don't have the energy for niceties.

'Elizabeth, how are you holding up?' Her voice is laden with concern. 'I'm sure you're aware by now that all the governors have been informed of what happened in the examination. What a horrible incident. Very vicious indeed,' she stresses the 'v's on each of the words.

'Yes, it was pretty horrendous,' I say.

'You poor, poor thing. I can't imagine what it was like.'

After the way she tried to pin the photograph issue on me, I was almost expecting her to twist the truth with this one too. But, of course, how can she? These are medical records. Private and secure. There is no way I would want anyone to see them. Not to mention the comment on my daughter. Maybe now they'll take these threats on me more seriously.

'I know today has already been unbearably stressful, but

would you mind having a quick meeting about this in person? Just so we get all our facts straight?' Florence asks. It's a polite and reasonable enough question, but I know there's only one answer I'm allowed to give.

'Yes, of course. I was planning on coming back into school this afternoon, anyway.' I glance at the empty wineglass. It was a pretty substantial measure, but it was still only one glass. There shouldn't be any problem with me driving in. Particularly not if I wait another hour or so. 'I needed to come back to check on my daughter, and make sure she's all right with me leaving again, but as long as it's quick?'

I know the way these things labour on. When I get there, I plan on giving a very firm time limit. Twenty minutes and then I'm going to be out of there. There's nothing I have to say that would warrant more time than that.

'Oh yes, it will be. I won't waste your time. I know how much stress your family must be under.'

My family. I haven't even told Jamie what's happened yet. Somehow, amid telling Sasha and accusing Alice, it slipped my mind. It'll be my next job, after dealing with Florence.

'I can come back to school to meet you. Whatever time you want,' I add, only as soon as I speak, a shudder ripples down my spine. The image of the children's faces giggling behind the glass doors forms in my mind. Looks and sniggers from the staff are bound to follow too. They'll all know by now.

'Perhaps after school hours?' I suggest, with a hint of hopefulness.

There is a pause.

'Actually,' Florence says. 'I was thinking it would be better if we do this off school property. Why don't I come to you? Or perhaps we could meet somewhere. Would that work?'

A house call from Florence? As a teacher, house calls are

reserved for the very worst of situations. Somehow, I don't think it's any exception when it's the Head involved.

'Sorry, yes, of course. Though perhaps not here. Sasha is at home today.'

'Of course. Yes, of course she is. Well, there's a little coffee shop in Bexley. That's not too far away from you, is it?'

'Yes, Bexley is good for me.'

'Great, and there's nothing to worry about. It's just a chat.'

'Right,' I say. 'Just a chat.'

If I hadn't been wary before, I definitely am now.

45

I don't ring Jamie straight away. I try to. I pick up the phone and stare at his name on the screen, but I don't know where I'd start. Whatever is happening, I'm the target. I'm sure of that. Sasha is just collateral damage. If it was the other way round, if it were Jamie who was being targeted instead of me, I'd be furious at him. Furious at him for bringing this pain onto our daughter, even if I don't know why. Then again, maybe it's just because I'm so angry at myself that I feel this way.

As I brush my hair and reapply my makeup, I find myself once again regretting that earlier glass of wine. It was only one glass, but I haven't had anything to eat this morning, and after the way Florence finished that conversation, I feel like I should be at my sharpest. I guess I just need to make sure I've had a couple of coffees and some food before I meet her.

Sasha is still in the bath and I have no intention of rushing her, so I wait until she's out before I tell her about the meeting.

'You don't mind, do you? I've made them promise it will be quick.'

Any colour that the hot bath added to Sasha's cheeks fades.

'Why do they need to speak to you? You didn't do anything?'

'Hey, there's no need to look like that,' I say, reaching out and taking her hand. 'The governors just need my account of things, that's all. After which, they'll hopefully piece together enough evidence to go to the police.'

'The police?' Sasha turns near translucent as she says this. 'You want to go to the police about this?'

'It's not just a case of what I want to do, it's what I need to do, Sash. This person is attacking me, not to mention the fact they've stolen medical information. That's a crime.'

'I get that, it's only... only...'

'Only what?' I say.

Sasha hesitates, and I can hear the thoughts whirring around her mind.

'Things end up in the papers when the police get involved, don't they?' she says finally. 'Isn't that what happens? When the police get notified, so do the papers. We'll end up on the front page somewhere.'

I want to offer her assurances, promise it'll be all right, but, until that moment, I hadn't even considered it. She's right, though. This would be a great by-line for some local rag in need of a quick story. *Catholic school teacher shares abortion story to school.*

I try to swallow back the images as they rise.

'We're not going to worry about that now,' I say, trying to sound confident.

'But if it ends up in the papers about you, then me and Christopher—'

'Like I said, we're not going to worry about that now.' I'm squeezing her hands even tighter, though I look her straight in the eye. 'I promise, your dad and I'll be here to handle every-thing. And if Singapore is what you want, then we can make it happen. Somehow. I promise, Sash, whatever is going on, we will find out and whoever is responsible will be punished.'

For a second, I'm sure she's going to call me out on making a promise that is entirely beyond my power to keep. She's certainly smart enough to know that I have no control over the situation regarding the police and papers, but I think she's holding on to whatever scrap of hope she can find, no matter how delusional.

'Okay,' she says, and nods her head. 'Okay, just don't be gone too long.'

'I won't. I promise you.'

46

I decide to wait until I know exactly what is going on before I call Jamie. That way, I won't have to give him half a story. Hopefully, this conversation with Florence will help figure out what our next steps are going to be.

The café Florence has chosen is old fashioned. Circular tables, wheel-back chairs and floral, vinyl wipe-clean tablecloths. Not to mention a vase of real carnations next to every menu. It's the type of place my mother would have taken me for tea, in the days when we still spoke, all those years ago. But, despite the dated décor, the place is bustling. Mainly with older people, enjoying toasted teacakes and sharing pots of tea, but there are a couple of mum-and-baby groups too. I can't imagine it's the type of place Florence frequents, but maybe that's the point. Perhaps she doesn't want to be recognised out in public, doing what she's about to do.

She's already there when I arrive. The second she sees me, her lips contort into such a tight smile, they're practically invisible.

'Elizabeth, Liz.' She stands up and adopts an expression of

devastation. 'What a terrible thing to happen. I've seen it, you know. Iris sent me the photo.'

I can't decide if the comment is meant to be a comfort or not. Of course, I knew the photo would be circulated. And Sasha has already shown me that. But knowing that it's getting to parents too, that's a different level of dread. And then there's still the question of how they got the photo. There were no phones in the exam hall, which means somebody either took a photo afterwards, when I left the papers with Nathan, or beforehand, meaning they're one of the people involved.

A flicker of hope ignites within me. If I can find out where the chain of messages started, maybe that will help find out who did it. I'm hoping that Florence's next suggestion is going to include something similar, along with a discussion about going to the police. Instead, she waves the waiter over, orders a pot of tea, and then looks at me solemnly.

'I want to be truthful with you, Elizabeth,' she starts. 'And that means there is no point in me sitting here, pretending that you were my ideal appointment for this position. I'll be honest, I thought you were too wishy-washy in your interview. Too soft. Not to mention too career-driven for a woman your age.'

I'm not sure how I'm supposed to respond to such unflattering remarks, or that she's insulted all women my age in one fell swoop. So I stay silent.

'We have definitely had our differences,' she continues. 'Different ways of seeing things. But I know the students think the world of you. And the parents find you very supportive. At the end of the day, it's the students and parents who matter in our line of work.'

'Personally, I think it's the students alone,' I correct her. 'But thank you, thank you – that means a lot.'

She offers a taut and awkward smile that falls into an expression of genuine relief as the waiter brings the pot of tea and places it on the table. Florence lifts the lid, removes the bag, and puts it on the side. She doesn't pour a drink. Instead, she takes the milk jug, and adds a dash to the bottom of her teacup, and lets out a long sigh.

'Elizabeth, you have done an admirable job, but what was revealed today—'

Revealed – I don't like the way she says that word. It's as if there's blame in it. Or the fact she called my work 'admirable.'

'The information disclosed this morning had some very real implications. We at St Anne's uphold our moral values. They are at the centre of all we do. Our core foundation.'

'I know, which is why we need to find whoever is doing this. This... the picture, my daughter, too – information was spread about her before today. And I think I know—'

'We will get to that, Elizabeth, I promise. I'm not dismissing your concerns, but, right now, my job is to nullify and control the most imminent threat to our community.'

Imminent threat to the community – it sounds like she's talking about large-scale terror attack.

'I have already had dozens of parents contact me who do not think it is right for you to continue in your position based on your history.'

Florence's eyes dart around the room, as if she's terrified someone may have overheard.

'My history? Do you even know why I had the abortion?'

It's a selfish line to use. When it comes to my abortion, I think it was the least traumatic that anyone who has to go through that situation can ever experience. But it's the fact that Florence would say such a thing without having a clue. All my form said was abortion. That could just have easily been for a miscarriage. She has no idea what other people go through, and it's clear she doesn't care. And, as for the dozens of complaints, what about the hundreds of parents who have no issue with me still working?

Her face flashes red, but only for a second.

'I'm afraid the reason does not matter,' she says, matter-of-factly.

'Oh my God, it really doesn't,' I say, feeling like I'm drifting out of my body, into another place or time. Somewhere with completely ignorant and harmful views. 'You don't care.'

'I can understand you're upset by this,' Florence says, trying again to smile. Although why is beyond me.

'No, no, obviously you can't. Because you would never have come here if you did. This is disgusting. You are disgusting.' I know I've pushed it too far but I can't help it. Now I've started, I can't stop. 'You think you can invite me to tea, throw a few false sympathies towards me, and I will give up a job I love? That's what your plan was, right? To get me to quit. To get me to give up on a career that I have spent decades building. I'm sorry, but if that's what you came for, you're going to be leaving here very disappointed.'

I stand up and place my hands on the tea table, hard enough to wobble the surface and knock some milk and spill the tea out of the teapot.

'If you want me out, you've got to go through all the proper channels, and you will have to drag me kicking and screaming through every one of them.'

47

This time, I don't hesitate. I'm straight in through the front door, pouring myself a glass of wine. I down it in one, top it back up, then call upstairs.

'Sasha, where are you? Grab your things. We need to go to the police.'

Sasha walks down to the bottom of the stairs to meet me. She's still wearing a dressing gown and, from the drowsy expression on her face, was asleep only a few minutes ago.

'The police? But I thought you said the governors were going to put things together first?'

'The governors aren't going to do shit. And I said we needed to do what had to be done, Sash. This needs to be done. Have you got the photographs on your phone? I need to know who sent them to you – every person. We need to trace them back to the first one. If we can do that, maybe we can find out who's responsible for all this.'

I hold out my hand, waiting for her to hand me her phone, but she doesn't. Instead, she's trembling.

'Mum, I can't,' she says.

'What do you mean, you can't? You have to do this.'

She shakes her head.

'It'll get out about Christopher and me. He could still go to prison, even if I don't want to press charges.'

'Sasha, you need to think about the bigger picture here.'

'I am! I looked into it, Mum. It's the CPS. The Crown Prosecution Service. They can still charge him, even though I don't blame him. He was in a position of responsibility. He could still go to prison.'

'Well, maybe that's a good thing.'

The moment I say it, I see the anger flash across her face, but I've kept these words in for so long now. Bitten my tongue for fear of losing my daughter. And what did that get me? Her needing an abortion at the age of fifteen, the stigma of it following us around. And now, a year later, a stigma of my own. No, I've had enough of playing whoever's game this is.

'Sasha, you know what he did was wrong. You know that.'

'He fell in love, Mum. That's not wrong. I was the one that wanted to have sex. He wanted to wait. Remember, I told you this. He's not a predator, Mum. The girl who dumped him in the summer was twenty-six. Older than him. Much older. He can't be a predator if he dates older women, can he?'

The more she talks, the more I see the pain in her eyes. With everything that has happened, I thought she was over him. I believed the way he'd hurt her, and shown the true extent of his manipulation, had made it possible for her to move on with her life. And I was pleased. I thought she would never pine for, or miss, a man who treated her that way. But now I see it's not the case. The passion is still there. The ardent love she felt for him and believes he felt for her. Not to mention the fervent denial that he did anything wrong, despite the evidence that's staring her right in the face.

'Darling, I know you loved him,' I say, trying a softer approach. 'And I know he made it feel like he loved you, too. Maybe he did. Maybe he really did, but that doesn't change the fact that you are still so young, and you don't understand how easy it is to be manipulated. You might have thought you were the one making the choice.'

'Great. Thanks for having so much faith in me, Mum.'

My fists are clenched by my sides. This isn't what I wanted at all. I wanted to get our lives back, not have them stripped away further.

'Sasha, it's not about you. We don't know what the person doing all this is planning next. They could be dangerous.'

'Because they know how to use a computer and a photocopier?' she says, snarkily.

My jaw clenches. There's no getting through to her now. I can tell that.

'If that's all you think they're capable of, then you really are more childish than I thought,' I snap. 'And forget about the phone. I'll get my own copies of the photos. I'll go to the police without you.'

The fury that clouded her face flickers, but, when it returns, her expression is like stone.

'You do that, and I'm gone,' she says. 'I'll leave here tonight and I'll go. I made a promise before; I'm making it again. And I won't break it. If you tell the police about Christopher, then you're dead to me. And before you try to tell me otherwise, I know exactly what I'm saying.'

48

All I can do is sit and wait for Jamie to come home. I've rung him so many times, but his phone is going straight to voicemail. Even so, I keep on trying. When he finally comes in through the door, it's quarter to five.

'Hey, I saw I had some missed calls, but my battery cut out. I only recharged in the car. What happened? Is everything okay?'

I don't say anything to him; instead, I just hand him my phone. The photographs have been circulated everywhere now. Katie got a copy, which means Alice also got a copy, which she forwarded to me, but only because I asked. There was no way she would have done it herself. I watch as Jamie studies the image in front of him, the same way Sasha did only hours before. The same way I did this morning, although it feels like a lifetime ago.

'Is this genuine?' he says.

I shrug. 'It was given to an entire exam class. I've never seen my medical records before, but all the dates look right. That was when I got the ear infection after a holiday in Turkey,' I say, taking the phone from him so that I can zoom in on several sections. 'That was a sinus problem I had after we did that ridiculous outdoor winter tobogganing. Everything is on there, straight down to the migraine I went for at the beginning of the holiday, for which they did very little.'

'What are you going to do? Are you going to the police?'

'Sasha says if I go to the police, it'll come out about her and Christopher, and she'll never speak to me again.'

'You know that's just her emotions talking.'

'I don't know. She's got my stubbornness. If anyone is going to do it, it's her. Oh yes. And Florence wants me to hand in my notice.'

'What!' Jamie's jaw drops so far it could be comical. 'What for?'

'Let's just say there's an action on there that doesn't fit in with their "Christian" values.' I put the word 'Christian' in air quotes. Let's be serious. Anyone who tries taking away someone else's power and does so in the name of beliefs is just using religion to hide what an arsehole they are.

'Shit, Liz. What are you going to do?'

I don't have an answer. Instead, we fall into a silence and when I speak again, my voice is so quiet, it barely sounds like me.

'I'm being targeted, and I know it's Nathan. It has to be. No one else has anything to gain by me losing my job. If I can just get the evidence together to go to the police, then maybe I can keep Sasha out of it altogether. After all, it's my medical record. That's the biggest piece of evidence. That's what I'm going to do; I'm going to the police, I'm going to give them everything I know, and that school is going to be grovelling for me to come back.'

He looks at me with a deep intensity.

'Maybe, for tonight, you should just sit down. You've had a few drinks. Have you even eaten anything today?'

I think about the smell of tea cakes and warm scones at the café I was at with Florence and my stomach growls. I managed a couple of coffees before I met her, but couldn't force myself to eat, figuring that I'd grab a sandwich or something at the café when my nerves weren't quite so shot. Instead, I had marched out of there before I'd even had a cup of tea.

'No,' I say as I realise. 'I haven't. It's fine, I'll get some toast.'

'Okay, as long as you're sure. I don't mind cooking.'

'No, it's fine. I'll be fine.'

The toast pops out of the toaster when my phone rings. Alice's name is on the screen. The guilt at accusing her remains. Whoever got access to my medical records could easily have looked up Sasha's as well. I don't know why I didn't think logically before flying off the handle earlier.

'Hey,' she says as I pick up. 'This might be the completely wrong thing to do, but I couldn't stand the thought of you staying at home, festering over whatever this arsehole is doing to you. So I wondered if you wanted to come over and watch a film? Or I could come to you if you don't want to leave Sasha. Or we could go out for drinks if you'd rather. You don't have to do any of those. If you just want to hunker down and shut yourself away from it, I'm fine with that, too. I just wanted to give you options, that's all.'

There's something about the way Alice says 'shut yourself away' that makes me pause. I get the feeling that's this person's plan. Whoever they are, they want me to hide away. To be too worried about what's coming next to live my life. I suspect they want me to quit my job just as much as Florence does. But I don't want to give them what they want. I don't want to give them anything else at all.

'Jamie,' I call across to him. 'Do you mind if I head out for a bit? Just for a couple of drinks, with Alice.'

He looks at me with his eyebrows raised.

'Are you sure you want to? Do you feel up to it?'

I think about Florence's smug face, her narrow-minded opinions. Whoever this is, whoever is trying to ruin my life. I won't let them do that.

'Absolutely, I'm up for it,' I say.

'Yeah, then sure, go for it.'

A second later, as I put the phone back to my mouth, I find myself smiling for the first time all day.

'I'll see you in town in an hour,' I say.

49

Given that I've already drunk past the limit, I grab a taxi into town. There are a couple of nice places to drink here, but they get busy, fast. And so, as we've done frequently, Alice and I meet in one of the large hotel bars. The décor is a little dated, but the music is quiet enough that you can have a decent conversation, and the bar staff are pretty liberal with their measures.

'I didn't think you were going to come out,' Alice says. I can't believe I saw her this morning. It feels like days ago. Then again, I can't believe how I spoke to her, or that someone has a personal vendetta against me. Apparently, it's a day for unbelievable things. 'How did the meeting with Florence go?'

'She wants me to resign,' I say.

At this, Alice's jaw drops open in a manner remarkably similar to Jamie's.

'What did you say to that?' she asks.

'What do you think I said to that?'

Her lips corkscrew into a half-smirk, half-grimace. 'So, I guess you didn't respond too kindly?'

'No, I need to get on to the union reps, find out the best route to go. I need to get the police involved, but Sasha is not too keen on the idea.'

'How is Sasha? Katie told me it's all going around her school, too. She's got a couple of friends who went there. I can't imagine how tough it must be for her.'

'It's tough. And horrible to watch.'

'And she's still set on moving to Singapore?'

'It doesn't feel like I can really say no to her. Tony thinks she can get a music scholarship and, with his staff discount, it'll be cheaper than where she goes at the moment.'

'But it's not about money, is it?' Alice says.

'No,' I agree. 'It's not.'

Silence wraps around us. A few giggles drift into the bar from the hotel foyer, but other than the clattering of glasses behind the bar, that's all there is. As a pressure builds in my chest, I wonder why I thought it would be a good idea to come out. All I'm doing is spreading my misery. I'm about to say as much when Alice clears her throat.

'I need to own up to something,' she says, quietly.

For a moment, I think she's going to tell me she lied. That she told Katie about the abortion and that's how Sasha's school found out. But, when I look up, I find there's a small glint in her eyes. She doesn't need to say another word. I know her.

'You've started seeing someone,' I say. Once again, my lips respond in the form of a smile. It's wide and genuine and the type I thought I'd never feel again. Alice has been single for years now and, whenever I brought up the idea of dating again, she would brush it off. For her to tell me means it must be getting serious.

'So, tell me about them. Tell me everything.'

'Okay, well, I want you to come at this with an open mind, okay? Because we've actually been together for quite a while.'

'If he makes you happy.'

'He does. He really does. But—'

I can't imagine what Alice is going to tell me. That he's younger, perhaps. That he's jobless, and she's been paying his keep. Maybe they met online, and she's never actually met him in person. Whatever it is, I don't find out as a shriek from by the doorway cuts across her.

'Oh my God, I can't believe it! Liz. Alice. This is amazing!'

50

Jo from reception heads towards us with her arms wide open. She goes first to Alice, hugs and kisses her on the cheek, then moves towards me. She hesitates for just a moment, but it's clear she's had a drink or two as she offers me the same tight hug. When she breaks away, she's grinning from ear to ear. If I had to guess, I'd say they came straight out after school and that's why she's looking so merry. But I can hardly judge her. For years, I did the same.

'If I'd known you two were going to be out, I would've sent you invites,' Jo says.

'Invites?' Alice replies.

'It's my birthday. We're doing a little pub crawl. And by little, I mean every single establishment that sells drinks, so that includes bars like this. Now, what are you having? It's Jessica's round.'

Jessica? It takes me a second to place the name, although when I turn and look at her, I immediately remember the trainee. So it looks like Jo really did send out invites to everyone.

It's not that I'm offended. I'm the headteacher; I don't expec to be asked out for drinks, but it looks like every other female member of staff besides Alice and I has been invited out for this birthday party, and that includes the trainee. It's not just Jessica. The mousey maths girl is also there, and though she's no longer wearing formal wear, she's still dressed up to the nines.

Along with teachers from almost all the departments, plenty of other people are in attendance. The other girls in admin are huddled together, though I'm grateful to see Sandra is not among them. There's a whole bunch of teaching assistants and even a couple of women from the canteen too. Obviously, I knew Jo was popular. She's always smiley and happy to everyone she meets, not just me. But I didn't realise she was this popular.

'What can I get you to drink?' Jessica says as she comes over to the table. 'The others are all on cocktails.'

Unlike when she's in the classroom, the poor young woman looks completely awkward. Like the last thing she wanted was to bump into her boss on a night out. And, as for buying drinks, she's not even on a proper salary yet. Still, it's not like I want to be here either. I can't help but wonder whether any of the women laughing and giggling away in the group know that I've been asked to resign. So far, the only person I've told in this room is Alice, less than half an hour ago, but I know how this world works. For all I know, Florence has already rung Nathan and all the other middle leaders to tell them they need to step up. She might've even told them before she spoke to me. Nothing would surprise me anymore.

'We were actually about to head off,' I say, looking at Alice for her to confirm.

'Yes, yes we were,' she says.

'Really?' Jessica's tone implies she doesn't believe us at all. 'Are you sure I can't get you one drink? I feel like we've invaded your night and I'm pretty sure, if you go now, the others will think it's because I said something to drive you off...' She pauses for a second. Hesitation twitches on her lips. I know what's coming.

'I'm probably out of line saying this,' Jessica starts. 'But all the staff were really upset about what happened this morning.'

I scoff. 'You mean that I broke the school's precious values?'

Her hand covers her mouth as she shakes her head.

'No. Absolutely not. No one thought that. Not for a second. Everyone was really upset someone had invaded your privacy. I'm so sorry, I didn't mean... I shouldn't have said anything.'

'No, it's fine. Thank you. Thank you for what you said. I appreciate it.'

She offers a tentative smile and for a second, she continues to hover. For a terrifying moment, I'm worried she's going to keep talking to us. That she thinks she has an open invite to join Alice and me. But, instead, she looks back to the group.

'Well, I should go get the drinks. Please, can I get you a cocktail too?'

I don't want to say yes at all. But I'm not ready to leave and, if Jessica's being truthful about how everyone felt after today's incident, then having these women onside could help in defending myself against Florence.

'A small one,' I tell her as I reach for my wallet. 'Here, take this.'

Jessica shakes her head. 'No, it's fine. Maybe you can get the next round. I'll just be a minute.'

A second later, she's at the bar.

'We're not staying for the next round,' I say to Alice. 'You know that, right?'

A smirk twists Alice's lips. 'I thought I heard someone say they're doing karaoke after here.'

'Please, please don't let me do karaoke.'

'But you enjoy it.' She smirks.

'The stakes can't get any worse. The last thing I need is videos of me singing up on the internet. That will get me fired.'

Rather than laughing at my joke, or offering another insult about my singing, Alice looks at me, her smile dropped.

'She's right, you know. That trainee. We're all on your side. We're going to fight this, all of it, together.'

51

It takes the bar staff a substantial amount of time to get the cocktails made, and when Jessica returns to our table, I am well and truly ready for my next drink.

'I hope these are okay,' she says. 'They look pretty green.'

That's one way of describing them. The drinks are practically fluorescent, and I'm betting there's going to be a sharp Midori melon hit when I take a sip.

'If it's really horrible, I'm sure one of the other girls will have it,' Jessica says, watching my face as I pick up the drink. 'I think these guys have had so much, their taste buds don't function properly.'

'Are you not drinking?' Alice says as I take my first sip. It's melony, that's for sure, but it's not unpleasant.

'I have to drive back,' Jessica says. 'So, I'll probably go in the next hour. I just need to stay for a bit, you know. Get to know people. Be polite.'

She lingers there and, for a split second, I think she's going to say something more about the exam paper incident. Or, worse still, ask me how I'm doing. It's fine when it's people you know well, checking up on you. But very few people know me well enough to have any insight into my state of mind. Which is why I find myself asking Jessica a question instead.

'So, how have you found your first fortnight?' I say. 'It's an amazing accomplishment to be taking your own classes already.'

'Full classes?' Alice interrupts, as surprised as I was.

'Well, with a supervisor in the room,' Jessica replies. 'But I love it. I feel so lucky to be in the school. It's such a shame it's only for one term. Hopefully, there'll be a position when I finish my training.'

'I'm not sure the current art team is going anywhere at the moment,' I say, not wanting to get her hopes up. 'But, you never know, we're always looking to expand. Where we can, of course. From what I've seen, St Anne's would be lucky to have you.'

Her smile broadens. 'Thank you, thank you so much for that.'

She glances over her shoulder, to where Jo, Lucy and several others are doing shots.

'I should probably get back to them,' she says, 'but maybe if you have a lesson at some point, I could come and watch? I heard you were great when you used to be in the classroom and I'm sure I could learn a lot from observing you.'

'Well, I'm not sure when I'll be back in the classroom,' I say, 'but, if I am, I'll let you know.'

She smiles, and a moment later she's gone.

'Oh, that's sweet. You've got a little fan,' Alice says, that smirk of hers firmly back in place.

'Yeah, a fan that doesn't know I'm not going to be allowed in the school, let alone a classroom, soon. Although, you know what, maybe there's something in that.'

'Something in what?'

'Maybe I should go back into the classroom,' I say. 'I'm sure Tony could find me a job somewhere abroad. He says international schools are always looking for good teachers. Obviously, his school wouldn't be an option. Not with Sasha wanting to be as far away from me as possible.'

'That's not true at all,' Alice counters. 'Sasha adores you, and you know that. This has been tough. She needs a bit of time, that's all. Wait and see.'

'Maybe,' I say. I take a sip of the drink; my initial judgement was far too generous. It's so grotesquely melon, I'm not even sure I can manage to drink it. From the other side of the bar, Jo calls loudly.

'What are you two doing? Come and join us!'

I look at Alice.

'I think I'm going to head back,' I tell her. 'I'll say I'm going to the loo. Can you make my apologies in a bit? You can say that I messaged you and you didn't know I was leaving if you like.'

'Do you want me to come? We can share a taxi.'

'You don't want to share a taxi with me; it's going in the opposite direction.'

'I know, but I can.' Alice looks at me intently, worry clouding her face.

'I want to give you a hug,' I say, 'but then the others will all know that I'm leaving. Love you loads, though, right?'

'Me too. Take care. And stay in touch, all right. We'll catch this bastard.'

52

My aim was to come into the house as quietly as possible. It's not that late, but I don't want to make a lot of noise, on the off chance that Jamie and Sasha are already asleep. As it happens, my keys get stuck in the lock, and by the time I get the front door open, Jamie is already standing there in the corridor.

'Good night?' he asks. I wobble my head back and forth.

'We bumped into a bunch from work, out for a birthday. I left Alice with them; I couldn't deal with all the pitying looks.'

'I'm sure people were just concerned,' he says.

'Yeah, whatever. How's Sasha doing?'

He offers me the same noncommittal shrug.

'I had a bit of a talk with her. She's been emailing Tony all day, finding out what she needs to move. You know, she's really serious about this.'

'I know, but there's a lot we need to think of. Like visas and accommodation.'

'Well, I'm sure she can get all those, but what we've got to decide first is whether we're going to let her go or not.' The way he speaks is like he's putting the decision entirely on me. And it's horrible. Either I'm the terrible mother who let her daughter go away to a different country because the daughter couldn't bear being with us, or I'm the terrible mother who made her daughter stay, despite all the horrendous things going on. It's lose-lose.

I'm tired. So tired, I ache all the way down my body. And I don't want to think. I've thought so much about what's happening and why it's been happening, and I don't want to do it anymore. But my gut tells me this is a decision I need to make soon.

'Let's talk about it in the morning,' I say.

* * *

When Sasha was little, I tried to make weekends as work-free as possible, at least while she was awake. I could squeeze in an hour or two here and there when she went to dance classes and music groups, but I would always make sure there was time for us as a family – cinema trips, visits to the beach or to country houses, dinners out. However, the older she got, the more life – hers and ours – got in the way.

For Sasha, weekends soon became the time for playdates; for catching up with friends, and then for catching up on homework, too. I won't lie, it fitted in well with me taking on more and more responsibility at work. It felt like a natural progression. Now, for the last year, while I've been headteacher, weekends have been almost solid work, with the exception being the evenings. We try to do something, especially if we can get cheap tickets or, if we can't go out, we curl up with a takeaway and watch a film. But this weekend is different.

'Why are you still doing work?' Sasha says to me as she comes downstairs. It's just gone six and I've been sitting at the kitchen table with my laptop out since ten this morning, sifting through emails and writing half-replies only to change my mind and start another one. I know I've got so much to do, but I can't seem to do any of it. Every now and then I've got up to make a cup of tea, or a sandwich. Only to find I don't really feel like it by the time it's made. I'm not sure how much work I've got done, but I reckon it would have needed less than a quarter of the time I've spent today.

'I feel like I need to do something,' I say.

Sasha nods and flicks on the kettle before she turns back and looks at me.

'I heard from Tony,' she says. 'I know you've asked him about me enrolling at his school. Does that mean I can go?'

I stare at my laptop for a moment longer, before closing the lid and turning so I can look her in the eye. 'This isn't going to be easy, Sasha. You are going to be on the other side of the world, and I know you think cutting all ties is for the best, but—'

'It is, okay? It's the only way out of it.'

'I just want you to think about this carefully. You'll have to fly out there on your own and live in a place you don't know while your uncle is busy with work. He won't have time to help you settle in.'

'I'm not a kid. I don't need someone arranging playdates for me,' she snaps.

'I know that. I just want you to think about this properly, that's all I'm saying. It won't be easy. You're going to be in a completely different part of the world, a completely different culture you know next to nothing about.'

'We spent weeks there on holiday, Mum.'

'On holiday, exactly. In nice hotels and restaurants. It's very different to living in a place.'

Sasha lets out a groan and I assume the battle is going to continue, but, when she speaks again, her voice is far softer.

'Look, I know what you're saying,' she says. 'I get it. I've never done a single flight by myself before, let alone a long haul, and I'll be giving up my place at the orchestra and you and Dad. I know all that. But we're already two weeks into this year. If you're going to let me do it, I need to go now, so I don't miss any more time. You're a headteacher; you've got to get that.'

'I do,' I say. 'I really do understand why you want to do this.'

She pauses, looking at me expectantly. 'So, does that mean you're letting me go?'

53

As much as I hate it, there's no point delaying things. Everything is good at Tony's end. Apparently, international schools are used to pupils starting at a moment's notice, which means it's up to us to get the ball rolling.

'There's a flight Monday,' Sasha says, looking at her phone.

'Monday? Don't you want a bit of time to say your goodbyes?'

'Not really. And it's four hundred pounds cheaper than any other flight going in the next week and a half.'

I take the phone off her, half expecting her to have made that up just so I tell her to book it, but she's right. The prices for these flights are as erratic as they are astronomical, and the only one that seems reasonable leaves in less than forty-eight hours.

'I don't like this; it's a long way for you to go on your own,' I say, handing the phone back. 'Maybe if you could wait until half-term, I could come with you? Or we could see if your dad can have time off work.'

I know what her answer is going to be before she says it, but I feel like I've got to try.

'Half-term is nearly two months away. I don't want to wait that long.'

'But it's a thirteen-hour flight, on your own. I hate the thought of you doing that without one of us with you.'

'It's fine, Mum. There are stewards and things on the flights to look after kids my age. It's not like I'll really do anything. Just sit there and watch a film. Well, loads of films. I promise I'll be fine.'

'She wants to do this,' Jamie says, offering me less than helpful support.

So that's it then. She's going.

As we head to bed a little after eleven, there's a feeling floating around the house. We always knew that having just one child would mean becoming empty nesters before most, but this doesn't feel like a choice. This feels like it's under duress. And it is.

I've taken a compassionate day off work for Monday. Mental health days were something I wrested for my staff last year, regardless of what position they worked in. The idea was that if they ever felt too overwhelmed by something – whether it was to do with work or not – they could take a day off with no questions asked. I didn't expect to be taking one myself, though.

As I email Nathan and June, I know everyone will think it's because of Friday and the exam, but they can think what they like. It's Sasha I care about right now.

Given this immense and unexpected change in our lives, Sunday is spent entirely preparing for the move.

'What about things like hot chocolate?' I say, as I look at Sasha's things, all spread out on the bed. 'You like having hot chocolate in the winter?'

'There won't be winter, Mum. Besides, I'm sure I can get i there.'

'But it'll cost a fortune. I don't want you taking advantage of your uncle. He's already going out of his way for you. We'll send money across; you don't need to use his or anything, okay?'

'Don't worry, I've got it,' she assures me.

I look at the suitcases – a glance turning into a lingering stare – before I find my voice and ask her another question.

'What about people? Aren't there people you want to say goodbye to? Friends from your school? From orchestra?'

I hope she doesn't take that to mean Christopher. I definitely don't mean Christopher.

She shakes her head. 'No, I don't need that. I don't want that.'

A beat passes. She knows what I'm thinking, but I have to speak up, ask the question first.

'Have you told him? Have you told Christopher that you're going?'

She purses her lips.

For the last year and a half, I've actively avoided saying his name, but, in a few hours, Sasha is going to be in an entirely different time zone to him; I don't think I have to worry anymore.

Still, the expression of sadness on her face tugs at my heart.

'I've messaged him. But he's not replied. I guess it's not that big an issue to him now he's moved on.'

I move across the room, wrap an arm around her shoulder and squeeze her tight.

'I thought he still cared,' she says. 'He told me he still cared.'

Her sobs are enough to break my heart all over again, but, as pleased as I am by this radio silence, I'm surprised. The fact that Christopher would go out of his way to pick Sasha up from school when she needed him, then not bother replying when she tells him news like this, seems contradictory. But it will help with the separation in the long run. I'm sure of that.

'In a few days, you'll be starting a whole new life. It's going to be incredible,' I say, trying to sound more upbeat.

'What about you? I feel bad leaving you with all that stuff going on at school.'

'I'm a grown-up. I can deal with this kind of thing,' I say, hoping to hell she can't see how much I'm lying.

54

It feels wrong not going into school on Monday. Then again, it feels wrong packing up my daughter's life into suitcases to move to the other side of the world and not going with her.

'It's not too late to back out,' I say at least a dozen times on the way to the airport. 'And if you get to your uncle's and decide you want to come back, you can. We won't judge you. We've already paid your school fees here for the next term, anyway.'

'Really?' Jamie's gaze leaves the road for a second to glare at me. 'That's what you want to talk about? School fees?'

'I wasn't talking about school fees. I said that it wouldn't matter if she comes back.'

For a second, I think about defending myself more, but instead I close my mouth and stay quiet. I know what I meant and I'm sure Sasha did, too. Jamie as well, for that matter. But we all react differently under stress. Last year, I was the one who had the weight of the world – or at least St Anne's – on my shoulders. To say I was irritable would be an understatement. But Jamie stepped up. The entire time he was there to offer me support, offering a distraction by regaling me with what was going on with him at work. Sasha is his baby girl, too. I'm not the only one losing my daughter today, and I know I need to cut him some slack.

She's flying from Heathrow, which fills me with almost as much trepidation as the actual move abroad. It's such a big airport, with people moving around in every direction thinking only about themselves and the plane they've got to catch.

As we park up, no one says a word, and it's not until the bags are on a trolley and we are in the elevators heading to the departure floor that I finally break the silence.

'Ready to check in?' I ask. 'We've got a bit of time if there's anything you want?'

Sasha's trying to act like she's not worried and maybe she'd get away with it if she was just with her friends. But I can tell how deeply her hands are dug into her pockets and how she's humming the tune to some big oboe solo, barely loud enough to hear.

'I should've brought a drink. I think I need some water.'

'You can't take water through into departures,' Jamie says. 'You'd have to drink it this side.'

I shoot him a glare. The way queues are here, it could easily be an hour before she's through to the other side.

'We can go to the shop; it's no problem,' I say. 'We've got plenty of time.'

Besides, heading to a shop and getting her a drink of water means I get to stay with her for a little longer.

'Why don't you see if there're any snacks you want too?' I tell her as we head into the shop. 'Or magazines. They've got some good offers on books. Why don't you grab a couple for the flight?'

'Okay.' She smiles, then heads over to browse the bestsellers.

I sidle over to the newspaper rack, feeling Jamie's presence behind me.

'Are you sure this is a good idea?' he says.

'It was a joint decision, Jamie,' I remind him. 'We both said she could go and she'll never forgive us if we change our minds now. It's happening.'

I don't want to have any more conversations, so I flick open the paper in front of me. I'm not even sure what paper it is. I flick through the pages mindlessly, until my eyes lock on one particular image. A photograph of a man. I squint, confused by the face that I recognise staring out at me. Next, I shift my attention across to the accompanying headline. And, just like that, my knees go weak.

55

I need to close the paper. I need to make sure she doesn't see it, but I've started reading now and my eyes scan down the page and the body of the text. Each word I read makes me feel more and more nauseous. That's when I see my name printed in black and white. My hand flies up to my mouth as I try to stifle a gasp.

'Liz? What is it?' Jamie says. 'What's wrong?'

I don't know how to respond. Instead, I step away from the paper.

With no need for further instructions, he takes my place. Silently, he reads the page. Judging by the time it takes, he's absorbing every word. Every putrid, false detail. When he's done, he turns to face me, his face white.

'Did you?' he says. They're the first words out of his mouth and they feel like a dagger in my side.

'No, of course I didn't. How can you even say that to me? I promised.'

He sniffs slightly before looking back at the paper.

'She can't see this. Go get Sasha. We need to go before she sees it.'

'Who can't see what?'

Sasha's voice makes both Jamie and I swivel around.

At the sight of her wide eyes, panic grips every muscle in my body. The fight-or-flight response wants me to grab her by the arm, drag her to the check-in, board that plane with her and never look back. But I can't do that.

'It's nothing, darling,' I say, smiling broadly. 'Your dad and I were just talking about something. Have you got your water? Let's go pay; we're going to be late for check-in.'

Sasha's eyes narrow on me.

'What do you mean we'll be late for check-in? You said we were early. We've got loads of time.'

'I know, but I was just looking at the queue, and it's building up. And you know how long these things can take.'

She doesn't even glance over at the check-in desks. Instead, her attention remains unwavering on me and her father.

'What is it you read?' she says. 'Is it about you? About the things at school?'

'Really, Sasha, it's nothing important,' Jamie joins in. 'Come on, we need to get going.'

'If it's nothing important, it won't matter if I read it, will it?'

'Sasha, please!'

She pushes past her dad to get to the newspapers. They are all stacked at different heights and I pray she picks up the wrong one, but the paper we were reading is obvious from the way the top doesn't lay flat. She flips to the first page, then the second, the third and then she freezes.

With every line she reads, her jaw drops lower, and the colour drains from her cheeks more and more. By the time she turns to face me, her skin is practically translucent, tears running down her cheek.

'You did this,' she says.

'No, I swear. I swear I didn't.' I can feel my own eyes welling now. Tears tumbling down towards my chin.

'You promised me.'

'Please, Sasha, you have to believe me. This is them. This is whoever is doing these things to us. I swear on your life it wasn't me.'

I reach out to touch her, but she flinches. The act alone is enough to rip pieces from my heart. With her eyes locked on me, she pushes back her shoulders and straightens herself up. I don't know when she finally hit the point of being taller than me, but she's there now and it makes me feel smaller and more helpless than ever before.

'I can see to myself from here,' she says with a snarl. 'Dad, if you want to come to check in with me, that would be okay.'

I look at Jamie pleadingly. He can't possibly think I did this. He can't. And he can't let her go without saying goodbye to me. I'm sure he's going to stand up for me. Tell Sasha that I would never do anything like this to her. But, when he looks at me, all I can see is disappointment.

'Maybe it's best if you go back to the car, Liz,' he says. 'I'll take it from here.'

56

I don't move from where I'm standing next to the paper stand with all its printed lies determined to rip my life apart.

I watch as Sasha queues up with her dad and inches towards the desk. Once or twice, I move when people try to get to where I'm standing, but a single side-step is the most I do. Not once do I take my eyes off her. Not as she winds closer to the front, or as she hands over her passport and gets her boarding pass. And, all the while, she's deliberately not looking at me.

When she's ready to go, I finally realise I need to move. In a half sprint, I run towards security and position myself right by the gates. The closest I can get.

Sasha strides straight up to me, with her bag slung over her shoulder, hugs Jamie tightly, then carries on as if I'm a stranger she doesn't even recognise.

'Sasha?' I call weakly, but she doesn't look back.

I don't know how long we stand there. Time has no meaning now. I've lost my baby girl, and not just because she's moved to the other side of the world. I've really lost her.

'We should go,' Jamie says eventually. I wait for a moment

longer, praying that she might reappear. That she might realise I would never do something like this and run into my arms full of tears and apologies. But we've been waiting so long, she's probably already through security. Finally, I force myself away, but I don't head straight to the car. There's a stop I need to make first. A stop where I buy every single one of the papers. It's a futile exercise. We are at Heathrow Airport. It's a national paper. Me taking ten copies out of circulation is going to do absolutely nothing in the grand scheme of things. But I need to do it for myself.

It's not until we're sitting in the car, with our belts on and the stack of papers piled up on the back seat, that Jamie speaks again.

'Did you do it?' he says.

My throat is swollen shut with tears, my vision blurry from trying to read the same grim print over and over. But this? Jamie's doubt? It causes an entirely fresh pain to surge through me.

'No, I didn't. How can you say that?'

'That's your name in there, Liz. How can they print a quote by you if you didn't give it?'

'How the hell am I supposed to know? I'm not a fucking journalist,' I snap.

I turn back to the article, this time focusing my attention solely on the title.

Protégé Musician Arrested for Statutory Rape

The picture shows Christopher playing his oboe, under which is a brief description of all his musical accolades, before it gets to the reason people want to read the article. A girl at an orchestra he worked with got pregnant by him at only fifteen years old. No names are mentioned, nor a timeframe. It might not even be referring to Sasha.

But I am named there, unmistakably.

Mrs Elizabeth Croft, headteacher of the esteemed St Anne's Catholic School near Potash, is acquainted with Mr Portland in both professional and personal capacities. She shared with us:

'It represents a breach of trust. To discover that someone you believed you knew can act so deplorably is to cast doubt upon your very own judgements. I am left only to hope that he receives a punishment commensurate with the gravity of his abhorrent actions.'

'It doesn't even sound like me,' I say to Jamie. '"Commensurate with the gravity"? When have you ever heard me speak like that?'

He doesn't reply, and he doesn't look at me either.

'This is what you wanted, Liz. This is what you wanted from the very start.'

'Yes. Of course, I wanted him punished for what he did to Sasha. We both did. Are you forgetting that? Are you forgetting that, more than once, I was the one who had to stop you from going to the police?'

'I'm not forgetting anything. I'm just trying to make sense of it.'

'Well, surely common sense will make you see that it's not me. Why would I do this? What would I have to gain?'

He shrugs as he looks at me.

'I don't know. All I know is that, with Sasha going, there was nothing to stop you going to the police.'

I can't remember a time Jamie has ever stunned me to silence with his words. Not like this. Not through pain.

My throat is clogged as I try to gather enough air to respond.

'Jamie, I did not do this. I need you to believe me. This is them. Whoever is trying to get me fired from my job. Who's sharing these things about my past. They're the one that's done it. You know that. Don't you? Jamie, you believe me, right? You know I didn't do this.'

The reply should be instant. We've been together for nearly twenty years, for crying out loud. Never in my life could I imagine doubting him. On anything.

A moment later, he turns his head to face me, his cheeks drawn inwards.

'Of course I believe you,' he says.

But it's already too late. I already know the truth.

57

I'm grateful that I'm the one driving home, because at least I have something to focus on other than the glaring silence that fills the car. Since the moment Jamie said he believed me, after the longest, most impenetrable delay and interrogation beforehand, we haven't said a single word. There's nothing I can say. After everything that's happened in the last ten days, I don't understand how he could doubt me, but there are a lot of things I don't understand right now.

As we pull up in the driveway, I cut the engine, but neither of us moves to even unbuckle our belts. We used to joke about when Sasha went to university and we'd get our home back. We used to laugh about how much fun it would be to have late-night parties, and not have to worry about keeping a teenager up, or have sex anywhere in the house we liked, from the kitchen table to the conservatory, without the worry of being walked in on. We had joked about how we wouldn't feel empty-nest syndrome at all, but would be grateful to get our lives back. There's no joking between us now.

After a minute, I open the car door and head inside. Jamie

has been on his phone for half the journey, probably reading sports things or doing anything to avoid talking to me. But, rather than follow me into the house, he stays there, lingering.

'I need to go into the office,' he says. 'I want to catch up on some things I've missed from today.'

'It's already three,' I say. 'Why do you need to go into the office? Surely that's what your laptop is for.'

He sighs a little and shakes his head. 'I just think I'll be able to concentrate better there, that's all.'

He doesn't make any move towards the house and it's clear he has no intention of coming in.

'Fine,' I say. 'I guess I'll see you later.'

I walk into the house and slam the door behind me.

Couples have rows, I get that. All couples argue, go through rough patches, doubt that they've made the right decision, and wonder if this is actually the person they want to spend the rest of their life with. Even Jamie and me. Some years have been brilliant, but some have been anything but. We've had months where all we've done is bicker and weeks when we've both spent extra hours at work because we haven't wanted to face the arguments we know are waiting for us at home.

But we haven't argued this time, and it's so much worse.

A glance at my phone tells me that Sasha is going to be boarding any second. I fire off a quick message, wishing her a safe flight and telling her I love her. Only after clicking send, I realise I need to say something else, too.

> I'll find out who did this. I promise.

Ten minutes later, the messages still all remain unread.

Not sure what to do with myself, I head up to her room and take a seat on the bed. To the untrained eye, the room looks perfectly lived in. There's still a duvet on top of the mattress, a pile of books by the nightstand and a few items of clothes scattered on the floor. But the pictures have gone from around the mirror and the oboe case has disappeared from beside the desk. The air feels different, too. Like it's missing something.

I sit in the hollowness and imagine what she's doing. I imagine her queueing up, staring at my texts but not opening them, then moving slowly forwards until she reaches the front of the queue and hands the cabin crew her boarding pass. I think of her needing help to reach the overhead lockers, then taking her seat and getting comfy before she starts looking through the films. Do they put all the minors together on these flights? It was one of the questions I was going to ask at check-in, but I didn't get a chance. I didn't even get a chance to tell her how much I love her.

Brushing away the tears that tumble down my cheeks, I look down at my phone to see it's already gone four. I've spent an hour sitting and doing nothing. An hour lost in my thoughts about Sasha.

Feeling like I should take a leaf out of Jamie's book and at least try to do some work, I drag myself onto my feet and head downstairs.

After fixing a glass of wine, I open my laptop. You wouldn't believe how many messages a headteacher gets in a day – hundreds. And I don't mean that in an exaggerative sense: literally hundreds. If I spent just one minute reading them all and another minute replying, I'd need to be glued to my desk for six hours solid. Still, there are a couple that need my attention, including a notice about the rescheduling of the Year 11 mocks, sent by Nathan, which I flick on just to see how it's been worded.

Due to unforeseen circumstances, the Year 11 mock timetable
has been adjusted.

Nathan's professionalism makes me laugh. *Due to unforeseen
circumstances.* I'm tempted to reply that they were most definitely
foreseen by someone, but I move past the email and look at some
others.

I'm surprised to see one from Jo there, checking up on how
I'm doing and hoping she didn't embarrass me at the bar on
Friday night. The anger I feel at Nathan's email is almost muted
by knowing there are good people like her out there. People who
support me. I've got quite a few messages of support that I wasn't
expecting. A couple of parents of students who've known me for
years have come forward and said how appalled they are by the
situation. Another from Lucy says the entire department is there
to help me in any way they can.

Yet, as much as I would love to only open the positive
messages, I know I can't hide under a rock. After polishing off my
first glass of wine, I bite the bullet and open the email that's been
staring at me since I opened my computer. An email from
Florence.

It's more than enough to have me reaching for a second glass.

According to the email, I am now on probation due to several
'unspecified incidents' and will have somebody coming in from
the governors and from OFSTED to monitor everything I am
doing. Anger pulses through me. I know how these things work.
They make sure you're in an unwinnable situation. They ply you
with so much paperwork and red tape, there's not enough hours
in the day to complete it all and, then, when they fire you, they'll
show you all the evidence they've collected to support your
incompetency. Even if you don't put a foot out of line, and work
all the hours God sends, they'll still find something to pull you

up on. They're on a witch hunt. But at least Florence is going down the proper channels to get me fired this time. That's something.

I go to see if there's anything I can reply to, but that's another rule I have. If you're not in school, you're not in school. Whether you're sick, on compassionate leave, whatever it is. If you've taken the day off work, then you don't start emailing people. And I need to stick to my own rules, especially now I'm going to have people monitoring my every action. So, instead, I head to the living room, close my laptop and turn on the television.

I can't even remember what series it is Jamie and I watch together. That's how little attention I pay to the television; I'm always tapping away on my laptop, doing some work or another. I find a thriller about a man who's lost his memory, and it's good, but I can't focus.

Switching the television off, I turn to my phone instead. My eyes are sagging from the weight of the wine, and all I can think about is that damn article. I didn't say any of that. I didn't speak to the police. I didn't give them a journalist's account of Christopher. Surely I must have some rebuttal. Surely the police can go to the paper and find out where they got this false quote from? A spike of hope ignites within me as I realise this could be what I need. I need to speak to this journalist. Then I can find out who's behind everything.

58

I wish Sasha was with me. If I put her on the task, she'd have every detail about the journalist up on her phone in a heartbeat. But Sasha's not here, which is what this is all about.

The journalist's name is Jeremy Petty, which, thankfully, is not too common a name. When I pair it up with the word *journalist*, there's only one professional profile the fits the bill. I click on it.

I'm faced with an incredibly plain-looking, white, twenty-something male in a sharp suit with a smile that looks even more false than the ones I give Sandra. A quick scan of his career history tells me what I probably could have guessed from the photo; he's a young highflyer from a privileged background What a surprise. A relatively attractive man who's working up the ranks of journalism, no doubt at double the speed of a more deserving female. One who doesn't t falsify quotes in the name o a story.

My cursor hovers over the word *follow*. I'd rather not have anything that links us. Sasha is smart. Knowing her, she migh have already looked up who wrote the article. But, after moment's more hesitation, I give up. The only way I'm going to get answers is by speaking to him, and this is the way to get me there. With a deep breath in, I hit that follow button.

The screen expands to give me yet more details about Mr Petty, but I'm not concerned about those. What I want is a way to contact him. Thankfully, that's provided in the form of a small button that says *message*.

It doesn't take me long to craft something. It's brief and to the point, but I have no desire to discuss personal details over emails.

This is Elizabeth Croft here. I need to speak to you immediately regarding your fabricated quotation in the paper. Please provide a contact phone number, or I will be forced to go to your editor immediately.

I hit send and close the laptop. After all, a watched pot never boils. I assume my bluntness will be enough to get his attention, though I have no idea how often people check their messages on things like that. Then again, if you're a journalist, it probably pays to check things constantly. The last thing you want is to miss that scoop.

Realising I haven't eaten anything all day, I grab a bag of crisps from the kitchen, then try again with the thriller. It's actually better than I gave it credit for and, though my mind continues to skip back and forth to Sasha, it helps pass another hour.

Six o'clock in early September is still perfectly light outside. It's a soft, dusky evening that would be the perfect opportunity to go out and stretch my legs. After all the time I've spent cooped up inside, a walk is probably what I need. I consider the other option – more television and more wine – but decide the walk is probably the more sensible idea. I'm just putting on my boots when the phone starts ringing.

I assume it's Jamie, perhaps saying he's on his way home and asking if he wants me to pick up any food, but, instead, it's an unknown number. My stomach twists and tightens. Unknown numbers aren't unusual. Sometimes, it's a miracle if I can go a week without a call from my phone provider telling me they can offer me a better deal. But something about this doesn't feel like it's one of those calls. Not so late in the evening.

For reasons I can't explain, my hand is shaking as I press answer and lift the phone to my ear.

'Hello?' I say.

'Hi Liz, it's me, Jem.' It's a young man's voice on the end of the line. One that fits perfectly with the image I just saw of the journalist on my computer screen. 'What the hell was your message about?'

59

It feels like all the air has been sucked out of the room. The hairs on the back of my neck rise and nausea billows through me.

'Liz? Is everything all right? I saw your message. What was that about?'

His voice brings me back to reality with a sickening thud.

'Who is this?' I say. 'And how did you get this number?'

My heart batters against my rib cage as I wait for him to respond, but he's quiet. Thinking, I assume.

'I'm sorry, I must have—'

'Jeremy Petty?' My entire body is trembling as I grip the phone so hard, my knuckles turn white. 'This is Jeremy Petty, right? How did you get this number?'

'I'm sorry, I think—'

'How did you get this number?' I yell. I'm practically rocking, I'm trembling so hard, but I don't move to sit down. Instead, I have one hand holding me steady against the hallway wall while the other holds the phone to my ear. The fact I've only got one shoe on probably doesn't help with the balance either, but I can't take it off. That would require moving and, right now, that's not something I'm capable of.

'There's obviously been a mistake,' Jeremy says. 'I'm ever so sorry.' His change in tone is all I need to know he's about to hang up.

'This is Liz,' I shout, hoping that he'll be able to hear, even if the phone isn't by his ear any longer. 'I'm Liz Croft. You wrote about me. Why? How? Where did you get this number?'

There's silence and for a second, I think he's hung up, but, when I look down at the screen, the call time is still ticking away. He's still there. It's probably the journalistic side of him. Where most people would hear a loon on the end of a phone line, he's hearing a potential story.

'Please.' I try a little softer. 'My name is Elizabeth Croft. I am the headteacher at St Anne's, and I want to know why you wrote my name in your article. You quoted me.'

Another pause follows, then I hear him clear his throat. My body tenses as I prepare myself for whatever is coming next.

'I quoted you because you said I could. Just like you gave me this number,' he says, his enunciation firm. 'So, if you'd let me repeat my first question, what the hell is going on?'

60

I slump down. I'm sitting on the hallway floor with my back against the wall. The evening's still mellow and light, but I'm freezing. Well, I'm shivering at least.

'Sorry, we need to back up a minute,' I say, my head spinning. While I have nothing to go on other than intuition, something tells me this man is telling the truth. Or, rather, he thinks he is. 'We have never spoken. I didn't even know you existed until today, until I saw that article you'd written. The one where you quoted me with something I've never said.'

'We have spoken. Not on this number, but you didn't want me to have your private number until yesterday.'

'Yesterday?'

'When you told me he'd been arrested. When you told me we were good to go to print. You gave me this number then, in case I needed to get hold of you.'

The nausea hits again, so much so that I drop my head beneath my knees.

'Liz, are you still there?' Jeremy says after a moment. 'I don't get what's going on.'

I pull in a deep breath of air, which I hold in my lungs for a second. I need to be rational. Or at least as rational as I can be. I need to think like Jamie.

'You've had emails from someone claiming to be me,' I say, thinking through the steps one by one.

'Yes, and we've spoken on the phone.'

'No, we haven't,' I remind him.

'No, I get that. Shit. I mean, I've spoken to someone on the phone. On a landline. Someone who said they were you.' There's a pause before he speaks again. 'Fuck.'

I hear the truth sinking in for him. As far as mistakes go for a journalist, I reckon this must be pretty high up there.

'You had no evidence of who I was?' I say, unable to hide my disbelief at the entire situation. 'You printed my name in a national paper, without even checking it was from the right person?'

There's another pause and a slight scraping sound, as if he's scratching at his head.

'We've been in discussion for months, Liz. You emailed me from your work account. That seemed enough.'

'I didn't email you.'

'I have all the contacts,' he says, sounding defensive, though he's got no right to be. He's the one who screwed up.

'Give me the address. Tell me what address they sent messages from.'

The thought of my emails being hacked causes my pulse to skyrocket. That poses a lot more issues than just mine and Sasha's private information being spread. That would mean whoever's doing this has somehow got access to school data. Thousands of details on minors and their families, which includes extremely sensitive material. This has to be enough to go to the police with.

'This is the email,' Jeremy says, bringing me back into the moment. 'Headteacher at Saint Anne dot co dot uk.'

'Say that again?'

'Headteacher at Saint Anne dot co dot uk.'

'Anne. You're saying Anne. Without an s. Is that right?'

'Yes, it's just Ann— Oh, fuck.'

The relief billows through me and my shoulders slump forward, suddenly released by the tension that has just flooded from them. My school is St Anne's. With an s. Whoever did this was smart enough to make the slightest alteration. Just enough to go unnoticed.

Though while I'm relieved as the school's system hasn't been hacked, the enormity of Jeremy's fuck up is still sinking in for him.

'I don't get it. I did my research. What you – she – told me about Christopher and your daughter, it all sounded so believable.'

'She told you about that? What did she say?'

He pauses, a sigh reverberating down the line, which blends into a sad chuckle before he speaks.

'Stuff that I fell for, that's for sure. She said they met at an orchestra and that Sasha was crazily talented. That he'd never heard anyone like her at that age before and she was undoubtedly going to have a career in music.'

It's true, but I don't interrupt to tell him that. I want to hear what else Jeremy has to say.

'She said that Christopher started giving Sasha extra oboe lessons, but you knew about that and it wasn't until a couple of months into them that she started staying later, lying to you about where she was so she could go back to his flat. And then... then...' He stops, and silence fills the gap. There's more he wants to say. He just doesn't want to say it to me. Ironic, really, considering he thought I was the one to tell him.

'What else did she tell you?' I ask. 'What else did this woman say about Sasha?'

Even though I know what's coming and even though I've faced it dozens of times in the last few days, it still doesn't make it any easier.

'She told me that Sasha got pregnant. Sasha got pregnant and Christopher dumped her. They stopped talking, but he knew she'd got rid of it. She got rid of the baby, moved schools, and you all pretended like nothing happened. You just carried on playing happy families. But now you'd had enough and you wanted him to pay for what he did.'

I feel sick again, and this time I cover my mouth, as if I might throw up.

'You didn't print that, though,' I say, finding only the smallest glimmer of relief in all this shit. 'You didn't print about Sasha getting pregnant, about me wanting him to pay. Why didn't you print that?'

'Because you – she, whoever she was – said she wouldn't corroborate the story if I did. And I liked you, her, whatever. I didn't want to drag your kid through any more stress. I just wanted to get the bastard the same way you did. She did. Fuck.'

Fuck seems about right. Whoever this is has enough decency not to want Sasha written about in a national newspaper, but didn't have any qualms in wrecking her school and home life so that she packed herself off to the other side of the world. And as for the fake email address, I'm sure most people over the age of fifteen would have little problem with something like that.

'You say she always spoke to you from a landline? Do you have the number, something the police can trace?'

This time, there's no pause before Jeremy replies. 'There's no need for that. I already know where she rang from.'

'You do.'

'Yeah, I'm not the shittest journalist in the world. Or at least, I wasn't. It's a pub. About a twenty-minute drive from your school. I did a quick search on it the first time I spoke to you. The location fit; all the pieces seemed to fit.'

I can hear him slipping into some well of wallowing self-pity that I don't have time for. This person isn't slowing down their attacks on me. If anything, they're speeding them up, which means I need to act.

'This pub, what's it called?'

'Why?'

'Because someone there might have seen her. You spoke to her more than once I take it.'

'Yeah, probably half a dozen times.'

'Which means she may well be a regular. They might know who we're dealing with.'

I expect my comment to be met with some sort of agreement. Perhaps even enthusiasm. After all, there's got to be even more of a story for Jeremy if he manages to catch this psycho bitch.

'Jeremy,' I say, still waiting for a response.

Finally, he speaks.

'It's called the Blue Boar. It'll take me about an hour and a half. I'll meet you outside. Don't go in without me.'

61

I've seen enough thrillers to know how this goes. The lead female, who is normally entirely rational and exceptionally intelligent, decides not to take the sage advice of the experienced professional and instead hurtles off on her own to her inevitable demise. I'm not saying Jeremy is a sage professional. From what I've already learned, there's definitely room for improvement, but the advice is sage. I should not be going alone.

The one thing I now know for certain is that there's a woman involved in this, but that doesn't mean she's working alone. There could be other people involved. Maybe people who work at the pub.

She might be behind the bar and have half a dozen burly friends who clock me the minute I walk through the door. And that's not a risk I fancy taking.

Still, I can't stay at home for over an hour climbing the walls. So I decide to walk there. It's not a short walk. According to the map on my phone, it's just under an hour, which should work out well. By the time I've got myself sorted and head out, I won't be there much before Jeremy. The fresh air should also help clear my head.

As I'm walking, I think about what I should tell Jamie. Whether to tell him where I'm going. It's not like I'm going alone, and it's not like I'd message him every time I go for a walk. There's that niggling feeling again. Not telling anyone where you're heading is the type of thing the dumb female in the thriller would do, meaning people can't get to her before disaster strikes. So I fire off a message:

> Gone for a quick walk. Might head to a pub,
> think there's a nice one in Bicknacre.

I read through the message to check how it sounds before I hit send. Should anything happen to me, and if it's actually Jeremy Petty behind these threats, then the police will know where to start looking for me, although I don't think that's likely. Not from the way Jeremy sounded. By the time he hung up the phone, he knew how much he'd screwed up. He'll be wanting to get to the bottom of this too. Besides, they'd be able to track my message on his LinkedIn profile, not to mention the telephone conversation we just had. Right now, meeting with a total stranger feels wiser than meeting with friends.

I take a thin coat, not because it's cold now, but because it might well be when I head home, and the entire way all I can think about is the conversation I've just had. This woman knew things about me and Sasha. She knew things about Sasha and Christopher beyond the simple abortion. She knew things that we only knew inside the family. Or close enough.

My mind goes back to Alice. She knew Sasha was dating Christopher. I told her that long before the pregnancy. I told her about the extra lessons and the lying that followed it. Alice was here for all of it. And what about Nathan? I'd been so convinced that it was him before. That his wife would have access to the medical data; it just made sense. But I'm doubting that now I know he's divorced. There are too many unanswered questions, and I don't like it one bit.

I reach the pub at seven-forty, ten minutes before Jeremy is due, and I find myself at a loss for what to do. I don't want to ring Jamie now; not with the mood he was in earlier. And I don't want to call Alice either. As for Sasha, well, Sasha's still on a plane.

But I need to speak to someone. Anyone who really knows me. Which is why I don't even think about the time, as I hit dial on the phone.

It doesn't ring for long, barely a moment before there's the click of the call being answered and the voice on the other end of the line. An exceptionally groggy voice.

'Do you have any idea what time it is here?' Tony says.

62

The sound of Tony's voice is all it takes for the tears to start tumbling down my cheeks, and he doesn't need me to speak to know that something is wrong.

'Liz? Liz, are you there? Liz? Don't worry, she's going to be fine. I promise you, I'm going to take care of her.'

I draw in a deep breath, which I exhale in staggers as I find myself unable to breathe without crying.

'Tony, it's all just so shit. It's so, so shit.'

'This is about Sasha?'

I don't respond. How can I give a succinct answer? It would take hours to go through everything. The thought of time finally makes me consider where in the world Tony is.

'Shit, it's the middle of the night for you, isn't it? I should go. It's probably three o'clock in the morning or something horrendous.'

'It's fine. I need to be up early to go to the airport. Do you want to tell me what's going on? Is it you and Jamie? Are you two okay?'

I continue to wipe the tears from my cheeks as I sniff more.

Sasha didn't want Tony to know everything. She told him as little as possible, focusing on bullying and how she wanted to be in a world-class school orchestra. Neither of those things are complete fabrications, but they're a long way from the truth, too.

'I just need you to do me a favour, okay?' My voice is still wavering. 'When she gets there, I need you to tell her it wasn't me.'

Tony lets out a slight hiss. 'You don't want to be a bit less cryptic than that?'

'No, she'll know what it means. It's important, Tony. I need you to tell her it wasn't me and that I'm getting to the bottom of it. You promise, right? You'll tell her I'm getting to the bottom of it?'

'Liz, is Jamie there? Alice? Somebody you can talk to? You don't sound good. I'm worried.'

I hold the phone beneath my chin for a moment so I can press my hands into my face as I take a deep breath in. When I put the phone back to my ear again, Tony sounds frantic.

'Please, Liz. This is scaring me. What can I do? How can I help?' he asks, in typical Tony style, trying to fix everything.

'I'm okay, honestly. I will be. I will be when I find out why this is happening. Right now, all I need is for you to tell Sasha what I said.'

'Why don't you tell her yourself?' he says, like it's the easiest thing in the world to do. 'You can speak to her yourself when she lands. I'm sure she'll want to tell you about the flight.'

I shake my head before responding. 'No, she won't want to talk to me. She won't, not now. So you're going to have to tell her instead, okay? I promise. I swear it wasn't me. You'll tell her this, won't you? Tell her I've found someone to work with to help figure it out.'

There's a pause, and I can almost see my brother's face and

the way he pulls at his hair when the stress gets too much. The way he did when Mum and I had that final falling out.

'Yes, I'll tell her. But are you sure you can't tell me what's going on? Maybe I'll be able to help. That's what big brothers are meant to do, you know – help.'

For a split second, I consider it. What harm would it do? Maybe it would be easier for Sasha if Tony knew the entire situation, but I need to honour her request. 'I'll be fine. I promise. As long as I know Sasha is happy, I'll be fine.'

I'm still speaking as I see a car turn into the pub car park. An old, silver hatchback with several dents and scrapes. Is that what a journalist like Jeremy would drive? It certainly doesn't seem high-brow. But he's young. Probably saddled with student debt the way anyone who got a degree in the last fifteen years is.

'Sorry, Tony, for waking you up and for this, but I've got to go now, okay? Message me when you pick up Sasha, right? Let me know she's okay.'

'I will, Liz, of course I will.' But I don't wait to hear what else he says. The silver hatchback has parked, and a man is walking out of it: a man who looks just like the photo on his LinkedIn profile.

63

We walk towards each other, meeting in the centre of the car park.

'Liz?'

'Jeremy.'

For a second, we stand there like we're not sure if we should shake hands or hug or extend our greeting so it's a little less awkward, but we don't, we just stand there.

'You didn't go in?' he asks. 'I'm glad. I thought that maybe you'd have decided you didn't trust me.'

'I don't,' I say truthfully, 'but I don't trust anybody right now.' I look towards the pub and motion with my head. 'Shall we?'

He nods. 'Do you want to talk, or do you want me to?'

'I guess we should just see when we get there.'

As we walk towards the building, I study my companion. I'd say he's mid-twenties. With his scuffed trainers and jeans, he's dressed casually, but I get the feeling that this is his go-to look. Just like the car, it's giving off the impression of someone who's strapped for cash, but maybe that's the fashion among younger people at the minute. Paying over the odds for a T-shirt that looks like it's already had holes patched over it. Regardless of his clothes, Jeremy is not looking as confident as I would expect someone in his profession to be. His eyes keep shifting back to me and, for some strange reason, I get the sense that I'm the one making him nervous.

'After you?' he says, holding open the door, only to hesitate and change his mind. 'Unless you want me to go first, that is? I can.'

'It's fine. I'll go in first,' I say, and stride past him confidently as if I'm walking into my assembly hall.

As it's a Monday night, I expected the pub to be empty, but it's not. Most of the tables are filled, and several people have vapes pumping clouds of steam into the air as they chat. The bar smells of smoke and beer, which is ridiculous considering how long there has been a smoking ban in place. Perhaps it's one of those places where rules don't apply after last orders.

'It's a popular establishment,' Jeremy says. 'Surprisingly.'

I know what he means. Dingy is the word. Dark and dingy. There are windows on one wall, but they don't seem to be letting any light in. Every other wall is occupied, mostly with brown landscapes that would look pleasant in the right environment, but this is not that. There are three large televisions, all currently showing football, along with a dartboard and a pool table, both of which have people playing on them. Several of the tables and all the stools by the bar are occupied, but none of the people sitting on them appear to be talking to each other.

'I guess we should go talk to a member of staff,' I say.

There are two people behind the bar. One is a middle-aged man with a small tattoo on his cheek, and several more over his hands and arms. He's staring fixedly at the football on the television and doesn't even acknowledge us. The other person is a woman, early twenties. I look at Jeremy and know we're thinking the same thing. Maybe this is the one he spoke to. Maybe this is the woman who pretended to be me. And, although I don't recognise her, I still wouldn't rule it out.

'Hey love, what can I get you?' Her voice comes out with the strongest of Essex twangs, which makes her sound a decade older than she looks. As far as identifiable voices go, this woman has one.

I look at Jeremy, who immediately shakes his head. I don't know if I'm disappointed or pleased.

'Hi yeah, please can I get a large white?' I say to her, smiling. 'Clive, what do you want?'

I don't know where the fake name came from. I wasn't even planning on getting a drink until the request came out of my mouth, though Jeremy replies flawlessly.

'A half of Neck Oil, please.'

She flashes him a smile before turning around and grabbing a wine bottle out of the fridge. This place clearly doesn't have such a thing as a wine list.

'I was hoping I could ask you a question,' I start, hoping I will find the words as I keep talking. 'You have a phone here, right? A landline?'

'Yeah, for taking bookings.'

'Bookings, right?'

I might be wrong, but it doesn't even look like this place serves food. I can't imagine anyone wanting to book here for anything other than a health inspection, but I keep that to myself.

'So, if that's what it's for, I'm guessing only staff can use it right?'

She lets out a scoff. 'Yeah, that's not the way it works. It's pretty much a free-for-all.'

'A free-for-all.'

'You know, for when folks have run out of battery and can't get a taxi home. Or when they're out of credit – by which I mean they don't pay their bills. Fair enough, though, if you ask me. Most of the folk here pay enough on drinks for us to let the occasional call slide.'

She places my wine down in front of me before picking up a half pint glass for Jeremy. As she pulls down the tap, I look at him, hoping he's going to have something insightful and discreet to say so we can find our woman.

'We're looking for someone who rang me from here, several times,' he says. 'I guess she'd be twenties to thirties. The last time she rang was yesterday afternoon.'

So much for discreet.

'Yesterday afternoon.' The woman rolls her lips. 'Yesterday was football. Spurs versus West Ham. It was crazy in here. Someone could have walked off with the phone and we wouldn't have seen.'

'Great,' I mutter, then pull out my card, ready to tap the machine she has waiting. 'So you can't think of anyone offhand. Any women who might have used the phone repeatedly in the last couple of months?'

I look at Jeremy to confirm this. 'About once every two or three weeks,' he adds.

She scrunches up her face as she rips off the receipt.

'Sorry, I'll be honest. We have a pretty high staff turnover here. I've only been here a month.'

'What about other staff? Are there any other women working here between your age and mine?'

'Your age and mine?' She says this like there are centuries between the pair of us, but I don't take offence. I would have probably felt the same way when I was her age. 'Mallory's the full timer over the weekends. But she's even older than you, I'd say.

Her daughter does a couple of shifts too, but you said she rang on Saturday right?'

'Right?'

'Yeah, well Maya's on holiday, so it can't have been her.'

I turn my attention to the barman with the tattoos and consider asking him the same questions, but his eyes are locked on the television screen and haven't moved since we came in. I doubt it's any different any other day.

'Okay, thanks for this,' I say to the woman as I pick up my drink. 'I appreciate your time.'

64

We take a seat in the corner of the bar, as far away from other people as possible.

For a minute, neither of us talk. We simply sip on our drinks, avoiding eye contact. The wine is drinkable, but that's not saying much, given my current state of mind.

'I need to apologise,' Jeremy says eventually. 'I'm so sorry, Liz. I've got you into this massive mess.'

'You think?' I say, before shaking my head and letting out a sigh. 'This isn't on you. Whoever is doing this is determined to bring me down. If you hadn't wanted to write the story, she would have found someone else to do it.'

'Probably,' he says.

Silence takes a hold again and, for the second time, Jeremy's the one to break it.

'Do you have any idea who it could be? Who would want to get revenge on you for something?'

'Honestly? No.'

I drop my head and stare into the wineglass. I'm a long way

from a saint, but I've tried to live life as a half-decent person. I do all the right things – buy the *Big Issue*, give money to people shaking charity boxes, go that extra mile in my job. But I must have slipped up at some point. Because people don't do things like this to others without a reason.

'Can you tell me anything else? Like what she sounded like on the phone?' I ask, hoping I might be able to pry something more out of Jeremy. 'Any accents, any mention of places. Anything.'

'Honestly, no. All she talked about really was Sasha and Christopher. Wanting to get back at him. Is there something that links the pair of you?'

'Christopher and me? Only Sasha. But we know this isn't about hurting her. Not as much. Otherwise, she would have let you write about the abortion.'

'Which makes it look like the sole target was Christopher.'

'Right, only I'm betting she knew exactly how Sasha would react. Or she had a fairly good idea.'

Once again, we fall into silence.

'So this article isn't the first thing this woman has done to you?' he says after an extended pause.

'No, it's not.'

'What else has she done?'

Given how this woman has screwed him too, it feels like there's an unspoken bond of trust between us and by the time my wineglass is empty, I've told him everything and by the end, he looks suitably shell-shocked. I'm also ready for another drink, though judging from the time, it would be better off if I had it at home.

'I don't suppose you can give me a lift home, can you?' I say 'It's about a ten-minute drive, though it might be the opposite direction. I'm happy to call a cab if you can't.'

'It's fine. Of course I can.'

I expect the car journey back to be silent, the way it was with Jamie when we came home from the airport, but it appears Jeremy isn't one for silence.

'Do you think she targeted me for a reason?' he says. 'Because I was young?'

'I don't know.'

'Maybe she knows me from somewhere. I don't know, school maybe. I didn't recognise the voice, though.'

I nod along, finding his constant chatter a wanted distraction to the whirring in my mind.

'It's just up here,' I say, pointing to the next turning.

Jamie's car is sitting in the driveway, though it's not a surprise. It's nearly half-past eight.

'Liz,' Jeremy says, cutting the engine as he looks at me. 'Don't go doing anything stupid, okay? We've got enough that we can go to the police. I'm sure of it. Let me go talk to some of my buddies at work.'

'I don't want more people knowing what a screw up this is,' I say, but he shakes his head.

'It's not your screw up; it's mine. And try to remember that I really believe whoever this is only wanted to make Christopher pay for what he did. But I'll keep your name out of everything, okay?'

At this, I let out a bitter chuckle.

'It's not really my choice in that anymore, is it?' I say, then open the car door. 'Thank you. Thank you for coming today. I appreciate it.'

'All things considered, it was the least I could do.'

'Yeah, you're right. It was.'

I take my keys from my pocket, although I remain by the front door until he drives away. Turning around, I see the front door is open. Jamie is standing there with his arms folded across his chest. A muscle on his jaw twitches.

'Why do I get the feeling I'm not going to like where you've been?' he says.

65

'Do you have any idea how much of a risk you took?' Jamie doesn't try to hide his anger. 'You met a strange man at a random pub when you've already got everything else going on. Surely you could have waited for me? We could have gone there together.'

'Would you have gone there with me?' I ask.

'Yes... maybe... I don't know.' He groans and rubs the bridge of his nose. 'What I do know is that I wouldn't have gone there without knowing more. You'd already spoken on the phone? Right, so why didn't Jeremiah Betty—'

'Jeremy Petty,' I correct.

'Whatever his name is, why wasn't his first port of call the police?'

'He's going to contact them. Once he's spoken to a couple of people he knows. He's a journalist. This was a chance for us to get ahead of this person, to catch them out before they realise we're on to them.'

'*He's* a journalist, Liz. *You* are not. You're a fucking teacher!' I don't know why he spits the words out at me, like it's an insult, but a moment later he's shaking his head and sighing. 'Please, beyond the possible risks, you need to think about this logically. If someone is targeting you, why would they give Jeremiah your real number, knowing he'd be likely to contact you and rumble it all as a ruse?'

'Jeremy,' I correct for a second time, my back teeth pressing harder and harder together with each inhalation.

'The only reason can be that they *wanted* you two to speak. Unless...' Jamie's head drops to the table before he shakes it and lets out a long sigh.

'Unless *what*, Jamie?'

'It doesn't matter.' He pauses before he looks back up at me. 'I should probably get an early night. I take it you're going into work tomorrow?'

'Of course I am. I haven't been fired yet.'

'I didn't say you had been.'

'Then why wouldn't I go in? Staying at home won't bring Sasha back.'

'No, it's just that...'

For the second time in as many minutes, Jamie doesn't finish his sentence. The tension around the table is the tautest I can remember for a long time. Even when the stuff was going on with Sasha and the abortion, Jamie and I tried to act as a team, for her sake as well as ours. Right now, it feels like we're on different fucking pitches.

As the pause stretches on, I wonder if maybe I should apologise for snapping at him, but then reconsider. He's not apologised to me. He should have supported me in front of Sasha. He should have told her I wouldn't have done it and at least persuaded her to say goodbye to me. When I think about it like that, I don't really feel like apologising after all.

'I'm feeling pretty congested,' Jamie says after a pause. 'I think I'll sleep in the spare room tonight.'

66

I wake up four minutes before my alarm and for a split second, I can't remember where I am. The bed next to me is empty. The house feels empty. Like the life and heart of the place has been siphoned off through the walls in the night. That's when I remember: she's gone.

I can hear Jamie asleep. Snoring away and, for a moment, I consider going into the spare bed and slipping under the covers with him. Perhaps silent apologies are the type we need now. Perhaps holding each other will be enough to repair whatever's causing all these cracks to form. But I don't. Instead, I have a shower, fix a coffee and am out the door before he's even awake. It's easier this way. For now, at least.

With no Sasha to get up and no breakfast or conversations to have, it's still dark when I park my car outside the main building.

The school has a thousand rumours of ghosts that walk the corridors at night when the children and staff are all safe at home. A small child in ballet clothes supposedly lingers on the staircase. The current rumour is that she was pushed down those stairs to her death. Another favourite is a young woman who roams through the halls, lost and fearful, her white gown trailing behind her as she sobs.

As I walk in through the front door and head to my office, I can't help but wonder what I would say to her if we bumped into one another. I feel we've got a fair bit in common at the moment. Not the ghost part, obviously, but the lost and fearful. That's how I feel too.

Jo's not on reception this early and Sandra's not at her desk either, so I slip into my room unseen, only to open up my calendar and frown.

Every appointment I had for the day has gone. All postponed. This would have to be Sandra's doing. No one has access to change my schedule except her, and I'm not sure if I should be mad or grateful. Either way, I don't dwell on it too long. I've got work to catch up on.

Jamie was right about one thing. Being at work definitely helps you focus. By the time Sandra lets herself into my office – without knocking – I've been sitting at my desk for forty minutes and have already answered a dozen emails and read through all the IEPs that have landed in my inbox since the beginning of term.

'Oh.' She jumps a little when she sees me. Obviously, she'd been expecting the room to be empty. I can't help but wonder what she did yesterday when I wasn't here. Maybe she took a nap on one of my comfy armchairs. Or listened to some music as she gazed out of the window. I'd bet my life savings that she didn't spend her day glued to her desk. 'I didn't know if you were going to be in,' she says, like I hadn't already figured that out.

'I just took one day's leave,' I remind her.

'I know, only…' Her words fade into the air, but I'm not going to let her get away with it that easily.

'Yes? Only what?' I fix my gaze on her. It's a challenge almost

A challenge to see if she's got the guts to say what she wants to. For a second, we remain there in a stalemate.

'I cancelled all your appointments,' she says finally.

'I saw.'

We're still there, locked in a staring match that I have no intention of losing, when she finally clears her throat and turns to go, only to change her mind. Instead, she twists back to face me and takes three strides towards my desk, so that she's standing in the middle of the room by one of the powder-blue armchairs.

'You know, if you would just get your head out of your arse for five minutes, you might see that some people here are trying to help you.'

'Excuse me?' My jaw hangs open, not least because I've never heard Sandra speak that way to anyone before and sure as hell not to me.

'People don't want you to fail. They want you to be good enough. That's not the same thing. They want to help you be good enough.'

My mouth closes, just long enough for me to grind my teeth together and spit my answer back at her.

'Are you saying I'm not good enough for this job?'

She shrugs and tips her head to the side.

'There are times when you do it well enough. There are some things you're very good at, but there are others you could do better.'

I shake my head, unable to believe what I'm hearing.

'You have no idea what this job entails,' I say.

'Actually, I do,' she replies. 'I see all the emails you have to deal with. All the demanding parents. All the constant requests and badgering. I couldn't do it. No chance. Not alone. I don't think anyone can do it alone. Not in the long run. Not without an unreasonable amount of sacrifice.'

'What are you trying to say, Sandra? Do you have a point, or are you just trying to ruin my morning?'

This isn't like when I had a go at her before. When there were professional standards and child welfare to think of. This is just because I'm pissed off. With Sandra, with the fucking woman who's leaking things. With the whole entire world.

But I'm not the only one who knows this is different. Unlike before, Sandra doesn't cower. She doesn't feel any remorse in the way she's spoken to me or concern over the gravity of her words. Just like for me. This is personal.

She stares at me for a second longer, before she finally takes a breath and speaks. 'I guess what I'm saying is, is the sacrifice really worth it?'

67

I don't leave my office all day, nor do I call Sandra in at any point. Even when lunchtime arrives and I'm famished from not eating breakfast, I stay where I am, not wanting to ask her to fetch anything from the dining hall. And it's not like Sandra's forthcoming either. The only time she enters is to place a pile of letters that need signing in the tray inside the office, after which she leaves without a word.

On the plus side, I've never read so many policies in one day in my life. It's all I do. Read policies, adjust the wording, then forward the email to the relevant member of staff for a final proofread. I'm in such a state of flow that the day soars by and, if it wasn't for the hunger, I could probably stay in that state long past the end of the day.

At three forty-five, the bell rings, and the children's voices filter through from outside. For a minute, I contemplate going straight home, but there are year group meetings on today, which means the teachers will be milling about. Facing the staff fills me with almost as much dread as seeing the students. Sure, I got emails from a couple of them, like Jo and Lucy, offering support, but there were plenty more that I didn't hear from. One or two I'm sure are elated at my current predicament.

It's just gone four when there's a knock on my door, and Alice steps inside.

'Hey you. How are you doing?'

For what feels like the first time in forever, I move my hands off my keyboard and let out a sigh.

'Well, I've got a lot of work done today.'

'That's not really what I was asking,' she says.

'I know.'

I stare at the computer, although I'm not reading anything that's on there. My eyes are blurred, the weight of my lids making me wish they could close then and there.

'Sasha's gone, and she hates me. Jamie is furious.'

'Furious? Why?'

'Because he thinks I had something to do with the newspaper article. I assume you've seen it?' There's no point lying to Alice; she knows me too well for that.

'Yeah, I have,' she replies. 'That quote about Christopher was weird. It didn't sound like something you'd say.'

'That's because I didn't say it!'

I groan. I know Alice means well, but I can't be dealing with anyone right now. 'Sorry, I don't mean to sound grouchy, but I've got a tonne of work to do here. You don't mind, do you?'

She offers me a sympathetic smile.

'No, course not. We'll speak later, right?'

'Sure. Course.'

A moment later, I'm on my own again.

Having told Alice I have work to do, I stay for another hour, most of which is spent putting signatures on a pile of letters Sandra has left out for me to sign. Any form of real productivity is gone, though I still bumble about until half-past four.

When I get in the car, I decide to change up my route home. Tapping on the car's sat nav, it only takes me a minute to find a detour that goes straight past yesterday's pub, so I decide to head there first.

When I arrive, I realise I don't know what I'm expecting to find that wasn't here yesterday. Maybe a member of staff's car parked in the car park. Maybe a group of them clustered inside, plotting my demise. Yet it's far, far quieter than yesterday. Probably because it's so much earlier in the day. It's the same man behind the bar, with the tattoo on his face, his gaze still fixed to the television screen. I stand directly in front of him, so I can't be ignored.

'A glass of red, please,' I say, hoping it might be better than the white.

It's not.

For half an hour, I sit there, on my own, nursing the glass, wondering if anyone is going to come in. I message Jeremy, who replies immediately, little good it does me. He says he's contacted people to find out the next best steps. I should just hang tight. Like I have any other choice.

It's just gone six when Jamie tells me he's going to be working late and that I should eat without him. I guess it's a meal for one tonight then.

68

Just like this morning, home is eerily quiet. Even more so without Sasha's music reverberating through the walls the way it normally does when I get home from work. I head straight to the kitchen and drop a couple of slices of bread into the toaster before opening the fridge and getting out a bottle of wine. The bitter, acidic taste of the cheap red is still adhered to my taste-buds so I pour a large glass and take a swig while I wait for the toaster to pop.

I don't know how I ended up here. Drinking alone at six o'clock on Tuesday evening, Jamie working late – probably to avoid me – and Sasha gone. I can feel myself slipping. Wallowing. But I don't know what else I'm supposed to do.

As I chew on the toast, I scroll mindlessly through my phone. Tony sent me a quick message saying that Sasha had landed hours ago. I know the plan was to go straight to school on that first day, even if it was only for a morning, to get a grip on the jet lag as quickly as possible, then spend the afternoon stocking up on essentials, like a new phone, the uniform and some clothes appropriate for the heat. I wonder how much of that she's actu ally managed to do. So far, Tony's only sent me that one text and I don't want to pester him. He's already done so much. Besides, Jamie will probably know.

Hating this isolation, I fire off a quick message to him.

> Don't mind waiting for you to get home to eat
>
> Have you heard from Sasha?
>
> Xxx

I type the kisses, then delete them, then retype them before I hit send. A minute later, his reply pings through.

> I've still got to do a couple of hours' work You should probably eat. Everything's good with Sasha. X

A single kiss in return isn't a bad sign. While Jamie can pull off good romantic gestures in real life, in the virtual world, his messages are always brief and to the point. I'd much rather have it that way. So, the single kiss is good. He normally doesn't even bother with that. But, as for telling me *everything's good with Sasha*, I was hoping for a bit more than that. Maybe he just wants to tell me in person, I think. Or maybe that's all she's told him too. Her texts are always brief when she's tired.

The two slices of toast have left me feeling utterly unsatisfied, and I open the fridge to see whether there's anything better or whether I should just bite the bullet and order a takeaway. I quickly decide takeaway is the only option.

I am topping up my wine glass when my phone buzzes again, although, rather than Jamie's name, it's an unknown number.

A surge of adrenaline rushes through me, as I think it could be Sasha on her new phone, but the hope is short-lived. There's a UK dialling code at the front of the number.

Swiping the message open, I frown at the grainy picture on the screen before reading the text below it.

> Cute couple. They look cosy, don't they?

I stare at the photo, queasiness twisting in my gut. There is no doubt who the people are: Jamie and Alice. Her hand is placed on his as he reaches across the table. She's dressed in a simple green dress, the same one she was wearing when she left my office only a few hours ago.

As I continue to stare at it, trying to make sense of what I'm seeing, the next message pings through.

> She's quite the actress too

> Certainly got you fooled.

> Remind me again why she got divorced?

> It wasn't because of an affair, was it?

69

Alice has got me fooled. That's the message I keep focusing on. *Alice has got me fooled.*

Her arms are stretched across the table, her fingertips placed on the back of Jamie's hands while he has his chin resting on his knuckles. Between them, a tealight is burning away.

I went down this route once before, I remind myself, grabbing my glass of wine and taking a hearty gulp. I accused her of lying to me and the pang of guilt still hasn't faded. But why would she be meeting with Jamie? And why would Jamie tell me he's at the office, when he clearly isn't?

The entire room is spinning, and it's not from the drink.

'You need to think about this,' I say aloud, hoping that my voice may carry some wisdom. 'You can't go in there, accusing her of something until you know for sure. But what else do I need to know?'

There's an easy way to solve this, of course.

I flick off the photo and navigate to my contacts list.

I hit call on Alice's name.

As the phone rings, my heart rate creeps up by a notch. Is she going to answer? Do I even want her to? And, if she doesn't, what exactly am I going to say? For a moment, I think she's not going to pick up, and I'm relieved. Only, before I can hang up, she answers.

'Hey, Liz. What's up? Is everything okay?'

I don't know whether her voice sounds forced, or it's just my paranoia, but I clear my throat and force myself to carry on talking.

'I was just home alone, that's all. Wondered what you were up to? Wondered if you fancied coming over for a drink.'

There's a pause. One that extends as I wait for an answer. Is she looking at Jamie, I wonder. Have they got me on speaker-phone as they secretly exchange sly smiles? All I need is for her to tell me the truth. To say that they're together. I'll work through the why later, but, right now, I need her to be truthful. But, even before she speaks again, I can tell that won't happen.

'I'm really sorry, I'm not feeling great,' she says. 'I'm already in my PJs. Pathetic, right?'

She offers a slight chuckle, but it's strained and tight. Still, I offer the same one back.

'Pretty pathetic. Okay, well, I'll let you rest. See you tomorrow?'

'Yeah, yeah. Bye, Liz.'

My hand drops to my side as the weight of the conversation pins me to the spot. Alice is lying to me. Jamie is lying to me. The two people I trust most in the world are keeping things from me and it feels like daggers through my heart.

I'm still standing in the same spot, utterly numb, when the phone buzzes again.

Wow, so I wonder what else she's been lying about.

You know, it's her, right? It's all her.

I don't know who this is messaging me. All I know is that they've made me see a truth I don't want to face.

Right from the beginning, Alice has been the only person it could have been. I was just too short-sighted, blinded by our friendship, to admit it. Maybe she doesn't have access to my medical records, but would it really be that hard to get them? I've told her about almost every doctor's appointment I've had for years. She could've gone in, pretended to be me, saying she forgot to get a printout. I wouldn't say we look alike, but with surgeries so stretched, and the fact there's been a new woman working on reception every single time I go in, how would they know it's not me? She knows my address, date of birth; she could get access to my NHS number too, I reckon.

It's her. It's got to be her. She knows everything about me. Everything to use against me, but for what? To take Jamie? It sure as hell looks that way.

The thought of them together causes another bout of queasiness. When have they been meeting up? How long? Was this the reason she and Philip got divorced? She never mentioned there being anybody else. She always just said it was his decision to walk out, but I never actually spoke to Philip about it. What if that's another lie?

I cut contact with him entirely when he left. It felt like the right thing to do after the way he treated Alice, but what if that's not the case? What if it was always her plan to stop us from communicating?

Realising there's one more thing I need to do, I pick up my

phone and scroll down the contact list to find a name I haven't called in nearly two years.

I'm amazed when he picks up.

'Liz?' The confusion is clear in his voice. 'Is everything okay?'

'Philip,' I say, not bothering with any sort of niceties. 'I need to know the reason you and Alice split up. And I need the truth, now.'

70

There's a pause and, for a second, I think Philip's hung up on me, but then his voice crackles down the line.

'It's been a long time. I didn't think I'd hear from you again.'

'I know. Look, I'm sorry about the way things went down. How we cut things off.'

'I was the one that left. Let's be honest, it's not like I made any effort to stay in contact.'

'No, but I should have tried. Jamie and I should have tried.' My voice has turned so dry, I'm struggling to speak. I swallow before I carry on. 'I need to know why. Why you and Alice split up? Why you left.'

At this, he lets out a low whistle. 'She still hasn't told you? Wow. That's impressive. Even for her.'

'She told me you were done being married, that you'd only stayed for Katie and, with her leaving, you wanted to move up north and be closer to her.'

'That's one way of wording it, I suppose.'

The knots in my stomach are growing tighter by the second, but I'm no closer to finding out what I want to know. I realise that my ringing after all these years has probably come as a shock to Philip, and the line of questions can't be much fun to talk about, but I don't have time for pleasantries. I rang for answers, and that's what I want.

'Philip, I need you to tell me the truth. Was there someone else involved? Is that why you left: because she was seeing someone else?'

'Liz, whatever is going on with you and Alice, I feel like these are questions you should be asking her.'

'For God's sake, just tell me, will you?'

Twenty years of friendship, and I've never snapped at him like that. The remorse floods through me, but I force it down. Can we even consider ourselves friends anymore if we haven't spoken for two years? I don't know. All I can hope is that he values the friendship we had enough to tell me the truth. If he can do that, then we're closer than most of the people in my life right now.

'Please, Philip, I've got a lot going on. There are some things happening that are really fucking confusing. I will speak to Alice. I'm going to speak to her. I just need to hear it from you first. Was she cheating on you? Is that why you split up?'

Silence follows my question, but it doesn't last forever.

'I found hotel receipts,' he says.

My knees want to buckle, but I'm clenching the arm of the sofa so hard, I can't go anywhere.

'And she admitted it?'

'She did.'

There's another question I need to ask, and my throat is so dry, it's as if I've swallowed sandpaper. Every syllable is an effort to scratch out.

'Was it with Jamie?'

'I don't know.'

'What kind of answer is that?' It's like I can't control how my words come out anymore. Like I'm on a knife edge, and it only takes the slightest thing to make me slip. I draw in a long breath, and try again. 'What do you mean, you don't know? Did you not find out?'

'No, I didn't want to know. I was being made redundant. I don't know if Alice told you that.'

'No, she didn't,' I say, wondering if I should start keeping a tally of all the things my best friend hasn't told me.

'Well, I was, so I had nothing left down south, anyway. I just wanted out of there. Look, if it was Jamie, then it's been going on an awful long time. I think you would've spotted it before now, don't you?'

I can't reply; I don't have the strength anymore.

'I hope you're doing well,' I say, my mind already drifting away from the conversation before it's even finished. 'I hope you're okay. Maybe we'll meet up again soon.'

'Maybe,' he says.

A moment later, I hang up. There's nothing more we have to say.

71

I open up on the picture on my phone again, and study it more closely, although this time I'm not looking at how close together the pair of them look, or how intently they are gazing into one another's eyes. I'm looking for other things. Clues as to where it is the pair are sitting. The seats are red. Non descriptive and absolutely no help.

It's only when I click on the photo and it asks me if I want to save it that I remember what Sasha showed me. What was it called? A reverse image search, something like that. Not that it matters what the name is. All that matters is if I can do it; maybe I can find out where the hell they are and get to them and catch them in their lies.

I'm sure there's some way of using my phone to do the search thing, but I don't know what it is, so I open up my laptop. A few clicks later, I'm inputting the photo of Jamie and Alice. A couple of moments is all it takes for dozens of related images to appear on the screen in front of me.

Straight away, I know some of them just aren't right. There's a bar in Edinburgh, for instance, and another one in Prague. And while it's true they do have the same kind of décor, I know there's no chance that's where Alice and Jamie are. I scroll down, and another one appears: Southend. I click on the link, and my pulse skyrockets. This is it. This is where they are.

I plug the postcode into my phone, then slam my laptop shut before grabbing my car keys.

As I drive towards Southend, I push my speed as much as I dare, racing down roads where I know there are no cameras, slowing down if there's any chance of them. As I reach the location, I can't see anywhere that hasn't got double yellow lines, but right now, after everything I've been through, a parking ticket is hardly a big concern.

I turn off the engine, but stay in the car.

A bolt of nausea rolls through me.

From where I'm waiting, I can see Jamie and Alice, still sitting there, in that same seat by the window. They're not holding hands anymore, but the way they're gazing into each other's eyes is enough to make me dizzy. They're not even hiding it. I have some staff members who live in Southend. If this is where they come to meet up and cheat on me, how many of my work colleagues already know?

It's been going on since Philip left; that's nearly two years.

I feel myself falling into a pit of tarnished memories. Jamie and I celebrated our twentieth wedding anniversary last year, and Alice was there... She brought us gifts. Told me how lucky I was to have found someone like Jamie. She *always* told me how lucky I was to have found someone like Jamie.

The anger of the memories is all it takes to spur me from my position, only I'm not concentrating. As such, I open my door into a passer-by.

'Fuck,' I snap at them. 'Why the hell didn't you look where you were going?'

The idiot has their black hoodie pulled up over their head like they're a fucking gangster and they're still in front of the door as I step out of the car. I consider offering them an apology, but before I speak, their shoulder slams into mine in obvious retribution.

If I had an ounce of rationality, it's gone.

'Watch what you're doing,' they growl before marching off.

'Hey, fuck you! It was a fucking accident you prick.'

It's only as they walk away that I see just how small the person's frame is. Then, as if they know I'm still watching them, they flip me the middle finger and a pale-purple nail is directed solely at me. I grind my back teeth together. Teenage girls can be the worst and this one's clearly a moody little bitch.

'Fuck you, bitch!' I yell again just for good measure.

For a moment, I worry that the incident would have attracted Jamie and Alice's attention, but they're way too focused on each other to see anything else.

Regaining my impetus, I stride into the restaurant.

'Excuse me, can I help you?' There's a maître d' on the door who's obviously meant to find me a seat, but I ignore them entirely. Instead, I march straight through, until I'm standing there in front of the table, looking at the two people I thought I trusted most in the world.

'Getting much work done, Jamie?' I say, before switching my smile across to Alice. 'Funny looking PJs.'

72

It could be comical, the level of shock on their faces. Comical, if it didn't mean my life has officially crumbled in front of me, that is. While Jamie sits there, gaping, Alice is immediately on her feet.

'Liz.' She stands up and wraps her arms around me in a hug, but I don't reciprocate. Instead, my entire body goes rigid in response. 'Liz, are you okay? I'm so sorry,' she says her voice so dripping with sympathy that I could almost fall for it if I didn't know what a lying, manipulative bitch she is. 'I didn't mean to lie. Jamie and I were worried, that's all.'

'Of course. That makes total sense,' I say.

Alice's eyes narrow on me, but it's Jamie who speaks next.

'Have you been drinking? Did you drive here after drinking?' His tone is so accusatory, it makes me laugh.

'You're going to turn this on me?' I say. The chuckle that reverberates from my lungs is so bizarre, I barely even recognise it. 'That's all you've got to say to me? You are unbelievable. The pair of you.'

There's a second of silence, in which Jamie's expression of confusion finally clears.

'I came here to speak to Alice about you; we are worried about you. You're not acting in your right mind.'

'Is that so? The two of you were just getting together so you could talk about me and how worried you are. Right. I'm so lucky to have such good friends.' I lay the sarcasm thick.

'Liz, this has gone far enough,' Jamie says, his voice exasperated, as if he's speaking to a schoolchild, not his wife. 'You're making a fool of yourself.'

'Blimey, making a fool of myself? How upsetting. At least it's me doing it to myself now, rather than you two.'

I look at Jamie, and then again at Alice.

'I spoke to Philip,' I say. 'He didn't just walk out and leave you. He didn't get tired of the marriage. You had an affair. You had an affair; that's why he left. Because you were cheating on him, cheating on him with my husband.'

Alice's skin goes so white, she looks ghostly. All three of us are standing now, though I don't know when that happened. I don't doubt that people are staring at us. The other tables in the restaurant are so quiet, I can hear the cutlery clinking against the plates. But I tune it out. It's Alice I'm looking at now. I've been around too long not to know that this happens. I'm hardly the first woman to have found out her husband has been cheating on her with her best friend. But this is Alice, who I thought of as a sister.

She holds my gaze for a second longer before she lowers it to the ground – the admission of guilt I've been waiting for.

When she looks up again, her face is emotionless. Calm. She throws a quick glance at Jamie before she looks back at me and speaks.

'You're right,' she says, pressing her lips together for a moment before releasing them. 'You're right, I did have an affair and I didn't know how to tell you about it. Two fucking years, and

I still haven't been able to tell you about it because you are so fucking judgemental.'

'There it is,' I say, a flicker of satisfaction on my face. 'Glad we're not still sticking with those false pretences. You know, I don't think I've ever seen this side of you before. It's nice to finally see the real you.'

Alice scoffs, the corner of her mouth turning upwards. 'You are so wrong here, Liz. So wrong, it's laughable. I had an affair, yes. But it wasn't with Jamie. It was with Nathan.'

73

I feel like I've fallen into a soap opera. Or a Telenovela, not that I've ever watched one. Perhaps it's just one of those prank TV shows, where any second now, everyone I've known is going to jump out from behind the bar with a 'surprise'. And Sasha, she'll be here with her arms wide, telling me she never got on a plane and left for Singapore at all. It was all just part of the joke. Only no one else is laughing. No one else except me.

'Nathan!' His name bursts from my mouth in an explosion of disbelief and clarity. 'Oh my God, it all makes so much sense now. That's why.'

I see a glimmer of relief in Alice's eyes as she looks at me questioningly, with a tilt of her head.

'What do you mean?' she says. 'You knew?'

'That's why you did it. That's why you shared the photo of me, that's why you got Katie to tell people at Sasha's school about the abortion, and made up some stuff to the papers for a quote about Christopher. It's all for Nathan. That was the problem when I first realised it was you. The only thing that didn't make sense was why you would do it. But now I understand. He made you.

Nathan made you do it. He used you so he could get to me. He used you to break me, so that he could get my job.'

Alice's gaze hardens as she bites down on her bottom lip. She's looking at me as if I've gone mad, and I've seen that look before. She gives it to children when they're misbehaving, and it works better than any reprimand. But I'm not one of her students. I'm not falling for her drama teacher skills.

'You can't honestly still believe I had anything to do with those things?' she says.

'Oh no, I'm positive. It can only be you. You knew when I had my doctor's appointments, you knew about the abortion, you had the photograph.'

'Elizabeth, this has gone far enough; we are going home now,' Jamie says, but I'm not giving in that easily.

'Surely you can see it,' I say to him. 'All the evidence is there. She is to blame for this. She is the reason Sasha has gone.'

He looks down at the table and shakes his head.

'Alice is your best friend. We've spent the last hour trying to work out how we can help you. She's the one who told me about what happened at the school today.'

'The school?' For the first time, I'm genuinely confused by what he's saying. 'What do you mean the school? I didn't leave my office.'

'Until you went home,' Alice adds.

'Yes, of course. I had to get home.'

They're both still staring at me in a manner I can't read. Actually, I can; I just don't want to. They're looking at me like I've gone insane.

'I don't know what you're on about,' I say.

'You don't remember what you said to Lucy in the car park?'

'Lucy? Head of Art Lucy?' My forehead's pinched so tightly, it's causing a tension headache. 'I didn't even see her.'

'Stop lying to us, Liz!' Jamie yells, before he drops his head. Alice, however, goes to take my hand, but I shift away from her.

Still, she softens her voice before she speaks.

'Lucy was broken. Crying because of what you said to her.'

'What I said to her? What did I say to her? I didn't see her.'

'She couldn't even drive herself home, she was that upset.'

'I don't get what you're going on about,' I say, shaking my head in disbelief.

This doesn't make sense. I didn't see Lucy, and I've never so much as made a student cry, let alone a teacher. That's not who I am. She should know that about me. She does know this. This is all just part of her game.

'She's lying about this, Jamie,' I say. 'Please, you have to believe me. She's lying about this.'

He's not able to meet my eye. Instead, he stares at the table, his hands wrapped around his drink as he rolls the glass between his fingers. When he finally lifts his head up to meet me, there are tears in his eyes.

'And what about Jeremy Petty? Was he lying too?' he says. 'Was he lying when he said you were the one who told him to print the article?'

74

I stumble backwards, the air freezing in my lungs as I shake my head.

'What are you on about? That's not true. That's not true. Jeremy, he knows. He knows it wasn't me...'

Jamie's fingers are back, pinching the bridge of his nose as he slowly shakes his head. 'I spoke to him, Liz. I know. Please stop this. Stop this lying.'

'I'm not lying. I'm not the liar here.'

I don't know how it's come to this. I came down here to confront the pair of them, and now it's all been twisted around to make me into the bad guy. How have they done this to me?

Neither Jamie nor Alice responds.

'I'm not the liar!' I repeat, this time at a yell.

I can see one of the wait staff walking towards us, probably wanting us to leave. They can ask all they want, though. I'm not going anywhere until I've got answers.

'I am not lying,' I say again, this time looking at Alice, but her head is down now, and tears are trickling down her cheeks.

Jamie's gaze shifts constantly as he avoids mine. But one thing remains consistent. The pain in his eyes. There's no glimmer, no light in them. Just absolute pain. Though whether it's because of what he's doing to me or what he thinks I've done to him, I can't tell.

'I rang Jeremy today, Liz. I got his number from your phone. He told me everything. How you had first contacted him last year, but then changed your mind and asked him to hold off on the story. Then how you rang him yesterday, all panicked about what you'd done. That's why he met you at the pub. There was no investigating, Liz. There was no need.'

'No, that's not true. That's not true.' I don't know why Jamie is saying this, or who he was speaking to, but Jeremy knows the truth. I know he does. 'We can ring him,' I say, grabbing my phone from my handbag. 'We can ring him and ask. He'll tell you the truth.'

Jeremy's number is still at the top of my recently called list, second only to Alice. I press call, then immediately flick it to speakerphone. Only the call doesn't ring. Instead, I get a computerised voice on the end of the line.

'The number you have dialled is no longer available. Please hang up and try again.'

I do as it says and ring again, only for the same message. The third time I try, it doesn't even do that. It just cuts out without a word. I may not know much about phones, but I'm pretty sure I know what this means. I've been blocked.

'He asked me to tell you to stop pestering him,' Jamie says with an expression of pure disdain.

'Pestering? Yesterday was the first time I spoke to him. Why don't you believe me? Please! Alice, Alice?'

I turn my attention to my best friend, although I don't know if I can call her that anymore. I don't think I can call her anything.

'You know I'd never do anything like that to Sasha. You both know I'd never do anything like that to Sasha. Please, you know that.'

The pair exchange a long look. Is it a lovers' look? The salacious gaze of two people who have been carrying on behind my back? I don't know, but what I do know is that this isn't good for me.

'We're not doing this any longer,' Jamie says eventually, grabbing his jacket from the back of the chair. 'I'm taking you home.'

75

Jamie spots my car, parked directly outside the restaurant, on double yellow lines. The front tyres are up on the kerb.

'Fucking hell, Liz, you're lucky you didn't kill anybody.' I don't know where his car is, but it doesn't look like he's planning on using it, as he takes my spare key from his keyring and opens the doors. 'Get in,' he says.

'I'm not going anywhere with you,' I spit. 'You lied to me.'

'Because I met up with Alice?' His eyebrows are so high, they're practically at his hair line. 'Because we wanted to discuss how to help you? That's how I lied to you? You just went in there and accused me of having an affair. You just outright said you don't trust me. And I'm meant to be okay with that? I'm meant to be okay with you accusing me of cheating?'

It's the one thing I've been wrong about in all this mess. It was Alice and Nathan, not Alice and Jamie, having an affair. One slight detail that has put my marriage on even rockier ground.

I get into the car without another word.

As is the theme now, most of the journey is in silence. It's only when we hit the dual carriageway after nearly ten minutes of driving I manage to speak.

'Jamie, I didn't do those things. I need you to believe me. I didn't upset Lucy, and I sure as hell didn't ask Jeremy Petty to print that article.' Jamie's eyes remain on the road, unblinking, but I don't stop. 'I don't know why Alice said that thing about Lucy, and I don't know why Jeremy lied about why we met or said he'd spoken to me before, but maybe they're in on it together. Maybe they're working together.'

Finally, Jamie tears his attention from the road to look at me.

'Please listen to yourself, Liz. What reason would Alice have for hurting you? For hurting Sasha?'

'What do you mean, "what reason"? Nathan has wanted my job for over a year. The fact it was him... I told you right from the beginning, he is the one behind this. I just didn't know how he was getting the information. Now I do.'

'And you really think Alice would hurt Sasha like that? She thinks of Sasha as a daughter. You're saying she would do all this just because she's in love? You can't believe that, not after how long you've known her.'

I shake my head. 'Please, I need you to believe me. Love makes people act crazy.'

Jamie snorts in response. 'You're honestly going to comment on other people doing crazy things? Right now, Liz, you look fucking insane.'

Silence fills the car as I take in what he's saying. I do. I see that. From his point of view, I must look crazy, but that must be Nathan's plan. Taking my job isn't enough. He needs to discredit me completely. To make me think I'm losing my mind and lose everyone that matters to me in the process.

When we turn off the dual carriageway, Jamie lets out a long sigh.

'I'm gonna call in sick tomorrow,' he says. 'I think the stress of Sasha leaving, it's causing you not to think clearly. And I think you need to do the same. Actually, I think you need to do more than that. I think maybe it would be best if you hand in your resignation.'

76

When we get into the house, I grab a bottle of wine, head up to the bedroom and slam the door, making it clear Jamie can sleep in the spare bed tonight. He always hated me having this head-ship job. He hated the way it took time away from him and Sasha. Maybe he's in on it with Alice, I think, only to change my mind. He would never do anything that meant being separated from Sasha. I might not believe much at the minute, but I believe that.

As I mull over everything Alice and Jamie said to me, it takes surprisingly little time for me to finish the bottle and pass out on the bed.

When I wake up, my head is pounding. I roll over, blink open my eyes, and then squeeze them tightly shut; the light blinds me and a low groan is the only noise I can make.

My mouth feels like I've been sucking on an old, dirty sock, and the back of my eyeballs feel like they've been doused in acid. It's not a good feeling.

'I didn't know whether I should wake you,' Jamie says. He's sitting at the end of the bed like I'm some sort of hospital patient and he's the visitor keeping vigil. 'There's water on the bedside table, some ibuprofen too.'

I twist my head to see it, and the small action causes a pain to shoot down the back of my neck, but I see he's right: water and painkillers.

It's only when I've taken both tablets that I can focus a little more and notice Jamie is still in the clothes he was out in yesterday. For a second, I think that maybe it's still night-time. Then I remember that there's light pouring in through the window. It's definitely morning.

'Have you not been to bed?' I ask.

He shakes his head. 'I couldn't sleep. I've had a lot on my mind.'

'You and me both.'

The sigh that rolls from his lungs is sad, resigned and utterly exhausted.

'Liz, I know you probably don't want to talk about this now, but I think we need to. Alice and Nathan wouldn't do this to you. I don't think anybody in their right mind would do this to you.'

'So they're not in their right mind. It makes sense, but it doesn't change the fact that somebody is trying to ruin me, to ruin my family, my life, and it's working, Jamie. It's working. They've taken my daughter from me, my job from me. They're taking you from me too.'

I expect him to say something. Like how nothing would ever take him from me. Like how we're too strong for that, and this is just a bump in the road. But he doesn't. Instead, he moves to my side of the bed and takes my hand in his.

'There are places you can go, you know. Places where you can talk to people. Work through your issues. We've been through similar before.'

'What, when?' I'm confused by how the conversation ha

suddenly switched. We were talking about who would be crazy enough to do this to me, and now he wants me to talk to people. The only people we should be talking to are the police because it's clear as hell Jeremy Petty isn't going to do that.

'Remember how you needed a bit of time to get sorted after Sasha was born? How you struggled, got paranoid about her falling sick all the time? You wouldn't leave the house because you were convinced someone was going to hurt her.'

'I had postnatal depression. I was fucking ill.'

'I know, but stress can do things like that to your body. It can change things. Chemicals and stuff. That can all affect how you perceive things.'

'How I perceive things? This isn't a case of how I'm perceiving things. These things a fucking happening to me, Jamie.'

'I know. I know they are. But—'

'But?'

He doesn't respond. Not with a single word. And that's when it hits me like a hammer to the gut.

'You think *I'm* doing this? You think I'm doing it to myself?'

77

He doesn't even try to deny it. He can't. It's there, written clear as day across his face.

'You think I did this?' I repeat. 'That I'm doing this to myself? Why?'

'I don't know, I don't know why, but Alice and I were talking, and it's the only thing that makes sense.'

'You think I would put myself through this?'

He presses his lips tightly together and reaches for the glass of water, only to change his mind. 'I'm not saying that you're doing these things deliberately. Maybe you're disassociating.'

'Disassociating?' I echo. 'Great, now you're fucking WebMD-ing me to find out if I'm psychotic. I'm not. I've not done anything.'

'Look,' he says, raising his hands as if he is approaching a rabid animal. 'I know you're upset about this, obviously, but I need you to consider the possibility. You've been stressed about work, stressed about a lot of things, but you need to look at this logically. You're the one person who has access to everything, photos, medical records; you're the one person who knew every-thing about Sasha.'

'And you think I spread rumours about my daughter around her school? What kind of mother would I be?'

'I'm just trying to figure this out the best I can,' Jamie says. He sounds desperate, which is ridiculous. What the hell does he have to sound desperate about?

'You're not trying to figure this out; you're trying to place the blame on me,' I say, 'and I'm not doing this to myself. Why would I?'

'I don't know, I don't... Maybe...' He pauses, and I hear something in the silence. There's something he wants to say, but he's too afraid to.

'Jamie, what is it? Why would I do this to myself?'

'The job is a lot of stress. I think it's too much. I think you know it's too much too, but you don't want to admit defeat. Your pride won't let you quit. This way, you won't have to. This way, it's just something bad that's happened to you.'

'You think I'd get my daughter's ex-boyfriend arrested and her sent to the other side of the world just because I don't want to quit my job?'

I shake my head, hardly able to believe what I'm hearing, when another thought strikes.

'What about the photo of you and Alice together? Am I meant to have taken it myself?'

'Photo of me and Alice?' he says.

I pick up my phone and flick to the image.

'Are you going to tell me that I just stood outside the restau-rant for an hour so I could take photos with a different number and send them to myself?' I say. 'There are messages, too. Here, read them.'

As Jamie reads through the texts, it's like he's forgotten I'm even there.

'These are from an unknown number?' he says.

'Yes, you can see that. I don't know who it is that sent them.'

Finally, he looks up and locks his gaze on mine.

'Well, have you tried ringing it?' he says.

78

My hands are shaking as I click on the number and prepare to hit call. I'm terrified. It's just going to give some long, painful, high-pitched ring, then say that the number can't be accessed or I'll discover that I've been blocked, just as Jeremy Petty has done. But I'm equally terrified that it's going to be answered. Will it be Nathan or Alice that picks up or have I got it wrong? Is it someone entirely different who's doing this to me?

For a split second, I'm not sure whether I want it to ring or not, but then the sound starts, and I have no choice.

'It's ringing,' I say to Jamie, flicking it onto speakerphone so we can hear. 'Now do you believe me? It's ringing. Somebody sent this message to me from a different phone.'

It rings for a while longer, before it flicks to a nondescript answer machine message. The relief is palpable, but so is the disappointment.

'Maybe I should ring from a different number?' I say. 'They'll know this one. Why would they pick up knowing they're going to be found out?'

Jamie's still staring at the phone and, for a second, I think he's

going to tell me this is just another of my disassociations. That's
we've tried once, and that should be enough. But then he looks
up and nods. For the first time, I feel a glimmer of hope. I need
Jamie on my side with this. I need him to believe me.

'You keep trying. I'll go get my work phone.'

I want to hug him. I want to hug him and cry and say I forgive
him for not believing me. But we still haven't got these guys yet.

'Alice doesn't have your work phone number?' I check.

He shakes his head. 'No. Not even Sasha does. It's downstairs,
though. I'll just be a minute. Keep trying.'

I don't need him to tell me that. I will ring this number a
thousand times if that's what it takes. As Jamie's footsteps pad
down the stairs, the phone starts ringing for a second time.

My heart's pounding at a pace fit to burst.

*This time they're going to answer, this time they're going to
answer.* I'm still saying the words over in my head when there's a
click on the line. I think it's gone to voicemail again, but there's
no machine. Panic surges through me.

'Hello, who is this?' No one answers me, but the line's still
open and I can hear them breathing. Quick, heavy breaths. 'Who
is this? Why are you doing this to me?'

Still, there's no reply, but I realise it's no good, me on the
phone like this with them, without Jamie here to hear. I lurch out
of bed and race to the hall.

'Jamie!' I yell, covering the mouthpiece of the phone. 'Jamie
they've picked up.'

I'm at the top of the stairs when he starts walking up towards
me. His pace is almost stoic. I don't know why the fuck he isn'
running. 'Please, quickly, before they hang up. Jamie, will you
hurry up!'

Despite my desperate pleas, he doesn't change his pace, and
he doesn't speak until he reaches the top of the stairs.

'They're not going to hang up,' he says.

I frown, confused, when he lifts up his hand to show me the phone he's holding.

It's a smartphone, complete with a camera on the back, but it's cheaper than anything I have and it's definitely not his work phone either.

'What is that?' I ask.

He shakes his head before he lifts it up to his ear.

'It was in your pocket,' he says, but I don't just hear the words come out of his mouth. I hear them come out of my phone. 'It's you, Liz. It's always been you.'

79

I stand there, silent, trying to make sense of what Jamie is saying. He's holding a phone I don't recognise and looking at me like I'm crazy. And then there's the fact that his voice came out of my phone when he spoke, although I was on a call to whoever is trying to screw up my life.

'Where did you get that?' I say, unable to hide the tremble in my voice. 'Why have you got that phone?'

'It was in your pocket, Liz. In your coat. I don't think it takes a genius to work out this is yours. That you sent the message from this other phone.'

I'm near mute with disbelief, first that the phone is there in my house, and second because I can't believe Jamie would think I could be behind this.

'Why would I have sent you downstairs to get your work phone if I knew that the one I was ringing was in my pocket?'

'Perhaps you thought you left in on silent.'

'Or it's because I'm entirely innocent. Someone did this. Someone planted that phone on me.' I shake my head, releasing a shuddering breath. 'This is all part of it, Jamie. Why can't you see that? I don't know how this happened. I've never seen that phone in my life. I swear. I've never seen it. It was planted on me.' A spike in adrenaline causes my pulse to rocket. 'Alice. She must've slipped the phone into my pocket at the bar. When she hugged me,' I say. 'It's always been her, working with Nathan. I know it has.'

Jamie covers his face with his hand.

'Liz, stop this.'

'She must've done it. You saw how she hugged me.'

'Like she always hugs you?'

'No, no, it was different. I didn't notice it at the time, but it was. I'm sure it was. Yes, that has to be when she put the phone in my pocket. It has to be.'

Jamie is pacing now. Moving back and forth on the landing.

'Alice didn't have another phone on her,' he says.

'You don't know that; it could've been in her bag.'

'So you're saying, when she saw you coming, she jumped up, hugged you and slipped it into your pocket and none of us noticed?'

'Yes, yes, that's what must've happened. I've never seen this phone in my life.'

I can hear the desperation in my voice. The begging. I hate it. It reminds me of all those years ago, when I begged my mother not to cut me off. To still see me as her same loving daughter, but she couldn't. I never thought I would have to beg the woman who brought me into the world to love me. And I never thought I would have to beg Jamie, either.

'Why don't you believe me?' I say.

He ends the call, stares at the phone a little longer.

'Liz, I don't know what's going on. I'm sorry. I'm sorry I didn't see that things were this bad before. I should have been keeping a closer eye on you. I should have been looking out for you more.'

I want to scream. I want to pound my fists against his chest and force him to see sense. But that'll only make me seem crazier.

'I didn't take that photograph. I didn't. I was here when I got that text message. I was here, at home.' My chest tightens. There must be some way for me to prove it.

'Liz, please, stop it. Everything you do just makes things worse. Surely you can see that.'

Maybe he's right, but I have no intention of giving up. I need proof. Proof that I didn't know where they were. Proof that it was that text message that sent me to the bar.

My heart skips a beat, causing me to gasp. I think I have it. I think I have the proof I need.

'This is the last thing. This is the last thing I will show you,' I say. 'I can prove to you it wasn't me. Please. Just let me show you this one last thing.'

He shakes his head and groans, and for a second, I'm sure he's about to refuse, to say that he doesn't want to listen to anything else I've got, but, instead, he offers a quick dip of his chin.

'Okay, what do you want to show me?'

I feel calmer now. No, not calm. Still far from calm, but calmer, and that's something. Somehow, Alice slipped that phone into my pocket without me noticing. And Jamie still isn't on board with believing that she is to blame, but I know I can prove it to him.

80

I take the steps two at a time as I race downstairs.

'Look, I can prove this wasn't me. The bar, I didn't know where the bar was. I had to search it up. Look at my laptop. It's on my laptop.'

'Please, I don't want to do this; it's upsetting you. I can see it's upsetting you.' Jamie puts a hand on my shoulder, probably to comfort me. But it does the opposite. I turn around and snarl at him.

'Of course it's fucking upsetting me; you think I'm going insane. Get my laptop from the living room. I will show you. I had to find the place you were. I had to search the internet with the photo. Please, get my computer.'

This time, he doesn't argue. He goes and grabs it from the bedroom while I pace the kitchen. I don't know how my heart hasn't given up, the way it's been hammering now. Not just today, but for weeks. But this will be the end of it. Jamie will see. Why would I have looked up a restaurant if I knew where they were? I bet it even has a time stamp on it, too. Everything we need to go to the police.

Jamie returns a minute later with the laptop in his hand.

'Have you checked?' I ask.

He shakes his head. 'No, I didn't want to go on it without you knowing.'

'You know what the password is?'

'I know, but it's yours.'

I open the lid, type the password in, and open up an internet browser.

'Fuck, fuck, fuck, fuck,' I mutter.

'What is it?' he says.

'I closed the browser. Just give me a second. Let me reopen the tabs. Please, give me a second.'

I'm tapping at the keyboard, but my hands are shaking so much, I keep hitting the wrong letters. Finally, I reopen my internet page with all the tabs and websites I had open the night before.

'See, I searched where the place was. I used the reverse image thing Sasha showed me, look.' I click on the back arrow, but it doesn't move. As far as the computer is concerned, there's nothing to go back and see.

'I promise. I don't know why it doesn't work.'

'Please, please, Liz. You need to calm down.'

'No, not until I prove this. I got the message, and then I came to you. I can go to tech. George will be able to find it. There'll be a time stamp on it, won't there? There has to be, right? You know, if the police need it to corroborate times or something. I can still take it to the police. I can do that, can't I? This will be enough for the police, surely. When I tell them everything else that has happened.'

'Please Liz, can you just listen to yourself? I don't know how can help you, but I need you to accept this. I need you to accep you need help. That's the only proof that I'm seeing right now. The proof that you need help.'

'Proof, proof.' I'm repeating the word as I close the laptop lid and recommence my pacing, only this time, it's not impatient pacing. It's the pacing of someone who feels like they are losing their mind. How do I get proof when everything I find just pushes Jamie further away from believing me?

Right now, though, I only have one concrete piece of evidence – one thing to prove that it's not me doing this – and that's how insane this whole situation is; he can't possibly believe I would choose to do this to myself.

When he looks at me, there are tears in his eyes. They well there, and I think he's going to let them fall, but then he sniffs and wipes his cheeks with his knuckles before he looks at me again.

'I think we both need a bit of space,' he says. 'You should take it easy. Get some more rest.'

'I don't need rest. I need to get to the bottom of this.' I don't know how else to word it so he'll listen to me.

'Please, Liz. You're not at work today, so just have a day off, right? Have a day off. I'll stay at a friend's tonight too. Give you a bit of space.'

The air freezes around me as his words sink in.

'You're leaving me?'

He shakes his head. 'I'm just giving you some time, that's all.'

I'm not sure what the difference is, but perhaps that's because there isn't one.

81

I feel like I've gone insane. Maybe I have. That's what all the signs are pointing to. I've lost my mind.

Jamie tried to say goodbye. He leaned in to kiss me on the cheek, but I jerked away and he didn't try again. Now he's gone, and the house is the emptiest it has ever been. What's scary is that it might be like this forever. Me alone.

By the time I drag myself up to make a coffee, it's gone eleven. I don't know where today has gone. Normally, by this time on a weekday, I would have been working four hours. Had half a dozen meetings and replied to dozens of emails. Now I'm not even dressed.

The smell of coffee dripping out of the machine hits my senses with a surprising bitterness. Normally, caffeine would be my go-to after more than a full bottle of wine the night before, but that's on days when I want to be awake and functional. That's not what I need. What I need is to shut the world away. Abandoning the coffee, I head back upstairs and crawl into bed.

On the off chance that something has changed, I try Jeremy Petty's number again, but I'm still blocked.

'Am I going insane?' I lift my hands up and look at the ceiling as if I'm talking to some higher being. 'Am I actually crazy?'

Talking to the ceiling and expecting an answer is probably a sure sign that I am, but I need something. I've watched films before, those sci-fi things, where people go to sleep and carry out all these nefarious plans they never would have dreamed they were capable of when they were awake. I always thought they were completely farcical, but now I'm not sure anymore.

At some point, I fall asleep. It's fitful and half a dozen times I start to wake, but each time, I force myself back. No matter how bad the sleep is, it's better than being awake.

It's my stomach growling that finally stirs me from bed. It must be the afternoon, and I still haven't eaten anything, though rather than heading downstairs, I move over to the window. Jamie's car is still gone.

I gaze out a bit, thinking about what he said to me before he left. He was going to stay with 'a friend'. Does he mean Alice? The thought floods my head, but I quickly quash it. I believe what Alice said about Nathan; it makes sense now, the way I've seen them chatting together in the corner of the staffroom, or in the halls when we were setting up for exams. That is the only reason, and it's still the only reason I can think of as to why someone would do this to me. She has to be the missing link.

I shake my head again.

'There is no missing link, Liz. It's you,' I say to myself. 'It's you, it's you.'

I repeat it over and over again, banging my knuckles against my head as I speak.

'It's you, it's you. You lost your daughter, you screwed up your job, you screwed up your marriage. It's you.'

I didn't ever expect going insane would feel like this, but then I suppose I never considered the possibility that I would actually go crazy, but if we are looking at the evidence, it's a pretty solid case.

I consider ringing Alice and apologising, telling Jamie he's right; I need to get help. I need to get help before I hurt anyone else.

I turn away from the window and finally head downstairs, but, when I reach the kitchen, there's the familiar crunch of gravel from outside as a car pulls into the driveway. Jamie. Of course he didn't leave me. He'd never do that. My heart leaps as I rush to the door to open it. I didn't realise how much his abandonment hurt until now. It hurts almost as much as knowing there's this sickness spreading through my mind. The fact that, when I needed him most, he left. But now he's come back. At least that's what I think until I hear the doorbell ring. Why would he ring when he has keys to let himself in?

With my hands trembling, I head down the hallway. I don't need to open the door to know who is standing behind the frosted-glass pane. I know her silhouette.

'Liz, I know you're in there. Please, Liz, can you let me in? I know you can hear me. It's Alice. Please let me in.'

82

'What are you doing here?' I spit, the glass still between us. Amongst all the mess in my head, the one thing I'm certain of is that Alice is a liar. She has lied to me for over a year and I'd be a fool to believe anything she says to me now.

'Please, can you let me in?' she says. 'I just want to talk to you. I just want us to talk.'

'You're supposed to be at school. You have exams to run.'

'Yes, well, I left an hour early. I had a free period.' I don't know her timetable well enough to know if that's true or not. Maybe Nathan's just covering for her. Again. Alice pauses for a moment before she carries on speaking. 'I spoke to Jamie. He told me about the phone.'

Anger surges through me. So that's why she's come, because I worked out her ploy and she wants to lie to me again so she can cover her tracks.

I open the door. Mainly so she has to look me in the eye as she lies.

'You have some nerve coming here.'

'Please, Liz, let me come in. Let me talk to you.'

'Why? So you can lie? So you can twist things?'

'I haven't lied to you, I promise. Other than about Nathan. And you're right, I should've told you about him. I should've, but I just wasn't sure how. I couldn't find the right time.'

'In over a year?' The laugh that cracks in my throat is harsh and bitter.

'I know. I know it sounds ridiculous, but... I didn't know how things were going to pan out between us. It was a drunken mistake the first time. That was what I thought. Then it kept happening even when we weren't drunk and then we were meeting up and it wasn't even about the sex anymore. Nathan was the one who suggested chatting on MySpace. He followed Leo's music on it, but we didn't think there was any chance of Philip or his wife finding our messages on there. We were wrong. Philip found out and left. Then Nathan told his wife. Later, Leo learned we were a couple too and, the longer things went on, the more ridiculous it seemed that I hadn't told you.'

'I was your best friend. I told you everything that happened with me. With Sasha.' I don't hide my exasperation.

'I know, and I didn't want to add to that. I knew how you felt about Nathan, and I didn't know where to start. Every time we've spoken, I've wanted to tell you. Honestly, it's been eating away at me. I kind of hoped you might just laugh about it and take the piss out of me.' She smiles hopefully, but I don't reciprocate it.

'Take the piss out of you for sleeping with the guy who's trying to single-handedly ruin my career? Well, not single-handedly,' I say, adding, 'I guess you're on his side.'

'He's not trying to ruin your career, Liz. He doesn't need to. He's got a new job as a headteacher in Rayleigh.'

'He has?' I flinch in surprise before shaking my head. 'No, that's not true. I would know; I'm his line-manager. He would've come to me for a reference.'

'He applied last year, asked Alan because he'd been his superior longer. I promise you. Nathan is not after your job. He doesn't need it. He's going to hand in his resignation. I can ring him now if you don't believe me. I can get him to hand in his resignation early if that's what you need?'

I know it's not a rhetorical question, and my instinct is to say it's because she's telling the truth. But that's what she wants. Of course, if I speak to Nathan, he'll back up her story. They'll have everything planned.

'Please, please let me come in,' Alice says again. 'Perhaps we can figure something out together. Work out why this is happening. I promise you, Liz, I'm always on your side. Haven't I always been on your side? Those training days, those drunken antics all those years ago. I never told anybody about the things that went down. Why do you think I'd say something now? Please, just let me come in for a coffee. I just want a chance to talk, that's all.'

I'm torn. Part of me wants to slam the door in her face and tell her to fuck off. I want to cut her out, the way she has done to me. But the house is so damn quiet, I don't want to go back into it alone. So I step back and let her in.

83

I gesture for Alice to follow me through to the kitchen, where I put the kettle on. The phone Jamie found in my coat pocket is sitting there on the table. I gesture towards it.

'Recognise that?' I say.

Alice looks at it and frowns. 'No, should I?'

'It's the phone you planted on me. In my pocket, when you hugged me at the bar.'

'A phone? I don't get it. Why would I put a phone in your pocket?'

'That's what I want to know.'

Alice stares at the cheap mobile, and I can see a thousand questions whirring through her mind as she decides what to say. Maybe she'll ask me about the messages that I got, or try to plead her innocence again. But she doesn't.

'How is Sasha?' she asks instead. It's not a great question to lead with.

'I've not heard from her,' I reply.

'Not at all?'

'Not a word. That's it. I'm out of her life now. Dead to her.'

At this, Alice's face creases with concern. 'She was obviously just angry. She wouldn't mean that. You're her mum; she adores you.'

'I guess we just have to wait and see.'

We fall into silence again, and I'm sure Alice is waiting for me to speak, but I'm not going to. She's the one who knocked on my door. She's the one who wanted to talk about things, so I'm giving her all the chances she needs to take the lead.

'Jamie thinks it's in your head, that it's the stress of the job causing you to act like this.'

'Wow,' I respond. I thought the first question was bad, but this is on a whole different level. 'Do you think the same?' I ask, hoping for an immediate answer. A quick response that would help convince me I'm not on my own here. But, instead, Alice's eyes train down on my table. The kettle has already clicked off, which means I should probably make her a drink, only I'm not planning on offering her one, and I don't think she's going to ask either.

'Liz, I swear on my life, on your life, on Sasha and Katie's lives. On everybody's lives. I would never, ever do anything to hurt you. Ever.'

'That doesn't answer the question, Alice,' I say.

She nods. 'I know. But you're the person who had access to the exam papers before they were given out. You have access to all the reprographics needed to print them.'

'As does every person in the school, including you and Nathan. He was the one who got the papers,' I remind her, only to see the muscles in her jawline twitch. Apparently, it's fine to accuse your best friend of over twenty years of being insane, but not a boyfriend of less than five per cent of that.

'You're right. I don't have a concrete answer yet, Liz. I can't get my head around it. But, whatever the outcome, I want you to

know that I'm here for you. If you want me to go with you, see a
doctor, talk to someone. I don't want you to feel like you have to
do it on your own. You're not on your own, okay? I'll always be
here for you. Always.'

How can she be so genuine and lying to me? I don't know. But
as the text message said, there's a reason she's a drama teacher.

'We've been through some shit together, the two of us, haven't
we?' I say quietly.

Alice lets out a sad chuckle.

'Don't you know it? But you know you saved me through
some of those times. You really did, and I want to be here. I want
to do the same for you. I've got to go; I need to pop back to
school, but I'll come by later, okay? I'll come and check on you. I
love you, Liz.'

'You don't have to do that.'

'Yes, yes, I do.'

I don't reply. Instead, I just stand there and watch her leave.

84

The house feels even emptier after Alice's departure. Is this how I'm going to be forever? I wonder. On my own, locked in my mind, seeing conspiracies in every corner? Alice seemed genuine, but that's the skill of the great liars and manipulators, isn't it? They make you feel like you're the one that's going crazy. Right now, that's exactly how I feel.

Could it really be true that Nathan has got another job? If that's the case, then him trying to bring me down would make no sense at all. He's competitive, leadership-driven, but he loves the school and the kids. If he goes, and I'm kicked out for being crazy, St Anne's is screwed. There's no way June could take over my role and no good Head is looking for a job at this time of year. I just can't imagine him being vindictive enough to do that. As I sit here, I realise that this is one thing I can verify. So I pick up my phone, dial the school, and hit the extension for my least favourite person.

'Saint Anne's, you've reached the headteacher's office.' Sandra's voice greets me. If Sandra's voice didn't grate on me normally, it does now. 'Mrs Croft's office' is what she's meant to say. Apparently, they've taken my name off the greeting. I guess that's a good indication of whether they think I'm coming back.

'Sandra,' I say with a tone of urgency. 'It's me, Liz.'

Despite my clear introduction, she takes a moment to respond, as if she's trying to figure out who's speaking.

'Elizabeth,' she says. 'I wasn't expecting to hear from you.'

'No, no, of course you weren't. Nobody is,' I say. 'Sandra, I need to ask you a question, and I need you to be truthful with me.'

There's another pause, this time even longer.

'I am not meant to be discussing any school matters with you. If it's an emergency, you should put in a request to the governors. They can be contacted by email.'

'They won't respond to me, not quick enough at least, and they probably don't have the answer to this question, anyway. This isn't a school matter exactly, not yet. It's more of a...' I pause, thinking how best to word myself, '...gossip matter?' As soon as I hear the word leave my mouth, I'm not sure I've made the right decision.

No one wants to be referred to as a gossip, and I'm pretty sure that includes Sandra, regardless of how true it is, but I don't want to beat about the bush either. This is the quickest way for me to find out my answer.

'I'm not sure what you're after,' she says tepidly, 'but I don't think I can help in this situation.'

'No, please, please Sandra, please. Please help me with this. It's a really simple question. I'm not... It's not... I just need you to confirm something for me. Tell me if a rumour I've heard is true. It doesn't harm anybody. Anybody at all, I promise. I just want to know whether Nathan has another job. Is he moving to Rayleigh to become a headmaster? Is that true? Alice is the one that told me. I assume you already know they're seeing each other?'

With this titbit of information, I feel the change. I wonder for a second if perhaps she didn't know about Alice and Nathan, and this is news to her, but then I change my mind. Of course, she knew, and she'd have loved having the upper hand on me like that.

'I'm not planning on doing anything,' I assure her. 'I'm pleased for him, I am. This is just clarification, Sandra. I'm just trying to rule out who might be doing these things to me, and if Nathan doesn't want my job, then I've been barking up the wrong tree.'

I hear her smack her lips together. It's possible she's chewing on the end of her pen. Whatever the noise is, I want it to stop, but I don't say as much. Not until I get a response.

'According to my sources, he is planning on handing in his resignation within the next couple of weeks,' she says.

'He is.'

'For a job in Rayleigh. Now, is there anything else you need?'

'No, no, thank you Sandra. Thank you so much.'

With that, I hang up.

85

Once again, the relief I feel is tainted. Nathan didn't want my job, which means my best friend probably wasn't helping him to bring me down. Which means I accused her unnecessarily. Several times. Worse than that, though, it means that she and Jamie are probably right.

This is me. I'm the one going mad. Mad enough to buy another phone and not even remember it. Mad enough to photo-copy dozens of exam papers with my abortion record printed on the inside. Mad enough to drive away my daughter.

The realisation is dizzying. Jamie was right. I'm the one person who had the resources and knowledge to make all these things happen. The why doesn't matter. There is no why when you've lost touch with reality. And that's what's happened. It's a strange feeling. That acceptance. Acceptance of yourself and how you're not the person you thought you were.

The fact that I'm still wearing my pyjamas and slippers barely crosses my mind as I grab my keys and leave the house. I need to be away from people. I need to be in a place where I can't cause anymore torment.

So far, the only person I've done real damage to is myself –
and Sasha, too. But that might change. If I don't remember doing
these things, who knows what else I might not remember doing?
I don't know where people like me belong. High functioning but
delusional adults, but I guess the hospital is the best spot.

I grab my keys, climb into the car, and go to type the name of
the hospital into the sat nav. Not that the quickest route really
matters. As I start to type on the screen, my mind stirs with
memories of last night.

I took the postcode for the restaurant off the computer and
wrote it on my phone before I typed it into my sat nav, didn't I?
Why would I do that if I already knew where it was? It would
have already been on the car's system.

Is this a memory I've placed in my mind? I wonder as I sit
with my hands on the steering wheel. If I've removed memories,
like buying the phone and doing the photocopying, then it stands
to reason I could place them in my mind too, but this one is vivid.
I'm certain of it, and if I'm right... If I'm right... A flurry of excitement fills me.

My hand is trembling so much, the keys are jangling. So far,
every bit of evidence has pointed to me being the one who's
going insane, but now I realise there's a piece of evidence I hadn't
even thought about. And, hopefully, if someone really is trying to
frame me, then they haven't thought of it either.

86

I don't know how to work all the various gadgets that the sat nav system is fitted with. The only functions I use are to get me to places and to ring people. But I know it does far more than that. I know it records all the journeys I've been on before, at least for a time. I remember the man in the showroom telling me as much.

'You are not going insane,' I tell myself, not sure if it's a statement or a plea. I need this. Concrete confirmation, either way. Undisputable evidence. And I get the feeling that it's only minutes away. I hit some more buttons, and the screen goes black, but I'm not giving up. A moment later and it's back to life, and I'm trying again.

After pressing a couple of random buttons, I'm on a screen I don't recognise. One of them changes the map so that it's now all in green and black – night vision, perhaps? The next takes me to something I've never seen before. It looks like a screen of code. Maybe Sasha could make sense of it, but I sure as hell can't. I keep pressing, using the back arrow, the menu key, any other combinations I can think of, and then, more by luck than judgement, something appears on the screen in front of me.

Previous routes.

Bingo.

My hand covers my mouth in anticipation of what I'm about to read. Either way, it's terrifying. I'm either insane or being tormented into insanity. Neither are great options.

With a deep breath in, I tap the screen one more time.

The first route that appears on the map is the trip last night, when Jamie brought us back from the bar. According to the sat nav, we were home at 9.36 p.m. That sounds about right, but it's the next one I'm interested in. What time did I actually leave home? The stupidity of drinking alcohol means that I'm not too sure, but that doesn't matter. I just need to read what it says.

A moment later, it tells me I left at 8.22 p.m.

I take my phone out of my pocket and open up the text message I'd received with the photo on it. The timestamp is there clear as day – 7.49 p.m. I received the message at 7.49 p.m. but I didn't leave here until 8.22 p.m. The only way that could happen is if I didn't send it. If I received the text then drove there. The way it happens in my memory.

The phone was planted on me. I have not gone insane. I can feel tears streaming down my cheeks. Like a jolt, I recall the moment I'd arrived at the restaurant and opened the door into a hooded passer-by. What if that hadn't been my fault at all? What if that had been their plan? To open the door onto me and slip the phone in my pocket that way?

Swiping across my phone screen, I navigate to the call list and hit Jamie's name. He needs to see this. He needs to come back now. If he sees it, he'll know I'm not lying.

When the phone goes to voicemail, I leave a message.

'Jamie, you can come back. I found it; I found the proof. I'm so sorry. But it's okay; it's not me. It's not me. Someone is doing this to us. Someone is trying to break us up.'

I hang up the phone after leaving the message. I check the time. He'll be at work still now, but it won't be long until he can message me back.

That's what I think, at least. I head back into the house and shower. For some reason, I feel grubby and dirty, and a shower is just what I need to clear my head. When I come back out, I see there's a missed call from Jamie. I go to reply, only to see there's a message too.

Liz, you need to stop this.

87

Liz, you need to stop this.

I read the message over and over again.

Does he mean he wants me to finish it? To find out who is doing this and put an end to it? That's what his message could mean, but I don't think it does. Tears choke in my throat. He still doesn't believe me. Jamie still thinks my last message was just another bout of my insanity, which means he's probably not going to believe me, even when he sees this evidence. He'll think I drove there, took a photo, and drove back just to cover my tracks. Or that I somehow found a way of hacking the sat nav system, even though that's well beyond my capabilities.

My heart is pounding against my ribs as I scroll down to another name.

Last time I rang him, he didn't pick up, and I'm not convinced this time is going to be any different. After all, if my husband won't pick up to me, what are the chances that my daughter's ex-boyfriend, who thinks I'm responsible for sending him to jail, is going to? Plus, there's the added complication that I'm assuming he's out on bail, awaiting trial, but that might not be the case. He might be locked up, with no access to his phone at all.

I press call and watch the screen. Waiting. Soon the phone's been ringing so long, I think it's about to go to voicemail, so I'm preparing to hang up when he answers.

'What the hell do you want?' he says.

My body is rigid with tension. I don't know why I thought this would be possible. Why I thought he would speak to me, but he's the only lead I have, however tenuous our relationship is.

'Christopher, I need you to know I did not go to the police. I never went to the police about you.'

'You're lying. You don't stop, do you? You've always had to have control of Sasha's life. And now you've pushed her away entirely.'

I can't take these insults to heart and I can't blame him for firing them at me. Not with what he thinks I've done. But maybe if I can prove that I'm not behind these other things, it might mean the police throw out his case, too. And if that's what I need to make happen for Sasha to talk to me again, then I'm willing to do it.

'Christopher, please, I need you to listen to me. I didn't do this. I didn't do this to Sasha and, if I was going to get you arrested, I would have done it to you a year ago when I first threatened it. Somebody is trying to hurt me and, to do that, they've been hurting Sasha. And you, too. I'm sorry, I really am, but I have to work out who is doing this. I have to work it out, and I need your help.'

'Why the hell would I do anything to help you?' he says. 'You've ruined everything. You've ruined my life.'

'Christopher, please, I didn't do it. I didn't. You don't have to do this for me, but do it for Sasha. Please. Sasha deserves to know the truth. Please, she deserves to know that I would never do this to her. Please... please help me,' I sob.

As I hold the phone out from me, I continue to cry – great, ugly sobs – hopelessly trying to sniff back the tears. I assume Christopher has gone, hung up on me the way I expected him to do the moment I spoke, but then he speaks.

'What is it you want?'

I try to recover myself as quickly as I can, wiping my eyes and nose on the back of my hand. I feel like I should've been more prepared for this conversation. Perhaps got some pen and paper ready to write things down, but, then, I don't know how much there is going to be to write, anyway.

'I need to know if you told anybody else about Sasha. About the abortion.'

'What do you mean?'

'You know what I mean. Sasha blames me, because Jamie and I are the only people who knew about the abortion, so I know why she thinks I'm behind it. But I'm not. You knew about it too.'

'Do you think I'm the one who told people? That I told people at her school?'

'No. No, no,' I say, though the thought hadn't crossed my mind until that point, but now he's put it there, it's hard to ignore. Christopher would want to ruin me, wouldn't he? He certainly would now, but then? He's the one who trashed his relationship with Sasha, not me.

'You didn't, did you?' I say hesitantly.

'God,' he says, and I'm sure he's about to hang up, so I shout, 'Sorry, I'm sorry. I'm sorry. I know you didn't. I know you wouldn't have told anybody deliberately. I know that. But is there anybody that you told? That you trusted to keep a secret? Another girlfriend?'

My mind races – Sasha said they reconnected because he had his heart broken over the summer.

'You had a girlfriend, didn't you? You were seeing somebody. Someone older. Did you tell them what happened with Sasha? I won't blame you, I won't. I know it's difficult. I know you need to talk to people about these things.'

'I don't know if—'

'I did,' I say, trying to make it easier for him to disclose it. 'I told my friend, too. I told my best friend. I needed to. I needed to have someone to talk to. We need to talk about these things. And I had Jamie. I can't imagine how hard it would be for you.'

Silence filters down the line, but I don't carry on talking. For the first time, I'm sure I'm getting through to him.

'I don't think she'd have said anything,' he says quietly. 'Why would she? She doesn't even know Sasha. It would make no sense for her to say something.'

'No, no, you're right. You're completely right. But just so I can talk to her, just to make sure. What was her name, Christopher? What was her name?'

I can tell he's torn. His life has already gone to shit.

'If we can find out who's doing this to me, to us, it might help your case against the police,' I tell him. 'If the article is discredited.'

There's another silence, but this one is shorter.

'Okay, I'll tell you,' he says. 'Her name is Alice. Alice Fortune.'

88

'Mrs Croft? Mrs Croft, are you still there?'

Christopher's voice is peripheral. All I can hear is my heart pounding, the swish of my pulse as the blood rushes past my ears at an ever-increasing rate. 'Mrs Croft, are—'

'Sorry, Christopher, yes. Yes. It was Alice Fortune, that's what you said? That's who you said you were dating?'

'Yes.'

'And how long was it for? I don't mean to pry, I don't. There's just a lot for me to unpack.'

'It was for a while. Six, maybe seven months, I think. Not as long as I was with Sasha, but long enough for me to believe it could be the real thing, I suppose.'

I can hear the sadness in his voice. He's obviously cut up about this relationship ending, but I really don't give a shit about Christopher right now. I'm thinking about myself. Jamie's got to take this seriously, surely. Everybody has. Alice dating the guy that my daughter had broken up with? That's not normal. She's twenty years older than him to start with. Nathan, my arse. It was all a fucking ruse to throw me off her scent. She's smart, I'll give her that.

I get ready to hang up when another thought strikes me.

'Can I send you some photos just to confirm we're talking about the same person here?'

'Sure, yeah, no problem.'

I'm about to hang up and send some photos from my phone to him when I realise there's a photo of Alice on the mantelpiece. I jump out of the car and fumble to unlock the front door.

'Hold on a second,' I say, sprinting through the house to the living room. 'I'll put us on video call. You can look at the photos that way.'

I switch the camera on my phone around to face the other way and hold it up against the photograph.

'Is this her?' I ask, pointing to the person next to me in the image. 'Is this the Alice Fortune you were dating?'

Putting Christopher on video call means I can now see his face too, and he looks terrible. His skin is grey, with dark bags beneath his eyes. I guess being arrested will do that to someone. As he squints at the camera, his nose crinkles.

'No, no, that wasn't my Alice.'

'You sure? I've got more photos of her dotted around the house. There's one of me, Sasha, Alice and Katie up by my bedroom. Hold on a second,' I say. 'Just hold on a second.'

I bolt up the stairs and show him the second photo.

'Here, there's another one here. I think you can see her face better in this one. Is that her?'

He shakes his head. 'No. I mean, she was older than me, but not that old. Like late twenties old.'

My insides are a mess, my stomach not knowing whether it should somersault or sink. So it's not my Alice Fortune, but what are the chances that Christopher was dating someone with the same name as my best friend? Someone he disclosed to about my daughter's pregnancy. These are not coincidences. They're not.

'Christopher, could you send me some photos of her? Do you have some photos of this Alice that you were dating? I just need to see.'

He bites down on his lower lip. 'I'm sorry, I don't. I only had a couple of photos on my phone, and it was stolen a week or so after we broke up.'

'Your phone was stolen?'

'Yeah, I mean, it wasn't a biggie, it wasn't too expensive, but you know, it was irritating. I lost all the photos.'

I race back down the stairs again, so fast I'm amazed I don't trip. In the kitchen, I point the camera to the phone Jamie found in my pocket.

'Is this it?' I ask. 'Is this the phone?'

'Looks like it, yeah. Where did you get it?'

I don't respond. Instead I pick it up and turn it over in my hand. 'Christopher, what was the passcode? What was the pass-code you used to get on it?'

'Zero, zero, zero, zero.'

I raise my eyebrows in disgust. 'Seriously? That has to be the worst password possible.'

But I type it in, nonetheless. It doesn't work.

'Whoever stole it must've changed the code,' I say.

I don't know how to get into it, but then a thought occurs. Whoever's behind this wanted me to believe the phone was mine, which means it might have a passcode I'm likely to use.

I try my birthday, then Sasha's birthday, then my wedding anniversary. None work. It doesn't matter though. I'll be able to find someone to get into it.

'Christopher, thank you, thank you, and I'm so sorry. If I can do anything to help, I will. I hope you know that, but I've got to go. All right, I've got to go.' I hang up and grab a hoodie from the peg by the door.

This time, I don't need to put the address into the sat nav. I know exactly where I'm going.

89

Wanting to draw as little attention to myself as possible, I park up on the main road a hundred or so metres away and walk into school. Part of me feels ridiculous. I'm wearing a baggy hoody that Jamie uses to go to the gym in the winter. The hood is pulled up as high as it will go. In my pocket is Christopher's phone.

Several students, straggling after lessons, walk past me, but pay me zero attention. There'll be a couple of staff still hanging around who have activities, but there are no meetings on a Tuesday. People try to make the most of their early evenings when they can, especially while the nights are still light. Meaning, hopefully, I can slip in unnoticed. That's the plan at least, and it works fine as I head in through a side door.

During the drive over, I toyed with the idea of going straight to the police, but the only evidence I have is the time on the sat nav, when I was drink-driving. Unless I have all the evidence I need to point the police in the right direction, then there's no point in me going. The little I do have is likely to get me in more trouble. And if I only know one thing about this person, it's that they have access to the school in some way. So I have a two-pronged attack in mind.

My first port of call is sorting out this phone. If anyone is likely to find any deleted photos on here, then I'm sure George is my best bet. So that's where I'm headed now. But as I weave my way across to the other building, a bevy of laughter reaches my ears.

'Elizabeth, Mrs Croft, we weren't expecting to see you in school. I hope everything is okay.'

Lucy, the Head of Art, is standing there with her trainee teacher, Jessica. Both these girls are young. Young enough to date Christopher. My skin prickles. Lucy is the member of staff that Alice said I'd upset. Who'd had to be helped off the school grounds because she was so upset by my words. And yet here she is, smiling straight at me. It's not exactly the reaction I would have expected. No, the way she's smiling at me is the response I would expect of someone who's playing a game and thinks they're winning. For a split second, I consider whether I can confront her here and now, but right now the only evidence I've got is that she lied to Alice. Still, with a little bit of luck and help, I leave the school this evening with enough evidence to put her behind bars and stop her doing anything like this to anyone else again.

As we stand there in silence, I realise Lucy has asked me a question and I've said nothing. I've just stood there, gawking. I clear my throat.

'Yes, yes, I just had to come in to do a few jobs. You know, no rest for the wicked and all that.'

'Well, I hope you're taking it easy on yourself,' Jessica replies. 'Is there anything we can help with?' she asks, with a glance at Lucy.

I consider the offer for a moment longer.

'It's fine, thank you. I'll be absolutely fine,' I say. 'It's just some boring admin, that's all. You girls go. Have a nice evening.'

'As long as you're sure,' she says again.

'Yes, thank you, Jessica. I'm sure I will see you all soon. Don't worry, I'm going to be back soon.'

I make a dart towards the admin building, keeping my head down, though thankfully I see no one else. A minute later, I'm standing outside the tech room.

'George,' I say the second I'm inside, 'I need a favour. And I need you to do it fast.'

90

George stares at me from behind his computer monitor. His desk is littered with hard drives and modems and other things I'd probably name wrong if I had to say them aloud.

'Mrs Croft. I wasn't expecting to see you,' he says. 'I thought... I... I, I thought you—'

'Sorry, George.'

I cut across him as he speaks. I don't mean to sound rude. Normally, when he's having one of his stuttering fits, I give him as long as he needs, but I'm on a tight schedule here. Besides, I'm not meant to be in school, and I still have to get up to the main building and face my biggest test yet. I'll be honest, this is the easy part. I just need it to happen fast.

'Are you any good with phones?' I ask.

'Phones?'

'This one,' I say. 'It's a long story, but it belonged to Sasha. Somehow I deleted a load of her old photos. I don't know how because I can't even get into the bloody thing now. I must have changed the code somehow, too. She's going to be furious. I know she is. I just wondered if there's any chance you can recover an of them. Just a few, maybe. I know it would mean the world to her.'

Am I outright lying? Yes. Do I think it is the wisest thing to do in this situation? Absolutely.

'Do you want me to see if it's linked up to any clouds?' George says, taking the phone in his hand.

'Can you do that? That would be amazing. Sasha told me you were the person I should see to get this sorted. She thought the world of you, you know?'

All lies and false flattery, but I can see it's working. George looks at the phone and takes it from me, before turning it over in his hand.

'Should be okay. I probably need to hook it up to a PC first. Clear all the caches, things like that.'

I've no idea what that means, and I don't need to.

'Whatever you need to do, George. Whatever you need to do. Do you think you can message me any of the photos when they come through? A text message rather than an email. That way, you won't waste any time waiting around for me. Have you got my number?'

'I'm sure it's on the system,' George says, rising from his desk.

'You're right, it probably is, but I'll write it down for you again anyway, just in case.'

I grab a piece of paper, not caring what is written on it, and write my number boldly at the top of the page. I'm scribbling down the last number when the door to the office opens.

'I didn't think you were in school?'

I spin around to find Carl looking at me, his normal snarl in place. It's hard to know if he's even capable of smiling; his face seems permanently fixed in a scowl.

'Just doing some admin,' I say, barely offering him the slightest glance before I turn back to George. 'As soon as you get anything, please message me, George. Or ring me if it's easier. Even if it comes through one photo at a time, that's all right, okay? I'm ever so grateful, and I know Sasha will be, too.'

With that part of my plan done, I walk out of the office and stride towards the main building, sweat slicking my hands.

I don't need a favour to pull off the next part of my plan. I need a miracle.

91

The first week I became head here, walking down the corridor that leads to my office, with its wooden floors and genuine oil paintings, caused an inexplicable flutter of nerves. I was going to sit in the headteacher's chair, have my email signature changed to say head teacher. I was going to be responsible for everything that went on inside the walls of St Anne's. And it was terrifying. Overwhelmingly so. Even with everything that was going on with Sasha, school was never far from my mind. My stomach was twisted so tightly together with knots that I could barely manage a coffee before the morning break, and I was up half the night, going over all my directions, making sure I hadn't messed anything up. Basically, it was imposter syndrome, big time.

But once I was past those initial weeks, and we'd already had our first few incidents of the year, I settled into the role. I didn't feel so much like an imposter. After all, I'd been working towards the job for the last two decades. The only time it would creep back in was during meetings with the governors. Where Florence would constantly speak over me, and veto any idea I wanted to put into place, railroading me at every turn. But, right now, as I step into the hallway and see Sandra sitting there at the desk, feel like I'm that new head again. Lost, with no idea what I'm doing.

'Elizabeth.' Sandra stands up as she says my full name in tha harsh tone of hers. 'What are you doing here? You're not meant to be on school grounds.'

I consider how to reply. I could lie, of course. Lie like I did to George, and say it's a personal reason, or go one step further. could say that everything has been cleared up, and that I'm now allowed to continue my job, but she won't buy it. She'd have expected an email thread discussing and confirming all this. If tell her I'm allowed to be here, she'll probably message Nathan to check, and then I'll have a whole more load of shit to face Besides, I've already spoken to her once today when I made her go out on a limb. Which is why I'm hoping that I have one othe option that just might work: the truth.

'Sandra, I know you don't like me, but regardless of any personal feelings, I know you are efficient at your job, and appreciate what you do, so thank you for that. But somebody i trying to frame me. Somebody shared my medical records and put images of me on the school screen. And they've done othe stuff too. I've lost Sasha.'

'Lost her?' Terror fills her face, and I realise the error in my word choice.

I shake my head quickly, trying to correct myself.

'She's gone to her uncle's, in Singapore. Moved there perma nently. She wants nothing to do with me. Somebody's doing this Sandra. And I think it's somebody in the school. I don't know who I can trust. I've accused everyone. Nathan. Alice. I even thought Jamie could be behind it, even though I know he'd neve do anything to hurt Sasha. Sandra, I know we don't get on and know that trust hasn't always been great between us. But you told me to ask for help, so that's what I'm doing now. I'm asking you, can you help me? Please.'

She looks at me with those birdy, beady eyes of hers, and I'm certain she's going to refuse. I'm certain she's going to pick up the phone and ring Nathan or Florence, or whoever else she can, to ensure I am as humiliated as possible.

Her nostrils flare slightly as she tilts her head up towards me, trying to make the most of her five foot two inches.

'You're right,' she says. 'We haven't always seen eye-to-eye. But I don't like people who sneak about doing things. You've got a problem with someone, you say it to their face, like you did to me. I respected you more for that, you know. Whoever is doing this to you is a coward. You need my help, you've got it. But I'm only paid till five-thirty; after that I'm clocking off.'

It's already approaching five, which means I need to move fast. I'm about to say as much when, for the first time, I see the tiniest hint of a smile twist at the corner of her lips.

'That was a joke, Liz,' she says. 'Come on. Let's get to the bottom of this.'

92

'I just want facts,' I say to her. 'I want to know who in the school has links to the medical profession.'

'The medical profession?' she asks.

'Yes, doctors, nurses, someone that could access my medical records. Recently too. That printout they put in all the exam papers went up to mid-summer, so they had to have accessed my records then.'

Sandra lets out a low whistle. It fills the quiet, but takes far longer than I would like.

'Well, there is Nathan's ex-wife. I assume you know that?'

'Lord,' I say, still finding it tough to shift my mindset after being so convinced for so long, but my reasons for suspecting Nathan just don't add up anymore. 'It's not him. What about anybody else? Lucy?'

'Lucy, the Head of Art?'

'Yes, her. Does she have a spouse who works in medicine perhaps? Or did she?'

Sandra pouts. 'Not that I know of. No, her wife's a teacher too I think. Yes, that's right. She definitely is. They met at art college on their second day, took all the same classes and even went to the same training college to become teachers, but now she's thinking of moving into primary. The wife, that is. Not Lucy.'

I have no idea how Sandra obtains so much information about people when she rarely leaves her desk, but, as impressive as it is, it's only useful if she can actually help me find the culprit. And, right now, I'm still not ruling Lucy out. I'm not ruling anyone out.

'Okay, so who does have ties to medicine?' I say again.

'Jo on reception trained as a midwife before she started working here.'

'She did?'

Now that Sandra's said it, I could see Jo in a position like that. Her constant smile would be just the reassurance someone in labour needed. Never in a million years would I have picked her as being someone behind something like this, but I'm learning that my instincts aren't something I can rely on. Perhaps never suspecting her should be a reason to make her a suspect.

'Could she still have access?' I ask.

'I doubt it. I don't think she ever did. I think she did six months and decided it wasn't for her. Not as happy a job as people always think it is. There's a lot of stress that midwives are under.'

I'm sure there is, but I really don't want to hear about it. I've got far more pressing things on my mind.

'Other people, then? There must be others. Students, staff. Anyone at all. Fathers who are GPs, mothers who are surgeons, psychiatry, perhaps? Yes, maybe somebody who has links to psychiatry, that would make sense. If anybody is going to manipulate someone and make them seem mad, someone with a background in psychiatry seems like an obvious choice.'

'Let's have a look at the parent database. Maybe we'll find something there.'

Could it really be a parent? A couple of them got upset with how I handled certain situations, like one student who didn't get the best exam results. But they just needed a place to vent their frustration. I can't possibly believe they would do something like that.

'Here, look,' Sandra says.

I scan down the names of children who have parents linked to the medical profession, including four nurses, two doctors and two pharmacists.

'I barely know these children. I've certainly not done anything that would warrant their parents doing this to me,' I say.

I want to cry. Not a very mature response for somebody in my position, but that's what I want to do.

Clearly Sandra can tell.

'I can keep looking,' she says. 'Maybe go through old CVs, things like that. I'm happy to stay and do it on my own for a bit if that helps. If you've got something else to do that would be more useful.'

I draw a deep breath in and force myself to smile. In terms of more useful things to do, I'm at a loss. I had two routes to go down, and this one has definitely failed. I just hope George has had more luck.

'Thank you, thank you, Sandra,' I say, and I mean it. 'You don't have to stay.'

'No, I know. But you never know what I might find with a bit more digging.'

93

My body feels heavy as I walk back down towards the tech office. I was certain that Sandra would come up with something – if anyone could see the links, it would be her. The fact that she hasn't has got me lost. I'm not barking up the wrong tree; I'm not going insane, but, if I can't find out who's doing this, then I might as well be.

If I can just get a photo. Something I can give to the police, to prove to them that the phone wasn't mine, that somebody planted it... that's got to be something, hasn't it? That's got to help.

I type in the code, then push open the door. For once, Carl is out from behind his desk, moving some large computer monitors to the side.

'Where's George?' I say, as I look around.

Carl looks at me and grunts. I'm positive he heard my question. There's no way he couldn't have done, but I repeat it, nonetheless.

'Carl, do you know where George has gone? He was doing a job for me.'

'I heard you when you came in,' he replies.

I can feel my back molars grinding together. By reflex, my mouth closes up into a smile, the way it always does in situations like this, but I drop it. I've no need for smiles right now.

'Carl, this is important. If you heard me speaking to George earlier, then you know that. Do you know where he went, when he's going to be back?'

Carl yawns as if I'm the most uninteresting person in the world, and carries on moving the computer monitors around.

'Said it was an emergency. Said he had to run.'

'Shit,' I say.

Given how important I told him this task was, the least he could've done was send me a text to say he had to go.

'Okay,' I say, talking to myself more than to Carl. 'It's okay. I'll just have to take the phone and find somewhere else to sort it out. There's a place in town; I'll try there.'

'Think he did it,' Carl grunts. The words are so guttural, I can hardly make out what he said, and I assume he wasn't actually speaking to me, but I respond out of politeness.

'Pardon?'

'Thought he did it. Thought he got what you were looking for. Pretty fast too. At least, that's what he said when he rang his girlfriend.'

Now my pulse is so fast, it's a miracle I haven't burst something. If George found the missing info on the phone, why would he have rung his girlfriend when I asked him to ring me? And why the hell would he have told her what I'd asked him to do?

I move across to George's desk, looking for my phone, but there's no sign of it.

I don't want to disrupt everything as I'm sure it all has its place, even if it looks a mess to me. I know how furious I'd be i someone shuffled things about on my desk, but the phone is my one piece of evidence. I lift a couple of notepads, a laptop that weighs four times as much as mine does and, still, there's no sign of the phone. Did he take it with him? Was he planning on sorting it out for me at home? It seems like the most logical option, and I'm about to ask Carl for his number so I can ring and check when I notice something else on George's desk. It's a photo.

'Carl,' I say, picking up the unframed Polaroid image from where it was Blu-Tacked beneath the monitor. 'Is this George's girlfriend?'

Carl glances over his shoulder. It's such a swift look, I doubt he actually sees the photo. He shrugs.

'Guess so,' he says.

I don't want to judge books by their covers, but this woman is attractive on a level that George is not. But that's not the first thing that attracts my attention. The first thing is the fact that I know her.

I feel a rush of adrenaline bursting through me as I pick up my phone and snap a photo of the couple and click send. I've no evidence for what I've just done, other than my gut instinct, and, rightly or wrongly, I'm going to follow it.

A second later, I type a message beneath the photo.

> Is this her? Is this your Alice Fortune?

I'm praying Christopher has his phone on him so he can see my message, but I've no patience and I'm about to ring him, when I notice the label underneath the message flick from unread to read. At the top of my screen, it tells me Christopher is writing a response.

My heart is all the way up in my mouth as I wait.

Yes, yes, that's her

You're sure? That's Alice Fortune?

Yes, that's her

94

My hand drops to my side, but the phone stays firmly between my fingers.

Alice Fortune is the trainee teacher, Jessica Smith.

'Carl, do you know anything about her?' I say, taking the photo over to him. 'Have you seen her much? She works in the school, right?'

'Dunno,' he says, shrugging.

'So, George didn't meet her at the school?'

'What is this, twenty bloody questions?'

'Carl, for fuck's sake. Can you just be a little less of a twat and help me with this? Do you know when George started dating her?'

His eyes harden, but it's clear he can tell he's dealing with someone at breaking point. 'He met her at some computer thing, I think. Or online maybe. It was on Discord I think. Yeah, that's it. I remember him saying. During the summer, you know when you teachers are having your holiday and we are still here.'

I don't have time to bother with the dig. All I know is the dates add up. She split up with Christopher once she got the information she needed from him, then moved on to George. But why? It's the why I just don't have yet.

I'm out the door and heading to my office when my phone buzzes in my hand. Sandra's name is on the screen.

'You've found something?' I say, assuming she wouldn't have rung me otherwise.

'Maybe. It might be nothing, but one of the trainees was working as a receptionist at a doctors' surgery before they started their placement here.'

'Let me guess,' I finish for her. 'Jessica Smith?'

I hear the hitch of her breath down the phone.

'How did you know? Are you all right?' Sandra says. 'Do you need me for anything?'

'Do you have an address for her? A home one?'

She pauses and I know I'm making her cross a line she doesn't want to cross.

'Please Sandra. I'm scared about what she's going to do next.'

Her silence lasts a moment longer before she speaks.

'I'll message it through to you now.'

'Thank you, Sandra.'

A second later, I've hung up.

I don't care if anyone sees me as I run down the school driveway and towards my car. The photograph is still in my hand. I'm not sure how I'm going to use it now. All I know is that I need every bit of evidence I can find. A link between Jessica Smith and Jeremy Petty would be useful too, and I'm sure I'm going to find it when I get home and start digging.

By the time I reach the car, Sandra has sent the address through yet, before I can open it, Jamie's name flashes brightly on the screen. I want to speak to him, tell him what I've found, but there are things I still need to know. Most of all, why Jessica's doing this. That's when I'll speak to him. I hang up, only for him to ring again immediately afterwards. There's a good chance he'll keep trying if I don't pick up.

'This isn't a good time, Jamie,' I say as I answer. 'I've worked it out. I don't know why, but I've worked out who is doing this to me.'

There's a pause. It grows and swells and stretches past the point of comfort.

'Good afternoon, Mrs Croft,' she says, the female voice a million miles away from Jamie's. 'I think you should probably come home now, don't you? Oh, and don't even think about ringing the police. You already know I have eyes and ears everywhere.'

95

'Where is Jamie?' Nausea sweeps through me as I hold the phone to my ear while I rest my other hand on the car, trying to keep myself upright. 'What have you done with Jamie, Jessica? Where is he?'

'James is here. I've just made him comfortable. Very comfortable, actually. I said I was coming to check on you and he was ever so grateful. Very worried about you. As was I, of course. He made me a drink – quite a stiff one – and obviously, I insisted he have one with me too. Then I slipped a couple of Valium in his. I'm sure it'll be all right, won't it? He's not allergic to anything?'

I can't get in a breath. Everything's just hollow gasps.

'What do you want?'

'Want?' My question is met with a silence that feels ponderous. As if she's the one confused by this situation. 'I thought that would be obvious,' she says eventually. 'I want to ruin you.'

I brush the tears from my face as fast as I can, trying to focus on what she's saying and not on the fact that this crazy woman has my husband.

'I don't understand. What have I done to you?'

'What have you done to me?' She laughs, bitterly. 'You took my entire life. You ruined everything for me.'

'What do you mean? How? What did I do to you?'

'I gave you the clues, too. I thought you'd get it straight away: the picture, the abortion on your medical records. But you didn't. Still, it was a nice touch that your daughter went away. Because that's what I really wanted. To ruin your family, the way you ruined mine.'

I open the car door and climb inside, but I can't get the key in the ignition. My hand won't stop shaking.

'Please, talk to me,' I say. 'Maybe we can put this right. Whatever I did, whatever you think I did, I'm sorry. I'm sure we can put it right.'

Her laugh is bitter and cold; it turns my arms into goosebumps. She's insane, completely crazy, and she's got my husband. I need to ring the police. I need to get him an ambulance, yet, as I pause, it's like she can hear my thoughts.

'Now, I don't want you to get any ideas about calling the police,' she says. 'Otherwise, I might give him something a little stronger and who knows how that might end?'

I grip the steering wheel so hard, my knuckles are white.

'What do you want from me?'

It's me she's after. Maybe if I can keep her focused on that, Jamie will be okay.

'You're going to come straight home,' she says. 'And when you're here, you're going to grovel for your life. And then I'll decide if I'm going to kill you slowly, or fast.' She laughs again, but this time, she sounds far younger, far more jovial. 'Now, don't hang up. I'm going to put you next to Jamie. You can talk to him if you want. You know, they say people can hear you talking when they're in a coma. I guess you'll be able to find out if that's true.

And I'm going to open a bottle of wine. You do have a lovely selection.'

'You're insane,' I say, not able to stop the words from leaving my mouth. The moment they do, fear floods through me.

'You're right,' she replies. 'And you're the one who made me that way. Now it's time you reaped what you sowed.'

96

I turn into the driveway; my phone has been on a call to Jamie the entire time. I tried to think of ways I could hang up without Jessica noticing, but every time I went more than a couple of minutes without speaking, I would hear her voice chime through.

'You need to speak up, Elizabeth. If I can't hear you, I'll think you've done something silly like driven to the police station. But you wouldn't do something like that, now, would you?'

'How do I even know you've got Jamie?' I said to her at one point. 'Send me a photo. You'll only need to hang up for a moment to send me a photo of him.'

Her chuckle was malicious and icy.

'Look at you. Thinking of clever ways to try to make me hang up the phone so you can call the police. But I'm sorry. You're right. You need to see that he's here.'

She flicked it onto a video call, which I accepted immediately.

There, slumped on the sofa, was Jamie. There was a large tumbler next to him, with coloured liquid – whisky, I'd guess – in a thin layer at the bottom. Not that he normally drinks at this time of day.

'Just setting the scene, you know,' Jessica said. She had the camera facing him, so that I couldn't see her face, but it was clear she was studying me.

'There now, aren't you happy I'm not lying? We can carry on as you were. You've been driving for quite a while now; you should really be home in the next couple of minutes. Accidents happen ever so quickly.'

She turned the camera round to where she'd set three candles up on the window ledge, despite still being light outside. The outside two were perilously close to the curtains.

Is that her plan? Is she planning to burn my house down with my husband and me unable to get out? I wouldn't put it past her, but I just don't understand why. What could I have done to make her act this way? She thinks I made her crazy. How is that possible? How?

As I park up, her voice chimes through again.

'No hanging up here either,' she says. 'Plenty of time to make a telephone call between the car and the drive. So I need you to leave your phone in the car, and step out with your hands above your head where I can see them. Do you understand?'

'Yes, I understand,' I say, glancing down at my phone, still trying to see a way out of this. All I need is to make one call, have one person hear me.

'And don't think about screaming for help either,' she says. 'It looks like Jamie's spilt an awful lot of his whisky, near the candles and on the curtains. If I were to knock one over, I hate to think how quickly that would go up. Certainly faster than you can get into the house with the front door bolted.'

97

Despite Jessica's previous comment, the door isn't bolted and my key lets me in with no issues, though I can smell the candles burning and the undertone of whisky the moment I step into the house. For a second, I go to take off my shoes, the way I normally would, but the voice inside my head tells me to keep them on. I might have to run.

'We're in here,' Jessica says, her voice chiming through from the sitting room.

As I step inside, she meets me in the hallway.

'You don't mind if I pat you down too, do you? Check for a phone?' she says, before proceeding to do so. She's dressed exactly the same as she was when I saw her at school. Barely two hours ago. Only she looks different. More manic. 'Excellent,' she says, then taps me on the arse like I'm some prize cow at auction.

I rush in to see Jamie there, still slumped in the same position. I drop down by his knees.

'What am I supposed to have done to you?' I yell. 'Jamie is not at fault. Let him go, please.'

His head is tilted to the side so I can see his chest rising and falling. At least that's something.

'Oh, he's free to go whenever he wants,' Jessica says, before letting out a loud laugh. 'You know, I thought the fact I was working in your school using my real name might be enough. I really did. When you came to my lesson and made it clear you knew my name, I thought that maybe this could all end differently. It could have been so different if you just acknowledged what you'd done to me.'

'How can I acknowledge it when I have no idea what you're talking about?' I say, my expression hardening as I suck inwards with a hiss.

'You don't want to get cross now, Elizabeth.' She points her finger directly at me as she snaps. 'Accidents happen when you get cross. And the way you and Jamie have been fighting lately, yelling in public even, who knows where people would place the blame?'

I glance down at her nails. They're painted a light shade of purple.

'You put the phone in my pocket,' I say, remembering the way the drunk had banged into me when I opened my car door. Only they hadn't been drunk at all.

'Oh my God, do you know that was the part I was worried about?' Jessica says with glee. 'I was worried I might screw that up. But it was so easy. You were so focused on Alice and Jamie, you didn't even notice. That's one of the bits I've been most proud of in this whole thing.'

'And Jeremy Petty. How did you get him to lie?'

'You make me sound so cruel. I was incredibly generous to Jeremy. Do you know how much debt people leave university with nowadays? Poor Jeremy was never going to pay that off. I wanted to help him.'

'So you bribed him.'

She grimaces. 'That's such an ugly word. I think of myself as philanthropic.'

'And Christopher? George?'

Her smile widens.

'How did you do it? How did you get George to do those things? To copy my medical records. To put my photo on the screen?'

'George?' At this, she looks surprised. 'Oh, George knew the truth. He knows what you did. And, once he knew, it wasn't difficult to get him on board. Not with his past.'

'George's past? What do you mean?'

I know George hasn't had an easy time, with his father taking his own life when he was at university, but I can't think how that would link to the situation I'm in right now. Still, I need to find a way out, and the only way I figure I can do that is by drawing this out long enough that Jamie wakes up. If there's two of us here, we could overpower her. But how long do those drugs take to wear off? How many has she given him? All of these are questions I cannot answer.

All I know is, I've got to keep her talking as long as I can.

'So Christopher, he was part of your plan too? You got to him?'

'I did. The statutory rape I already knew about. Let's be honest with each other, Elizabeth. This has been a long, long time coming. I've had eyes on your little family for years, and I couldn't believe my luck when your perfect little daughter started sneaking around with an older man. I think I knew before you did, and I knew that was something that was going to have to go in my arsenal. Something I'd come back and use later on, but when he told me about the abortion...' She claps her hands in front of her, something between a prayer and an exclamation of delight. 'That just shows the beautiful synchronicities in life, doesn't it? It's like the whole universe is conspiring to make all of my wishes come true. And to give you what you deserve.'

I know I need to keep on talking. I know I need to do things that don't upset her, but it's damn hard.

'Why? Why do I deserve this, Jessica? Can you please tell me that?'

She turns and passes the living room, stopping at the candles to blow them slightly. Not enough to extinguish them, just to make the flames flicker.

I want to reach for Jamie, grab hold of him. But then what?

Before I can move, Jessica spins around and looks at me.

'Well, perhaps we should start at the beginning. The beginning for you, at least. The photo, this photo.' She holds her hand out. Between her fingers is a copy of the photograph that was shown to the sixth-form assembly. 'Do you remember that night, Elizabeth? Because that's the night you did it. That's the night you ruined my life.'

My hands are shaking as I take the photo from her. It feels like this is it. Whether I live or die depends on what I can recall about that night, but it was twenty-odd years ago.

'Do you want me to jog your memory a little?' Jessica says with that same singsong voice that makes bile rise in the back of my throat. 'You were a trainee teacher, much the same as I am now. No, actually, that's not true, is it? I'm very good at my job. Very conscientious. I don't think you were the same, were you? No, by the look of this, you liked to spend your nights out partying, didn't you? Seducing men?'

'This is to do with a man?' I say, trying to make sense of the pieces she's given me. 'You're angry because I did something with a man?'

'Something,' she says. 'You got pregnant and had an abortion. You aborted his child. My father's child.'

'Your father? This is about your father.'

As I stare at her, the memories of that night flood back to me. That was the night Alice and I didn't share rooms. The night I started an affair with a married art teacher.

'David Smith,' I say, his name bursting from my lips the moment I remember it. 'You're David Smith's daughter.'

'Bingo.'

98

I know who she is now or, at least, I know how I'm very vaguely linked to her. It sure as hell doesn't explain why she's hell bent on destroying me.

'You're David Smith's daughter?' I repeat.

'No one calls him David,' she snaps. 'That just shows you didn't even know him.'

'I didn't. I didn't know him. It was a one-night thing.'

'That's not true; don't lie to me,' she yells.

I flinch; her breath is enough to shake the flames on the candle dangerously close to the curtains. One mishap is all it would take for this place to go up in flames.

'I'm sorry. Dave, you're right. Dave, he... he was a nice man. An artist. A fabulous artist.'

'He was. He was the best man in the world, and then you ruined it.'

'I'm sorry, I'm sorry. I didn't know he was married.'

'You are such a lying bitch,' she hisses. 'It went on for weeks and weeks. You can't be seeing someone for weeks and not know that they're married, not know that they have a fifteen-year-old daughter at home. He even had that fucking photograph of you.'

My chest is burning. Tears welling up through me. So that was why the photo was different from Alice's: because it was never hers in the first place. Dave was the one who took it. As I continue to swallow back the tears, I get it. I get why she hates me.

'I am so sorry. I am so sorry if what I did broke up your family.'

'Broke up my family? You really don't know the half of it, do you?'

Tears run down my cheeks. This is all because of some fling I had over fifteen years ago. All this pain because of a silly couple of nights. It doesn't make sense.

'Tell me,' I say, my voice little more than a crackle. 'Tell me what happened to your dad. To you.'

She laughs again, but I hear the tears choke her.

'Like you actually care.'

'I do, I do. Believe me, I really do. I want to know.'

She huffs and I have no idea what she's going to do. I want her to sit down. The way she's pacing makes me nervous. I'm about to ask her if she wants to take a seat when she starts talking.

'Okay, well, after your little fling, my dad decided he needed a chance to live his life. He'd been with my mum since she was sixteen, and she got pregnant. Unlike you, they decided to keep the baby. They didn't just throw me away like some piece of trash.'

'Jessica, I'm sorry, I'm sorry for this...'

'He left us.'

'I understand. He left you and you're angry. I understand. I would be angry too.'

I want to be getting through to her. I feel like I should be. Instead, she looks at me and sneers.

'Wouldn't that be nice if that was all? Wouldn't it be convenient if that's all that's on your conscience? But I'm afraid it got a little worse than that. You see, you remember me saying that George was happy to help me? That George understood? That's because the same thing happened to his parent. She killed herself.' Jessica's voice drops. 'After my father left her, my mother killed herself. That's what happened.'

'Jessica, I am so, so sorry,' I say. There is no lying now. There is no attempting to appease her. All of this is genuine. It feels as though my heart has been ripped to shreds for this poor girl. To go through something like that, I can't imagine.

'Are you?' Her voice is even more sceptical. 'Are you really sorry?'

'Of course I am. You should never have had to go through that. No one should ever have to go through that.'

'He was nothing to you. You didn't even remember his name, but he was everything to her. Everything. For three years, she deteriorated. Drink first, other things later. Do you know I was a good student? I tried to be a good student, but it's pretty hard when you don't know what you're going to be coming home to each night. Whether you're going to be on your own, whether your mum can even remember your name or whether she just sits there constantly...'

She stops. Whatever she was going to say, I don't want to know. I don't want her to carry on, but she does.

'Then, when I was eighteen, she decided she'd had enough. She ended it. She hung herself. I was the one to find her. But, you see, I already knew who you were. I knew who you were and what you'd done to my family. And I made it my mission to do the same to you. To take away everything that ever meant anything to you. Now I've done it. Your daughter despises you, your husband thinks you're crazy, you've pushed away your best friend, you'll never work in education again and, oh yes... I'm going to take your home from you now.'

99

Some strange part in the back of my brain wants to laugh at the situation. This is what's going to ruin me. An affair with a teacher all those years ago – it would be amusing if it wasn't so catastrophic.

'Jessica, I need you to think about what you're doing here.' I use my calmest voice, the one I've practised on the most troubled of students. 'You could have a good life now. You're a good teacher. I've seen that. Outstanding. You can finish your training and have a whole life ahead of you. I'll move to Singapore to be with Sasha. You'll never see me. I promise. I'll be gone.'

She shakes her head like I'm the one who's gone insane.

'No, don't you get it? It's got to be everything. You have to lose everything.'

'Right, you're right. And I have. I have. You're right, Sasha won't even answer my calls. It's true, you can look at my phone. You can see she hasn't replied to any of my messages. She wants nothing to do with me. You've done it, I promise you. You've broken this family up for good.'

Her head bobs up and down a little. She likes hearing how

much she's ruined things for me. So maybe if I can just focus on that, I'll find a way out.

'I think Jamie just came back here to get some of his clothes,' I say, only realising as I speak that it might be the truth. 'He wants to leave me, you know. He said that this morning. It's not working anymore. He doesn't like this person I've become. He doesn't like what he thinks I did to Sasha with Christopher. He wants nothing to do with me. Nothing to do with me ever again. I won't see him again. You let him go and I won't see him again, I promise. And the job, I'll write my resignation here, I'll write my resignation with you watching.'

'And then what will you do?' she asks. It's the simplest of questions, but this is the answer that matters.

'I don't know, I... I don't know at all. I've got no friends, nothing. No Sasha. No job. I don't know what I'll do.'

I feel the tears streaming down my cheeks because it's true. I don't know what I'll do. Somehow, I need to get to the police, but I can only do that if we're all alive.

'What about Alice?' she says. 'She came and saw you after lunch.'

She looks satisfied at seeing the surprise cross my face.

'I saw her leave school this morning,' she explains. 'I think the only place she could have been going was to you. Did she want to make things right? Repair your friendship?'

'No. She hates me. Really hates me. She won't forgive me; she can't forgive me. Please, I'm on my own. I'm all alone. Just take Jamie away from here. Let me take Jamie away from here. Please, I'll go now. Just let him be.'

'You know, you remind me of her a little bit,' she says slowly.

'Her?'

'My mother. The way she begged and pleaded with my father

to stay. It's similar. He held her life in his hands, too. Not quite so directly, but this feels rather like poetic justice.'

'Jessica please,' I say. 'Please, I—'

'No. No more.' She lifts her hands to me like a stop signal. 'I'm tired of talking.'

Before I realise what's happening, she's strode towards the windowsill. In one large sweep, she knocks the candles to the side.

It's instant. The flames engulf the fabric, rising towards the ceiling, catching along the top of the curtains. It's a perfectly framed border of flames, but it doesn't stay there for long. She wasn't lying about spreading the whisky; a trail catches light down the side of the wall, leading straight towards the sofa. Straight towards Jamie.

'Please don't forget, you're the one that made this necessary,' she says as she walks past me. I go to stop her, not sure what I'm hoping to do, but it makes no difference. She grabs something from her back pocket and thrusts it through the air into me. 'You only have yourself to blame,' she says.

100

I've been stabbed. For a second, I can't believe it. Not until I press my hand against my side and it comes back dripping and red.

'Fuck! Fuck!'

The front door slams shut. Jessica is gone.

Smoke is filling the room. I can't believe how quickly. It's so dense, it's stinging my eyes, making it impossible to see. I used to do all these fire safety talks with the children about what you should do in a situation like this. Get out of the house. That was the obvious one, but what else did they have to do? Stay low, that was it. I need to stay low. I go to crouch down, but the pain sears up through my side like I've been stabbed all over again.

'Jamie! Jamie, wake up! You need to wake up.'

Staying low doesn't seem to make that much difference. My lungs are still filling with smoke. My eyes streaming. I need to move fast, but I can feel the blood pooling on my top.

With my arms reached out, I grab hold of Jamie's ankles. I can't lift him; there's no way, but I could drag him.

It takes three yanks to get him off the sofa and onto the floor. His head cracks backward on the carpet. It doesn't sound good, but I can't think about that now. Instead, I use all my weight to drag him out with me. The flames have spread now, around the doorframe, the frame that we have to go through.

And I'm trying. I'm trying my hardest, but, with each yank, I pull him less and less far. I don't think the knife went in deep, but I can see the blood dripping down the side of my leg, and the weakness spreading through me. There's no way I can do this. There's no way I can get him out of the house. I don't know what to do.

In that moment, I see my future flash in front of me. The choice I'm left with. This was the real choice Jessica left me. I've got enough energy in me to run, enough strength to get me out of the house. And then what? Do I leave my husband in here to burn? Do I leave Sasha's father to die? How can I do that? But the only other choice is I stay here and die with him.

There's so much pain in my body, from my lungs, which are burning from the smoke, to my side, which is throbbing, to my arms from trying my hardest to get Jamie out, but it's my heart that hurts the most. Thinking of Sasha hearing the news. It's almost enough to make me turn around and run out the door on my own.

They're going to blame me, I realise as the flames engulf the ceiling. It'll all be blamed on me. And there's nothing I can do. I try one last tug at Jamie's arms, but he doesn't move at all this time, which means there's nothing I can do.

My knees go weak, and I'm about to drop to the floor when I hear her voice call out to me.

'Liz! Liz, are you in there? It's me! It's Alice!'

101

I duck my head down and run out into the corridor. 'Alice! Alice!'

'Get out!' she shouts. 'Get out of there!'

'Jamie. Jamie's inside.' I'm coughing out my words. 'He came back for me. It was Jessica. It was Jessica. Jamie is in there; we need to get him. He can't move. She drugged him.'

'I'll get him.'

'You can't, you can't,' I scream, but she pushes past me, anyway. 'Alice, Alice, no, please, no!'

The smoke is billowing out of the door now. I don't know how far in she is, but she won't be able to see him. The only way she's going to get to him is if I guide her. I take a deep breath of air, cover my mouth with my top, and run back into the smoke.

'Alice,' I call her name once before I start choking. 'The living room, the living room.'

'I've got him,' I hear her say, coughing and choking, too.

Squeezing my eyes closed, I pray I know my way around my house well enough. I go to touch the wall corner, only for my hand to recoil from the heat. As I step closer, I hit something softer. Alice is back.

'I've got him. I've got his arms,' she says. 'But I need you to help me. I need you to help me with directions.'

I don't know where I get the strength from. A moment ago, I'd lost it all, but I use every bit I can muster. It doesn't matter if this is the end of me, I realise. I just need them to be okay. I just need them to get out of here.

'We're nearly there, we're nearly there,' Alice says and I can hear sirens in the distance, getting closer and closer.

Please let them be coming for us, I think. Please let them be here. Let them save Jamie, let them save Alice. Please let the sirens be for us.

My back heel slips outside the front door and a blast of cold air stings my cheeks. A second later, I collapse onto the driveway.

* * *

When I come to, I'm in the back of the ambulance. Every inch of my skin feels as if it is on fire, and my lungs feel as though I've swallowed burning embers.

'Jamie! Alice!' I twist around, ignoring the searing pains that shoot all the way through my body. Jamie is there on the gurney next to me, not moving.

I try to climb off my bed, only to be halted by the firm hand of a paramedic.

'You need to stay where you are,' he says, but I shake him off.

'Is he okay? Is he okay?'

He ignores me, but there is another paramedic working on Jamie, whose eyes meet mine, full of sympathy.

'We're not sure at the minute,' she says. 'He's breathing, but he's not waking up. He inhaled a lot of smoke.'

'He was drugged,' I say. 'She drugged him, the woman Jessica. She drugged him. She said it was Valium.'

The paramedics exchange a look and offer a nod.

'Okay, let's get him to the hospital. Sirens on.'

'Wait, what about Alice?' I say, stopping them. 'Where's Alice? Where's Alice? I can't go until we've got Alice. Where the hell is she?'

I scramble towards the door and the paramedic tries to stop me, but I push her away. I'm not sure how I push her off, but it's badly thought out. A second after she moves to the side, I tumble forward and onto the ground, the scrapes on my knees adding to the thousands of other places on my body that already hurt.

'Liz?' Her face is black from the smoke and there's an oxygen mask over her face, but she's alive. 'Liz.'

She takes the mask off her mouth and she hugs me. I wince from the stab wound. I don't even know if I told the paramedics about that. Perhaps they saw it anyway.

'I'm sorry, I'm sorry I didn't believe you,' she says.

'It's okay, it's okay. We're all okay, right?' I say, wiping the tears as they streak down her cheeks, and ignoring the ones that fall down mine. 'We're all okay?'

She nods. The siren on the second ambulance blares out.

'Get in,' the paramedic says, and this time I do as she says.

EPILOGUE

George is the one who found Jessica for us. I gave my statement after the hospital, after which I had no hope that they would find her. It had been hours, and I assumed she'd be lost in the wind. And she was, in a manner of speaking. On her way up to Scotland. There's no chance the police would have caught her on their own. Only George had placed a tracking app on her phone.

It's creepy as far as a boyfriend goes, but I'm not surprised. Instead, I was incredibly grateful. He gave her up to the police in order to lessen his sentence time. Jeremy Petty was quick to throw Jessica under the bus, too. All it took was for the police to locate several unusual bank payments to him to corroborate my story. He wanted a big story to get the scoop on. I guess he's got it now.

The board of governors sent me a long email, explaining how horrific it was that I had suffered so, at the hands of a crazed woman. The email said lots of things, about my tenacity, my trustworthiness, my devotion to the school, but it didn't say sorry for how badly they had treated me. I suppose I shouldn't have been surprised. And it didn't matter. I couldn't go back to St

Anne's. Not if they tripled my wages and doubled my holidays. There was only ever one place I wanted to be. With my daughter.

It was Alice who rang Sasha from the hospital, updating her on everything that had happened. I could've done it myself; I was there, listening in on the conversation, but I wasn't ready to speak to her. I wasn't ready to hear that she might still hate me anyway.

What actually happened was that Sasha wanted to get on the next flight home, but we didn't let her. She'd had the right idea from the beginning; we needed to get as far away from our old lives as possible.

Unfortunately, mine and Jamie's move required slightly more planning than just booking a ticket, getting on a plane and saying goodbye to our old lives. There were things to deal with: insurance companies, the police, court dates. We needed to lay everything with Jessica to rest.

And, now, it's done. That chapter of my life is closed. At least in terms of the police and the paperwork.

In reality, it's far harder to feel like I'll ever truly escape the fear and paranoia I felt during those weeks. Even as I sit on this plane, flying across the ocean, it's hard to believe that I don't have to keep looking over my shoulder.

'Do you think she'll come to meet us?' I say to Jamie. A plastic tray full of food sits in front of me. It's the third meal I've been offered this flight, but, even if I was hungry, I don't think I'd manage to eat, given how intensely the nerves are bubbling away inside me.

'She said she was coming last night, didn't she?' Jamie replies. 'When you spoke to her.'

'Yes, but she might have changed her mind.'

In the three months since the fire, I've spoken to Sasha almost daily, and some weeks, it was like the old days. The days before Christopher. We laughed and chatted and she told me how school and the orchestra were going as easy as anything, but, at other times, there was an unspoken tension filling the silences.

I didn't make the accusations against Christopher, but that didn't stop them from being true. Just like it doesn't stop me being glad that there's no chance of him getting out for at least four years.

In one conversation we had a couple of weeks ago, Sasha actually sounded pleased about this. It was like she finally understood the gravity of his actions, but then, two days later, she was defending him to the hilt, begging me to do all I could to help him.

For the last hour of the flight, my nerves are shot and, by the time we step off the aeroplane, my hands are slick with sweat.

'I wish we'd booked a hotel,' I say as we collect our luggage. 'She might feel like we're trying to be on top of her otherwise.'

'Don't be so silly; she wants us there. She said the same to both of us. It's going to be okay, I promise you.'

Mine and Jamie's relationship has had its own healing to do. The guilt he feels for not believing me is probably even more intense than the guilt I feel for all I put him through. Just like Sasha and me, we are taking it one step at a time and right now we are feeling good about things. We wouldn't have made this move together if we weren't.

When our final bag is sitting on the trolley, Jamie takes my hand and squeezes it tightly.

'Look, we'll go back to Tony's place, and if, for some reason or another, Sasha is stressed or upset by our presence, we can book a hotel room when we get there. But I don't think you need to worry. It's going to be just fine. Wait and see.'

I glance down at my phone and the last message I received from Sasha.

Safe flight. Can't wait to see you. Love you.
Xxxxx

I'm sure Jamie's right, but, when I get to the final set of automatic doors that lead into the departure hall, I still stop.

'Just give me a minute,' I say.

When they open, I'm going to see one of two things: either Sasha, standing there waiting for me, or Tony on his own. I know which thought terrifies me the most, but it's still the one I want.

Jamie takes my hand, and I'm about to say I need another minute when a passenger strides in front of us, and the doors open. Instinctively my eyes snap forward. There directly in front of me is my baby girl. Only, she doesn't look like a baby anymore.

Her skin has darkened from the sun and she's cut her hair shorter than ever before. I knew this of course. She's sent me photos and we've spoken on video calls, but she looks so much more grown up in person.

With my legs trembling, I take a step forward and then another and before I realise what's happening, I'm running. Sprinting towards my little girl.

Before I've even reached the barrier, she's climbed over it and is racing towards me. The moment we meet, I wrap my arms around her, unable to stifle the sobs that are set free from my lungs. This.

'Mum...' She's crying too. Trying to wipe her eyes without letting go of me.

'I'm here. I'm here,' I say, wishing I could pull her in even closer. 'I'm here and I'm never leaving you again.'

ACKNOWLEDGEMENTS

Thank you so much for reading *The Head Teacher*. I really appreciate that out of all the books out there, this is one you chose to pick up and read. It is never lost on me how lucky I am to be in this career and that is only possible because of you. So as always, my greatest debt of gratitude goes to you, my readers. Thank you.

If you are someone who has read my works previously, then I want to thank you so much for taking a chance on this book. I know it's a departure from my normal feel-good reads or my Greek mythology retellings and I am very grateful that you came along with me on this newest part of my journey.

I also need to offer a very heartfelt thanks to my editor Emily Yau and Boldwood Books for taking a chance on me and believing that I could write in this new genre. I hope I haven't let you down!

Lastly, I have to mention my husband, Jake. My decision to write this book, alongside my normal genres means that I have spent even more time pinned to my desk than normal. (And that's saying something!) It would not have been possible without the unwavering support that you have offered behind the scenes. You are always there to bounce ideas off, to help me hone my plots and to pick me up on my down days. It might be my name on the cover but this publishing journey has always been a team adventure. Thank you.

ABOUT THE AUTHOR

H.M. Lynn writes tense, gripping psychological thrillers with her signature engaging and emotionally rich storytelling. She also writes in many other genres including romance, as Hannah Lynn.

Sign up to H.M. Lynn's mailing list here for news, competitions and updates on future books.

Visit H.M. Lynn's website: www.hannahlynnauthor.com

Follow H.M. Lynn on social media:

facebook.com/hannahlynnauthor

instagram.com/hannahlynnwrites

tiktok.com/@hannah.lynn.romcoms

bookbub.com/authors/hannah-lynn

ALSO BY H.M. LYNN

The Head Teacher

H.M. Lynn writing as Hannah Lynn

The Holly Berry Sweet Shop Series

The Sweet Shop of Second Chances

Love Blooms at the Second Chances Sweet Shop

High Hopes at the Second Chances Sweet Shop

Family Ties at the Second Chances Sweet Shop

Sunny Days at the Second Chances Sweet Shop

A Summer Wedding at the Second Chances Sweet Shop

The Wildflower Lock Series

New Beginnings at Wildflower Lock

Coffee and Cake at Wildflower Lock

Blue Skies Over Wildflower Lock

THE

Murder

LIST

**THE MURDER LIST IS A NEWSLETTER
DEDICATED TO SPINE-CHILLING FICTION
AND GRIPPING PAGE-TURNERS!**

**SIGN UP TO MAKE SURE YOU'RE ON OUR
HIT LIST FOR EXCLUSIVE DEALS, AUTHOR
CONTENT, AND COMPETITIONS.**

SIGN UP TO OUR
NEWSLETTER

BIT.LY/THEMURDERLISTNEWS

Boldwⓞⓞd

Boldwood Books is an award-winning fiction publishing company seeking out the best stories from around the world.

Find out more at www.boldwoodbooks.com

Join our reader community for brilliant books, competitions and offers!

Follow us
@BoldwoodBooks
@TheBoldBookClub

Sign up to our weekly deals newsletter

https://bit.ly/BoldwoodBNewsletter

Printed in Great Britain
by Amazon

46185765R00218